An Indian child danced along the sidewalk.

She looked like a wood sprite, or a flower swaying on the wind.

Grinning at her unselfconscious beauty, Luke paused to watch her. Black hair flowed in satin ribbons to her hips. Her limbs were lanky, promising willowy height one day. In the dusky rose of her cheeks, a dimple flashed. She was the spitting image of his sister at that age.

Luke stepped forward, intending to ask the little girl about her clan. She spun around, and Luke's attention was snared by her exquisite, unusual eyes.

Pure topaz.

In that split second, Luke's world shifted. He blinked. Took in a breath and looked again.

His jaw hardened. Only one person in the world had eyes that precise color. Jessie.

This beautiful child was not just related to Luke's clan.

She was his daughter.

Dear Reader,

Welcome to Silhouette **Special Edition** . . . welcome to romance. We've got lots of excitement in store for you this April—and, no fooling, it's all about love!

Annette Broadrick, the author of over thirty-five novels for Silhouette Books, is making her debut in the Special Edition line with a book in our THAT SPECIAL WOMAN! promotion. *Mystery Wife* is a tantalizing, compelling tale about a woman who wakes up with a new lease on life—and a handsome, charismatic husband she doesn't remember marrying. . . .

And that's not all! *Shadows and Light,* the first book in the MEN OF COURAGE series by Lindsay McKenna, is due out this month. It takes a special breed of men to defy death and fight for right! Salute their bravery while sharing their lives and loves!

Loving and Giving by Gina Ferris, the new addition to Gina's enormously popular FAMILY FOUND series, is due out this month, as well as work by other favorite authors Nikki Benjamin, Natalie Bishop and Ruth Wind. April is a month not to be missed!

Sincerely,

Tara Gavin
Senior Editor

Please address questions and book requests to:
Reader Service
U.S.: P.O. Box 1325, Buffalo, NY 14269
Canadian: P.O. Box 1050, Niagara Falls, Ont. L2E 7G7

RUTH WIND
WALK IN BEAUTY

Silhouette®

SPECIAL EDITION®

Published by Silhouette Books

America's Publisher of Contemporary Romance

With love to Aggie, Robert, David, Tex, Jimmy 1 and
Jimmy 2, Ed, Bill, Cheyenne, Danny and all the others.
And for Luke, with many thanks. Bon voyage,
my friend.

 SILHOUETTE BOOKS

ISBN 0-373-09881-2

WALK IN BEAUTY

Books by Ruth Wind

Silhouette Special Edition

Strangers on a Train #555
Summer's Freedom #588
Light of Day #635
A Minute To Smile #742
Jezebel's Blues #785
Walk In Beauty #881

RUTH WIND

has been addicted to books and stories for as long as she can remember. When she realized at the age of seven that some lucky people actually spent their days spinning tales for others, she knew she had found her calling. The direction of that calling was decided when the incurable romantic fell in love with the films *Doctor Zhivago* and *Romeo and Juliet*.

The Colorado native holds a bachelor's degree in journalism and lives with her husband and two young sons at the foot of the Rockies.

Luke and Jessie's journey: — — —

Chapter One

A blue jay feather lay on the sidewalk as Luke Bernali climbed from his truck. He almost stepped on it. A flash of iridescent blue caught his eye in time, and he bent over to pick it up.

Jessie.

The feel of her and the sense of warning were so strong, he had to resist the urge to look over his shoulder. Luke twirled the feather in his fingers, admiring the shimmer of color banded with sharp black stripes. Blue jays had been her favorite birds. Luke once made her some earrings from a pair of tail feathers.

He half smiled at the bittersweet memory. With the respect usually reserved for the feathers of eagles and hawks and other such birds of power, he nestled it between the folds of a paperback science fiction novel on the front seat of his truck. Jessie had cared little for traditional explanations of the qualities of feathers. Even if no one else in the world valued blue jays, she'd told him, she did. She liked their colors and their sass.

For just an instant, he felt another small wash of warning. He brushed it away. Silly. She'd been gone more than eight years.

With a quick glance at the dark storm clouds gathering in the November sky, he lifted a pile of Navajo weavings from the back of his truck and flung their solid weight over his shoulder. Mountains towered behind the bank of shops along the street, their deep blue color shadowed beneath the clouds obscuring their summits. Luke breathed deeply and smelled snow.

A young Indian girl danced alone on the sidewalk in front of the store he was about to enter. Against the wintry background of the approaching storm, she looked like a wood sprite or a flower swaying on the wind. Grinning at the unselfconscious beauty she projected, Luke paused to watch her.

Long black hair flowed like satin ribbons to her slim hips. Her limbs were lanky and long, promising willowy height one day. In the dusky rose of her cheeks, a dimple flashed, elusive and charming.

She was the spitting image of his sister, Marcia, at this age. Luke stepped forward, intending to ask the child about her clan.

She spun around and saw him watching her. Luke caught a swift impression of beaded earrings flashing in her great mass of hair before his attention was snared by her unusual, exquisite eyes.

Pure topaz.

The color alone was startling in her powerfully Navajo face, against her dusky skin and broad cheekbones. Together with their enormous size and calm expression, they were astonishing.

In that single split second, Luke's world shifted abruptly. He blinked, took in a breath and looked at her again. She had stopped dancing to look at him with those beautiful eyes.

His jaw hardened. There was only one person in the world who had eyes just that color. This child, beautiful against the dark day, was not just a relative to his clan, as he had first suspected.

She was his daughter.

"Hi," the girl said. "You must be the guy they're waiting for." She pointed with her lips toward the shop selling rugs and pottery and various other Southwestern artworks.

Luke took in another slow, deep breath, trying to keep his emotions soft, quiet, fluid. "Are they waiting?"

Her lids flickered over the topaz irises, then swept up again. Mischief flashed in her dimple. "Not too long. The man in there said you were probably on Indian time."

Luke chuckled. "Just another kind of time."

"Where's Daniel?" she asked.

"He's—" he cleared his throat "—he's not feeling well. Is he a friend of yours?"

She nodded.

"I'm Luke. Daniel's a friend of mine, too—or he used to be, a long time ago."

"Luke?" The child measured him. Her gaze flickered toward the rugs he carried over his shoulder, then narrowed on his face. "Luke Bernali?"

If he'd had any doubt that one of the people he'd find waiting for him inside would be Jessie Callahan, it was now erased. "That's right."

She shook hair from her eyes. "There's a picture of you in my mom's office," she said, as she glanced

through the windows of the gallery and then back to
Luke. "My mom's inside."

"Don't go away," he said and pulled open the door.

Jessie shifted impatiently. She wore no watch at which
she could glance with pointed severity, so she folded her
arms and sighed. Loudly.

The man on the telephone didn't even look up. He'd
been absorbed in his conversation since five minutes after her arrival, and it was no accident, she was sure.
Geoffrey Wilkes wanted Jessie to know he was a powerful, important man, a force to be reckoned with.

At moments like this, she really wondered why she had
given up cigarettes.

She shifted, strolling away from the man at the desk
and into the showroom. Just beyond the window, her
daughter, Giselle, danced to the imaginary tune playing
in her mind, as she always did. Jessie smiled. What a kid.

Her smile faded, though, as her attention returned to
the inner walls, where Navajo weavings were displayed to
best advantage on adobe-colored walls. Tasteful arrangements of Hopi pottery reclined on pedestals scattered around the natural clay tile floors, and several
understated collections of silver and native stone jewelry
were exhibited in glass cases. Everything in the store ca-
tered to the hunger for original Southwest art that swept
the country, and every last article was genuinely Ameri-
can-Indian made. Guaranteed.

For a price, of course. The huge rug on the wall dan-
gled a tiny handwritten price tag in five figures. Un-
doubtedly worth it—the wool had been sheared from a
sheep the weaver owned, then combed and dyed by hand,
then spun and woven over many, many days and weeks
of work. The highest possible quality.

Too bad the weaver had received less than a tenth of the price for her efforts.

A familiar burn welled in Jessie's chest as she glanced at the man behind the desk. This time, he caught her eye. His expression, to her surprise, showed not the worry or coldness she expected, but a very definite male appraisal. He lifted his eyebrows in suave acknowledgment of her catching him.

Annoyed, she shook her head. Where was Daniel? She could handle the confrontation on her own, of course, but it all went so much more smoothly with someone from the reservation to back her up—someone with fresh, lovely products to display.

Wilkes ended his phone conversation and glided toward Jessie. "I'm sorry, Ms. Callahan, but you must know how temperamental some artists are."

Dryly, Jessie inclined her head. "One thing after another."

The glass door of the showroom whispered open.

Jessie murmured a prayer of thanks and turned toward the door. The showroom was dim in the cloudy afternoon, and all Jessie could make out was that the man in the doorway was not Daniel. Daniel wore his hair in a long braid, and he was not as tall as this shadowed man. As he shifted the rugs on his shoulders, Jessie felt a jolt over the way he moved his head, just so, as if—

She frowned, waiting for the man to come forward where she could see him clearly. He paused a moment, then moved toward them with a lazy, loose-limbed grace. His hair caught and reflected all the light in the room. Her knees shivered dangerously. Oh, please, she muttered to the universe at large. Not this. Not now.

But her plea went unanswered. In a softly accented voice, the man spoke. "Jessie," he said. "I knew there was something familiar about that little girl out there."

Only Jessie would have picked up the fury in the dulcet tones. And even after eight years, she was intimately familiar with that voice. Not deep, not rumbling, not loud. Indian men rarely had deep voices, and Luke was no exception. His was a voice rich with promises, a tenor of deceptive gentleness, musical with the accents of his first language.

Jessie clutched the fabric of her shawl tight in her fist. A roar of white noise filled her ears as Luke stepped into the light. For long moments, Jessie stared at the once-beloved face, unable to breathe or move or blink. When she felt a prickling blackness at the edge of her vision, she forced herself to breathe deeply.

Her mind cleared. "What are you doing here?" she asked, and her tone was more perplexed than she had intended.

His gaze locked with hers, straight and dark and penetrating. "Daniel is sick. My sister called last night to see if I'd pick up the rugs and bring them over. I drove up to Denver this morning and got them."

"You think we could have old home week later, folks?" Wilkes cut in. "I've got work to do here."

"No problem," Luke said. The undertone of anger was now channeled toward the man in front of him. "It's pretty simple, Mr. Wilkes. Unless you start paying a little bit more up-front, you won't be selling any more rugs."

For a pinch hitter, Jessie thought in some surprise, his opening remarks were pretty strong.

Wilkes pursed his lips, eyeing the weavings Luke carried over his shoulder. "I think there's room for discussion," he said reasonably.

Jessie swallowed a smile. There was always room for discussion, at first. The gallery owners knew they were soaking the weavers. Another grand wouldn't cut into their profits much.

If it had been Daniel standing next to her, Jessie would have shot him an amused glance. Since it was Luke, she pressed her lips together.

"Why don't we all sit down in my office?" Wilkes suggested, signaling a clerk. "Have a cup of coffee?"

"Fine." Luke lifted his chin toward the window, where Jessie's daughter peered anxiously inside. "What about your daughter? It's gonna snow."

Jessie lifted her eyebrows, about to comment on the intelligence levels of a seven-year-old. She thought better of it and lifted a hand to indicate Giselle should come in. The girl bounced in eagerly, her eyes alight with curiosity and excitement as she came to stand beside her mother. She threw a coquettish glance toward Luke.

In turn, his icy calm melted and he grinned almost helplessly at the child. His daughter. A fact both father and daughter had obviously figured out.

Great.

Once again, Jessie thought she'd like to faint. Or grab Giselle's hand and run as fast as she could away from this man, away from the past, away from the confrontation she could feel brewing.

But she'd made a commitment to this project, so she dutifully followed Wilkes into his office and took a seat in one of the richly upholstered leather chairs. Giselle sank gracefully to the floor, her hair surrounding her like a cape. Luke took the chair next to the girl, winking at her as he sat down.

Luke's physical presence, so vivid and close, slammed Jessie suddenly. In the strong light of the office she could see him well. His hair was the same thick, heavy black, a little too long. It flowed like river water when he moved. His eyes were the same—penetrating, dark, expressive beyond measure. A few time-etched lines fanned from the corners into his broad cheekbones.

The yellowish cast to his skin was gone, and he no longer carried the extra weight around his middle. All she smelled was the curiously foresty scent of his skin. The booze, then, was gone.

She wondered with a pang how long it had been.

The hands and mouth were still much too clear in Jessie's mind. She'd seen them in miniature every single day since Giselle was born and didn't care to renew her acquaintance with those details.

Wilkes sat down behind his broad desk. "What kind of money are we talking here?" he asked, cutting straight to the chase.

Luke folded his hands loosely. "Half the price you ask for the rug. And we'll deliver."

To his credit, Wilkes didn't erupt in outrage as so many of the gallery owners had done. He absorbed the information for a minute, then looked at Jessie. "And I imagine your presence here signifies a little inducement?"

"You imagine correctly," she replied and handed him a list. "These are the artists who will pull their work from galleries that refuse to pay a more equitable price for the weavings."

"Has anyone given any thought to what will happen to all these artists if they can't display their work?" He gave her a measured stare. "Your paintings, for example, Ms. Callahan. They've only been selling well for what—two, three years?"

"There are other methods of displaying our work," she returned calmly. "And other ways of earning a living." But he'd struck at her secret terror. What if, after all this was over, she could no longer sell her own work? It was a dream that had been long and hard in coming, and she'd hate to see it die.

"What about all those little old ladies out there weaving on the reservation?" Wilkes asked, leaning back in his chair. "Anybody ask them how they feel about giving up the tidy little sum they're already getting for a rug? I understand it goes quite a ways out there."

"In the first place," Luke said in a deadly quiet voice, "they aren't little old ladies. They are young women and old women and in-between. Many of them are the primary breadwinners in their families—as they should be with such talents. In the second place, you stand to make a profit of eight to ten thousand dollars on every one of those big rugs. And all you do is put it on your wall."

Jessie knew she should be concentrating, but Luke's dark honey voice flowed seductively around her. In the four years they'd spent together, she'd never once heard him raise his voice, except to call a dog. Grimacing in wry amusement, she remembered, too, how alarming that had been to her at first. Her own family had been unable to discuss the weather without a boisterous, loud argument.

She sobered as Luke continued. "Even at the new rates, you'll make almost obscene profits."

Wilkes dropped forward, arms on the desk. "I'll tell you something. There's no way I'll pay a dime over twenty percent of my gross on those rugs. And from what

I've been hearing through the grapevine, I'm not alone."
He gave Jessie a cool glance. "No artist on that list of
yours will cause me any real loss of revenue, so you can
take all your toys and go play somewhere else."

Jessie shot Luke a glance. A thin smile curved his lips.
"I forgot to mention something else," Luke said, shifting the weavings on his shoulder. "We've taken an op-
tion on a shop around the corner here. You've got six
months, and then we open—just in time for tourist sea-
son. When your customers find out they can get the same
rug for half of what you charge, I bet I know where
they'll shop." He stood up and tossed a card from his
shirt pocket onto the desk. "You know where to find us."

Hastily, Jessie scrambled to her feet, gesturing toward
Giselle.

Wilkes laughed. "It's been tried before, you know. It
never works."

"This time it will," Luke promised quietly, and walked
out.

Giselle skipped after him, leaving Jessie behind. Jessie picked up her scarf and purse from the chair. "I hope
you'll give this some thought, Mr. Wilkes," she said. "It
is going to work this time."

"We'll see about that."

Lifting her purse and scarf to her chest like armor,
Jessie headed outside—for the second confrontation of
the day.

Luke patted his shirt pocket for the bag of tobacco he
kept there, wondering if he had time to roll a cigarette
before Jessie reappeared. He could use one.

He decided to try and pulled the makings out—a single thin sheet of paper, a perfect pinch of moist tobacco,

a deft roll and quick lick. Done. He stuck it in the corner of his mouth.

"You shouldn't smoke, you know," said the little girl beside him. "My teachers told me it can give you cancer or heart attacks. I convinced my mom to quit."

. Luke pursed his lips, then squatted beside her. Such a beauty, he thought again with a twinge in his chest. His child.

"I don't smoke a whole lot," he told her. "That's what's hard for people to remember—a little tobacco, a little beer, a little cake, they're all okay. If you smoke a pack a day or drink a bottle of whiskey or eat a whole cake, then you get sick."

Her enormous topaz eyes rested on his face. "You're my father, aren't you?"

Luke held her gaze. "Yeah. I think so."

"Are you mad at my mother?"

He took a kitchen match from his pocket and scratched the tip with his thumbnail. Mad? He lit the cigarette and inhaled deeply before he spoke. "No," he lied, to spare the child who had nothing to do with anything between her mother and father.

The door swung open and Jessie pushed outside, a swirl of color and glitter and fragrance. Luke saw her spy him and Giselle cozily talking together on the sidewalk; then he watched as she planted her feet and crossed her arms in a fighting posture. Squatting as he was, Luke was at a disadvantage.

There was also the small matter of his breath, which seemed to have deserted him.

Damn. He searched for his fury. She'd hidden from him for eight years, not only herself, but her daughter. There should be nothing but fury in him.

He had loved this woman once with an almost scorching intensity. Seeing her again so suddenly unnerved him, tangled him up inside like a can full of rubber bands.

How could anyone remain so unchanged? She was as beautiful as she had been the first time he'd seen her, almost twelve years ago. It was a beauty as wild and tender as the stubborn roses that grew by the sea in her father's California garden. Her skin was pale and pure, her hair a rich chestnut that spilled in abundance over her shoulders, catching around the rise of one breast as if in a caress.

But it was her eyes that had bewitched him the first time, so many years ago, the same extraordinary eyes her daughter had inherited—eyes the color of the first golden fingers of morning sunlight. They bewitched him again now.

"Come on, Giselle, let's go," she said, and turned.

Luke was on his feet instantly. "Jessie," he called in a harsh voice.

She whirled, ready to battle. He could see it in her stance, in her fisted hands, in the blaze of her eyes. She was scared stiff and as unsettled as he, but battle she would. "What?"

"You can't just walk away."

Her lips twisted in a bitter smile. "Can't I?"

That brought his fury rushing back, clean and pure as a mountain stream. "Well," he said quietly, "I guess you can. You've done it before."

She just looked at him.

He crushed the stub of his cigarette under the heel of his boot, exhaling in an effort to curb his anger. "I'm asking you not to." He touched Giselle's hair in wonder, and she looked up at Jessie with hope, a hope and pleading that broke his heart.

Jessie saw it, too. Luke saw her swallow—and for an instant, he felt pity for her. He and Giselle had nothing to lose, everything to gain. For Jessie, quite the opposite was true. "Giselle," he said quietly, "give me a minute with your mother, all right?"

"I don't want a moment with you, Luke," Jessie whispered fiercely, but Giselle had already skipped away.

He set his jaw. "Looks to me like you got caught red-handed, me and her in the same place at the same time."

She refused to look at him.

"Look, Jessie, we can let sleeping dogs lie or we can have a bloody, screaming fight in the middle of the street. I don't really give a damn about the past, but you can't expect me to just walk away from my only child without a second glance." He crossed his arms. "Be fair."

"Fair!" She spat the word.

Light glowed like wine in the rippling fall of her hair, danced like moonlight over her nearly translucent skin. Luke could smell her perfume, a deeply exotic mix of frangipani and sandalwood and something he couldn't name. It made him dizzy. "Well, maybe fair is the wrong word," he admitted.

Her gaze, frightened and wary, met his. Luke felt the impact as a fist to his gut and he glanced away. "I'm sober now, Jessie," he said, looking at a piece of mica caught in the sidewalk just beyond the toe of his boot. In his ears, his voice was rough.

She didn't say anything for a long time, and in the silence between them Luke felt a rush of things spring and whirl like dust devils. "I can see that."

"Just come with me now for a little while," he urged. "We'll get a hamburger or something. You've had a long time to know her, Jessie. Give me an hour or two." He licked his lips. "Please."

For a moment, he thought she would refuse. Her chin jutted stubbornly toward the mountains. Suddenly, she capitulated. "All right. But only an hour."

He found his gaze on the curve of her cheek, at once intimately familiar and completely strange to him. A sword of that old, familiar grief stabbed his gut. In a harsh voice, he asked, "You want to go in my truck?"

"We'll just follow you."

In the instant before she turned, Luke thought he glimpsed a tear.

Chapter Two

Jessie had experienced some very strange moments in her life, but the first half hour sitting with Luke and his newly acquired daughter in the worn booth of a downtown Colorado Springs café counted among the strangest.

There were, after all, few guidelines for her to follow. Dear Miss Manners, she imagined writing.

I wonder if you might offer a few rules of etiquette for coping with the unexpected reappearance of the love of one's life who's also the father of one's child—a child he didn't know existed, by the way— after an eight-year separation.

She stabbed a french fry into a pool of ketchup. Miss Manners would no doubt urge civility and ordinary courtesy. Unfortunately, Jessie thought, chewing the dredged fry, civil was pretty far down on the list of the things she felt.

It seemed a rather cruel trick of fate to send him at this late date. The life she had built from the ruins of her relationship with Luke Bernali was a peaceful one, free of the wild peaks and valleys she had known with him.

She'd finally forgotten him, if not forgiven. She had finally stopped dreaming of him, except once in a great long while. She had finally come to believe there might be a chance that someday, somehow, she might love another man.

One glance at him in the middle of the gallery had been enough to show her how foolish her illusions had been. One glance, and there was a quick humming in her veins ... something strong and lusty and full of sex, but deeper than that, too. It was a lyrical sound, a song in her soul. As if she had known him always, as if—

She set her jaw and grabbed the ketchup bottle. Get real, she warned herself. Luke Bernali was just that kind of a man. Sleek and lean, with those rich, deep eyes. Eyes that promised he knew all there was to know about women—and he liked every single bit of it. No woman in her right mind could fail to respond to those signals.

The ketchup bottle, fairly cooperative a moment before, refused to release its contents. Aggravated, Jessie shook it. Three small drops fell from the mouth.

Across the table, Luke chuckled softly.

Maybe she could punch him. A good solid left to the jaw would probably do wonders for her mood.

Giselle seemed to be having no trouble with the rules of a first encounter with her father. Nor did Luke seem at all handicapped. They dove headfirst into the apparently unequaled joy of acquainting themselves. Giselle chattered about her second-grade class and her reading, divulged her preference for dogs over cats and the fact that she had just completed her first beadwork project. In his turn, Luke told Giselle about his carpentry business and his sister, Marcia, who was Giselle's aunt.

After their hamburgers were finished, Giselle asked for quarters to play pinball. Jessie had taken a breath to tell her no when Luke passed a dollar bill over the table.

"We really do need to be going," Jessie protested.

"I need to talk to you," he said. Seeing Jessie's rebellious glare, he added, "About the project."

"Fine," she said to Giselle, who bounced away.

As if Giselle had provided the strings of the surreal puppet show being staged, the conversation abruptly collapsed with her departure. From the window, cold gray light spilled between them. Jessie looked outside to watch fat snowflakes drift down toward earth, unable to bear the painful reality of Luke's harsh and beautiful face.

"I can't believe you kept her away from me all these years, Jessie."

Sudden tightness clutched Jessie's throat. If she let him lead her back to the past, she would be lost. "I thought we were going to talk about the project."

A flash of anger tightened his mouth. "God knows we wouldn't want to have three minutes to talk about all this."

"God knows." She lifted her chin defiantly.

He stared at her, his eyes filled with seething emotion. Then his jaw went hard and he shifted his gaze away, toward the light snow falling beyond the window.

Jessie wanted this over with. "Why don't you tell me what's going on with the project?"

"All right." He looked at her. "I took Daniel's place today because he was poisoned."

"Poisoned? Like food poisoning?"

"Strychnine." He slipped a toothpick into the corner of his mouth—an old habit that stirred up curiously painful associations. "He was lucky—he only ate half his meal. While he was eating, a snake spooked one of his horses and he went to check it out. The dog got his supper." He looked at her. "The dog died."

"I can't believe it," Jessie said. "Is he all right?"

"My sister said he was pretty sick, but he'll live."

"Who did it?"

"Nobody knows right now." He shifted the toothpick to the other side of his mouth. "The next day, Mary and her son lost their brakes on the way into Gallup. They found signs of tampering."

"Are you suggesting some kind of conspiracy?" Jessie shook her head. "Don't you think that's a little paranoid?"

"Maybe." He eyed her steadily. "There's a lot of money at stake for these people. We've reached almost all the major dealers in the Southwest the last few weeks. Do you really think it's surprising they'd try to find a way to push back?"

"I guess not."

For a moment he said nothing, and Jessie could see unease in the way he twiddled the toothpick in his fingers. Finally he asked, "Do you still want to go ahead with the appointment at the other gallery in the morning?"

"Of course. If we run at the first sign of intimidation, it'll guarantee the situation won't change."

"That's not what I meant."

Jessie, stung, looked at her paper napkin, crushed into a tight ball in her hand. "I knew what you meant," she said quietly. "I'll still go."

"How did you get mixed up with this project?" he asked.

"I could ask you the same question. I thought I knew everyone involved."

"My mother was a weaver, Jessie—that would be enough to catch my attention by itself."

"I haven't forgotten. It's just that it seems I would have heard of you or something."

"It's Marcia who is really into the project. They couldn't get ahold of you on the phone last night, so she called me and gave me a crash course."

"Marcia—the Denver contact, right?" Jessie had heard Daniel speak of her, but never with her last name. "How is she?"

"Good." His expression softened. "She's a violin teacher—teaches Suzuki method to inner-city kids."

Jessie found herself chuckling. "That fits. I bet she's good at it."

"She is." He lifted a brow. "So, what about you? How'd you get involved?"

Jessie moved her plate out of the way so she could fold her arms in front of her on the table. "I met Daniel when I was pregnant with Giselle, and he sort of took us under his wing." Carefully, she pushed a stack of bread crumbs into a neat little pile in front of her. "It was important to me that Giselle have Navajo people in her life, so she'd know who she was. I couldn't give her that, and Daniel—"

She chanced a peek at Luke's face. He stared fiercely at his hands. A long muscle along his jaw stood out.

Jessie hurried on. "When Daniel started this project last year, he knew I was involved with a lot of other artists. He recruited me to get the support of the local art community."

"You know," Luke said, his voice oddly flat, "he used to be my best friend."

"He was?" Jessie frowned. "He's never said a word about you."

Luke shrugged.

"He's been a good friend to me," Jessie went on. "And Giselle loves him."

As if the knowledge pained him, Luke looked away from her to Giselle. An expression both hungry and joyful crossed his face. Jessie recognized it. It reflected the astonishment she still felt sometimes, watching Giselle at some ordinary task.

Nothing had prepared her for the love she felt for her child, something so deep and gripping and unfathomable Jessie couldn't even define it. In loving Giselle, she found herself unable to keep even a corner of her heart aloof, as she'd always been careful to do with everyone else. Even Luke. Maybe especially Luke.

"I can't believe it," he said softly. "Look at her. She's so beautiful and smart—she looks just like Marcia." He turned a harsh gaze to Jessie. "Was it so terrible that you couldn't have given me this small thing? Just to watch her grow?"

A vision of her alcoholic mother, drunk and incoherent, flashed across Jessie's imagination. To spare Giselle that horror, Jessie would have done a lot more than simply leave Luke. "When I saw you last," she replied quietly, "you were hardly father material."

His lashes, black and straight, swept down. Dusky color stained his cheekbones and for an instant, Jessie was ashamed.

He cleared his throat and shifted, pulling a twenty from the front pocket of his jeans. He stood up. "I have some things I need to do before dark."

Jessie nodded.

He paused at the tableside. When he spoke, his voice was rough. "Maybe I'm still not what you think she needs." His eyes, dark and luminous in the cold light, were somber. "Don't run away again, Jessie. Please."

Her throat tightened dangerously and she bit her lip hard. "No. I won't."

"I can't make the past right, but I really am sorry things turned out the way they did." He swallowed. "I'm sorry—" he shook his head "—that's all. I'm sorry."

On the way out, he paused to murmur something to Giselle, his graceful, long-fingered hand flat on her back. Then he ambled out, waving toward the waitress in a friendly farewell.

It was still a full sixty seconds before Jessie could absorb his words. Then she buried her face in her hands, fighting back tears of rage and loss and mourning.

Once she'd had to choose between the child growing in her belly and the love that had healed her. It had been the hardest struggle of her life. For years she had mourned him, tortured herself with "what ifs" that had no bearing on real life. What if she'd been stronger? What if she'd seen the signs of his alcoholism in time to help him? What if she'd given him a chance and he'd been able to kick his habit?

Now he appeared, sober and strong, a perfect fulfillment of her most fervent "what if . . ."

What if he stopped drinking?

She looked at Giselle, bent over the pinball game with intense concentration. Eight years ago, Jessie had chosen to be this child's mother, alone. She had chosen to devote herself to motherhood the way her own mother had not.

Through the window, she watched Luke's truck pull into the street and drive away, feeling a plucking sorrow. There was terrible irony in all of it, she thought. If she'd never known Luke, had never reveled in the unconditional love and support he'd given her, she would never have been strong enough to leave him the way she had. Without the healing of his love, she would never have known how to love her child, to be the mother she was.

But she lived with the irony. For Giselle, she could bear the guilt.

The thought made her feel much stronger. Briskly, she stood up, gathered her daughter and paid the bill. Then she took Giselle out to explore Colorado Springs.

In the still of the evening, Luke bent over a bureau he'd bought at a flea market. Below the chipped layers of paint, he'd seen the extraordinary beauty of it, and now he lovingly sanded the ridges of the carved drawers, gently so as not to mar the delicate grain of the maple.

The smell of sandpaper and dry wood eased the tension he'd been carrying with him all day, as did the repetitive motion and the simple beauty of the wood itself. At sixteen, he'd landed his first carpentry job and fallen in love with the profession. Over the years, he'd learned almost every aspect of it, from framing buildings to making drawers that moved smoothly on their rollers to this delicate kind of refinishing work.

Recently he'd found a huge market for the work he loved best—recreations of Victorian-era woodwork for the stately homes built during the heyday of "Little London," and now being reclaimed by up-and-coming young professionals. He made banisters and baseboards and wainscoting. On weekends he browsed flea markets and garage sales for pieces like this that would be sold to the same people who contracted reproduction spindles for their stairways.

Luke's enormous black cat wandered into the room, meowing plaintively. Luke chuckled as Nino bumped his shin and scooped the animal into his arms. "What do you think, hmm?" he said to the cat. "I bet someone is going to pay a pretty penny for this one."

Nino meowed loudly in answer, his Siamese blood showing in his protesting tone.

Beyond the cozy warmth of the kitchen, the storm that had threatened all day was breaking. Wind moaned around the corners, rattling the dry branches of a vine outside the kitchen window. The sound was lonely. It underscored Luke's sense of being haunted—by Jessie, by old specters of himself, by the past.

Nino jumped down and meowed to go outside. Luke crossed the tiled floor he'd laid himself and let the cat out. His dogs, hearing the click of the door, bounded up, tongues lolling, ears alert in hopes of being let in. "Forget it," Luke said with a scowl. "I've had enough of animals tonight."

Tasha, a wolf-Malamute mix, grinned and leapt for Nino, who crouched with annoyance at the dog slobber dripping onto his ears. Nino then reached up with one massive paw and slapped Tasha's nose. No claws, of course. There were rules to this game.

Shaking his head, Luke closed the door and fetched a can of coffee from the fridge. There on the shelf rested a single bottle of beer. It had sat there now for nearly four years, ready in case he chose to fall. For one aching instant, Luke wanted to finally break down, twist off the top, gulp it down. He wanted to take refuge in one ice-cold beer to blunt the memory of Jessie's golden eyes, staring at him with such fierceness this afternoon.

Instead, he made a pot of coffee and rolled a cigarette while he waited for it to brew. He leaned against the counter and flicked a kitchen match with a thumbnail, watching the reflection of the flame in the window. Beyond, snow floated down from a sky as cold as the past.

Had there ever been a man as stupid as he'd been with Jessie? That single, lonely beer in the fridge summed it up. He'd traded the greatest love of his life for booze.

As a boy, he'd lived on a reservation near the border of New Mexico and Arizona. There had been no drinking there, not ever. But sometimes his family would go into Farmington for supplies, and Luke's father would sadly point to Indians standing in clusters at the doors of certain bars, fighting, sleeping on the blacktop roads out of town for warmth. "See?" Luke's father said, over and over. "Don't let yourself be an Indian like that."

Luke was ten when the family moved to Colorado Springs, and the image of those drunks faded. By the time Luke joined the army at eighteen, he drank beer along with the rest of the young, homesick soldiers. He dismissed his father's warnings as the overly rigid advice of a traditional—quaint but not altogether useful in the world beyond the reservation.

But even just the beer had sometimes given him hangovers that scared him. He would awaken with a swollen head and a clutching fear in his chest, feeling as if he couldn't breathe, as if he were on dangerous ground. He'd go on the wagon for a while, but the problem never seemed that serious. With practice, he learned his limits and stayed within them. Only beer. Only a few.

In his kitchen, on this cold winter night, Luke shook his head over the illusions he'd built so carefully, the lies he'd told himself. He poured a cup of coffee, stirred in a generous measure of sugar and reached for the milk in the fridge. His gaze caught on the bottle of beer once more, but his hunger for it was dissipating quickly.

In the living room the stereo paused as a new record fell into place, then Jackson Browne was singing about the lengths a man would go to forget a woman.

Jessie. Not a woman he'd been able to wash from his mind, though God knew he'd tried. He had buried himself in the arms of other women, in work, in projects. Another man would have used liquor. Luke didn't have the luxury. His father, it seemed, had been right—at least about Luke. This was one Indian who couldn't drink, not if he wanted to have a life.

He rubbed a restless palm over his chest, trying to ease the ache there. *Jessie.* Her name echoed through his mind, over and over, like a lost voice borne through a canyon by the wind. It seemed impossible that she'd just dropped into his life out of nowhere today, with no warning whatsoever.

He hadn't forgotten her. Even after so much time had passed, a song or a certain kind of sunset brought his memories of her rushing back. He'd hear someone laugh, or turn a corner in the grocery store and see some woman with long hair, and he'd be instantly back in the past.

They'd met twelve years before, when Luke worked for her father in California, building an addition to the lawyer's house by the sea. One morning he looked up toward the house and there she was, standing in the window of her bedroom, a soft white gown floating around her, her long, wavy hair lifting in the sea breeze. At lunch, she brought iced tea to the crew.

He told himself to be careful in the beginning. She was young, only a little past twenty, and somehow fragile—he didn't want to hurt her. At the time, he'd been in no mood for settling down with one woman, and for several weeks, he kept her at arm's length.

But somehow, he found himself seeking her out. They walked along the beach for hours in the evenings, talking and talking and talking. He learned her tragic story, shared his own losses, fell in love with her. And still he didn't kiss her, didn't even hold her hand.

Tired of waiting for him, she simply came to him one night in his tent on the beach. And Luke, for all his reasoning and caution, had not been able to resist the vulnerable way she offered herself. His will collapsed under the force of her innocent seduction, collapsed to the greater lure of his hunger for her.

As long as he lived, he would never forget the power of that joining. It had shattered him, and when the pieces came back together, he wasn't the same man he had been before. Even now, he could see it—her long hair tangled by his fingers, her skin translucent and white in the moonlight. The sound of the sea underscored their passion, a passion so violent and moving and deep he still never thought of it without feeling her against his chest, smelling her skin and tasting her mouth.

From that night onward, they had been inseparable. When Luke grew restless in California, Jessie wandered with him, and for three years, they had lived an almost idyllic life—traveling and working and loving.

Luke picked up the sandpaper and eased a corner under the lip of the bureau, sighing. Their last year together wasn't as easy to think about.

He wished sometimes he could point to that single moment when his control over his drinking had unraveled, but he couldn't. His father died, and Luke and Jessie traveled to Colorado Springs to be close to Marcia, who needed her older brother. The death was sudden, unexpected, searing, and left Luke feeling unbalanced. His drinking, always present but never dangerous, took a day-by-day turn for the worse.

No drama. No searing pain. Nothing he could pinpoint. He simply learned he could blunt the lost places inside himself with booze. He knew he was losing Jessie. In the cold light of morning, he sometimes hated himself, but it didn't help. He couldn't stop.

She left a year later. Packed her bags and disappeared. It was the first bracket on the worst period of his life. Shortly afterward, his ten-year-old dog had to be put to sleep. Marcia finished high school and went off to college. Luke lost a job, and then another one. Through it all, he drank. And drank some more.

One morning, he awakened in a public park at dawn, unable to remember how he got there. He sat up slowly and saw an old man staring at him as he rubbed grass marks from his cheek. A crippling shame seized him, and Luke realized he'd become one of those men his father had pointed out to him in warning so many times. Instead of going home, he walked straight to detox and checked himself in.

The phone rang, abruptly shattering his reverie. Luke stared at it for a moment, then grabbed it on the second ring.

"You better back off." The voice was young, Indian, unfamiliar.

"What are you talking about?"

"The weavers' project."

"Who is this?"

"A concerned party. We ain't gonna give up those profits."

The line went dead. Luke replaced the handset with a frown.

He dialed his sister's Denver number. "Marcia," he said when she answered, "have you heard anything from the res today?"

"Luke, do you know what time it is?"

He glanced at the clock. "Sorry. It's important."

"I was going to call you in the morning." She yawned. "Somebody shot a bunch of sheep again."

Luke swore.

"Yeah. Only a few were killed, but it's pretty ugly anyway. Why?"

"I just got a weird phone call."

"There was bound to be some harassment. We knew that when we started. Daniel thinks maybe after you talk to the people tomorrow, we'll back off for a month or so."

"Good." He paused, considering the plan that had just bloomed in his mind. It wasn't fair to Jessie, but then, she hadn't been fair to him. For seven years she'd raised their daughter, kept her hidden away from him. "Marcia, can you get down here tomorrow night? There's someone I want you to meet."

"Who is it?"

He smiled to himself, thinking of Giselle's dimples and the thick aura of mischief she carried around. Even Marcia would instantly see the resemblance between them. "It's a surprise."

"Hmm." In his imagination, he could see her eyes lifting in curiosity and anticipation. "Okay. I don't have repertoire classes tomorrow, so I can be down by suppertime. How's that?"

"Perfect."

"Can I stay for the weekend?"

"You know you're always welcome here."

"See you tomorrow, then."

Luke hung up. For a long moment he stood by the phone, staring at it as if it could foretell the future.

Once, he had known the answer to everything. Once, he had moved with smooth, clean confidence in every situation, sure he knew what was best. Life had shown him how foolish that assumption could be.

He poured himself a second cup of coffee and finally identified the hollow feeling in his chest. He was scared. Scared cold. For years his life had been as predictable and dry as the Southwestern plains where he'd spent his first ten years. He wasn't quite sure how the rains of this day's events would change him. He wasn't sure he wanted to know.

Damn her! He slammed his hand against the counter, feeling anger and pain and sorrow and something so big and buried so deep he couldn't put a name to it.

Leaves rattled against the window. If it had been Jessie alone who had walked into his life today, Luke knew what he would have done. He would not have spoken except in business. He would have avoided looking at her, shut her out until the business was done.

But Giselle changed everything. For his child, the only child he had, he would risk blowing open his defenses. For Giselle, he would risk it all.

Chapter Three

The next morning, Jessie awakened late. Giselle had already washed and dressed, boiled water for Jessie's tea and now sat impatiently by the heavily curtained window.

"What time is it?" Jessie asked.

"Seven-fifty-seven," Giselle replied, swinging her legs. "I tried to be quiet."

"You didn't wake me." Jessie pulled the pillow over her face with a groan. "I just wish they'd invent a later morning."

"I'll make your tea while you're in the shower."

"How did I end up with such a cheery morning person?"

Giselle raised her eyebrows coyly. "Maybe my dad is a morning person like me."

It was the sort of thing she said often, but this time it was a plea for information. Jessie propped herself on her elbows and pushed her hair out of her face. With a scowl, she said, "He is. A crack-of-dawn morning person."

"I think he seems really nice, Mom."

By unspoken agreement, neither of them had mentioned Luke's name after leaving the restaurant, but Jessie hadn't been foolish enough to believe the subject would remain closed. She considered brushing it away now, at least until she woke up a little.

Instead, she found herself saying, "I'm glad you like him."

There wasn't a cup of tea in the world that would make any of this easier. Giselle had grown up with the portrait of Luke that hung on Jessie's studio wall, but there had not yet been occasion to tell her much more than they had differences that led to their separation before Giselle's birth.

"But you need to understand that I don't have to like him just because you do."

Giselle said nothing for a minute. The physical appearance of her eyes had come from Jessie, but the stillness behind them was Luke through and through. "Do you think he loves me, Mom?"

"Yes." Jessie plucked at the bed sheet, unable and unwilling to confess that she had left Luke, giving him no chance to decide how he felt about his child. "He will love you even more when he gets to know you like I do."

"Are you going to let me visit with him?"

Jessie swung her feet off the bed and sighed. "It's not that easy."

Giselle pressed her lips together, seemingly acquiescent. Jessie gathered clean clothes and headed for the bathroom. As she reached the door, her daughter spoke. "It would be really nice to have more people in my family."

"I didn't know you minded that it was just you and me."

"I don't mind." She dipped her head and a fall of hair flowed forward.

Leaning against the threshold—one foot on carpet, the other on tile—Jessie waited. This was something else that belonged to Luke, Giselle's way of considering her words, weighing them out before she spoke them into reality. Jessie had always found it odd that a child could inherit mannerisms and gestures from a parent she had never seen, but she had. Giselle walked like Luke, too, and carried herself with his unconscious air of pride and calm strength.

The child lifted her head. "When we go to powwow, I always wish there was a grandma that was really mine, or cousins, or uncles. There's always so many people in every family except ours."

"Why didn't you ever tell me?"

"I don't know." Giselle swung her feet, and the silver-threaded double strings on her high-topped tennis shoes swept the ground, back and forth.

Jessie bit her lip, the tiniest bit wounded that she hadn't been enough for her daughter. Intellectually, she knew that was a ridiculous response—children always want a broad network of family. Alone with her father, Jessie had longed deeply for the wild Irish Catholic cousins they had left behind in Ohio when her mother died.

"You don't have any grandparents, sweetie. Luke's parents are dead, too." It was one of the things that had drawn them together so long ago; both carried the wound of losing a mother at a vulnerable age. When Jessie was twelve, her mother had finally succumbed to her alcoholism. Luke lost his at sixteen to complications of tuberculosis. At least, she thought now, Luke's mother had gone of more or less natural causes.

"But I have an aunt now," Giselle said. "And a father."

"Yes, you do." She shivered in the cold room. "We'll talk about it, honey. I promise."

"Okay."

This time Jessie hurried into the bathroom, closing the door firmly behind her to forestall any more discussion. Under the hot spray of the shower, she wondered how life had grown so complicated in less than twenty-four hours. Pursing her lips in a frown, she cast her eyes heavenward in mock severity. Some people sang in the shower. Jessie had long chats with the heavens.

"Thanks a lot," she said dryly. "I've gone two whole months without smoking and now you drop Luke Bernali in my lap?"

No lightning split the sky to strike her dead, but a distinctly uncomfortable prod from her conscience was nearly as effective. "I'm only kidding," she muttered, picking up a bar of scented soap. As she worked it into a lather over her face and shoulders, she sighed. "I'm sure you've got your reasons."

A more religious or superstitious woman might have sworn that she heard a distinct, powerful chuckle. Jessie figured it was gurgling in the drain.

A good cup of scalding hot tea couldn't stop the curious questions of a seven-year-old, Jessie thought as she inhaled the steam of her second cup, but it could certainly make other things appear in a much kinder light. Giselle had asked that they wear the same hairstyles today, and after French-braiding both sets of long hair, Jessie was energized.

"It's a beautiful day," she said, yanking the pull on the drapes. A thick scarf of mist draped the mountains. "I've always loved this city."

"It's pretty," Giselle agreed. "Before we go home, do you think we could go to the mountains?"

"I wouldn't think of leaving without taking you up there." Impulsively, she hugged her daughter. "I'm so glad you got to come with me."

"Me, too." Giselle returned the embrace fiercely. "I love you, Mom."

"I love you, too." Straightening, she glanced at her naked wrist and realized she still didn't have a watch. After three days without smoking, she'd taken it off. Time passed much more slowly when she glanced at her wrist every two minutes. "I think we're supposed to meet Luke pretty soon. Did you have enough to eat to tide you over, or should I stop to get you a junky fast-food breakfast?"

"I can wait."

"Let's hit the road then, kiddo." She draped a wide, fringed shawl over her sweater in lieu of a coat and opened the door.

On the way down the stairs, Giselle asked, "You used to live here, right?"

"For almost a year." A terrible year, except for the fact that Giselle had been conceived. It was the year Jessie had lost everything but her mind—and even that had been a close call. The thought took a little of the sheen from her mood. Resolutely, she took Giselle's hand. "Your dad was raised here."

"I thought he lived on the res when he was little."

"He did, when he was small. I think they moved here when he was nine or ten. His mother had tuberculosis, and they moved here for the climate." She glanced at

Giselle. "You can ask him. I'm sure he'd be happy to tell you."

It was the right thing to say. Giselle looked at Jessie with a brilliant, beaming smile. They rounded the corner toward the car, holding hands in friendly accord.

So the sight of the car was a doubly sickening shock. Jessie froze in her tracks, instinctively pulling Giselle back.

"Oh, yuck!" Giselle cried.

The small blue economy model was nearly unrecognizable, so smeared was it with a substance that gruesomely resembled blood. It covered all the windows, the hood and trunk and doors. Scrawled over the windshield were the words, Go Home.

Nothing could have induced Jessie to drive the car until it had been inspected engine to trunk.

They needed to meet Luke at the gallery in a half hour. Mentally, she raced through the choices available. She could call a cab, the police or Luke, who had given her his number the day before.

It wasn't a tough decision. She needed help. "Let's go call Luke."

They waited in the hotel coffee shop. By the time Luke drove up in his well-preserved but very old pickup truck, snow had begun to fall lightly.

Jessie spotted the truck first and gathered her shawl. She dropped several dollars on the table for the coffee and Giselle's muffin, then glanced out the window again to see Luke slam the door behind him.

She was braced for his appearance this time, but it didn't help much. For a long, long moment, she was utterly riveted to his powerfully male beauty against the mountains and snow. Wind whipped the tails of his long black duster around his calves and caught at the hair on his collar, tossing black strands over his angular face. Firmly, he brushed the offending locks away and pressed a worn black cowboy hat down upon his head.

Dipping his head a little against the swirling snow, he headed toward the coffee shop, moving with the careless grace of a cougar or a gunfighter.

He looked, Jessie thought, like a legend.

At her side, Giselle urgently tugged her hand. "Let's go, Mom!"

Jessie allowed herself to be led outside. Even then, with the cold wind circling her neck and snow lighting on her cheeks, she couldn't seem to pull herself together. Especially when Luke stopped a few feet away and simply waited, looking at her with a sober expression. She found herself noting small details about him—the slim, elegantly beaded hatband, the gleam of a silver chain around his neck, the evidence of recent polishing of his long broken-in boots. In those things, she realized he had recovered his careless, small vanities, and it was a good thing that he cared again.

The strangeness of knowing his secret vanities so intimately struck her forcefully. All at once, it seemed absurd they should be standing here like this, so many years too late. How could she make small talk to a man with whom she'd been wholly intimate? Someone with whom she'd shared not only the deepest secrets of her body, but of her mind and heart and soul.

"Where's the car?" he asked.

"I'll show you," Giselle volunteered. She rushed forward, bouncing. "It's right over here." It was impossible to miss the worshipful expression on her face.

Jessie was grateful when Luke reached out his hand to take Giselle's and bent his head toward her with a gentle smile. "Good morning," he said.

Giselle's eyes shone. "Good morning."

Jessie trailed behind them, trying desperately to find a way to put things in perspective.

At the car, Giselle said, "Pretty gross, huh?"

Luke nodded. "Did you call the police, Jessie?"

"Not yet. I wanted to wait and see if you thought it was connected to what we talked about yesterday."

"Probably." He rounded the car, his duster catching the wind as he walked. "I'd even venture a guess that that's sheep blood."

"Why?"

He glanced at Giselle, then back to Jessie. "Long story."

She nodded, again grateful for his thoughtfulness toward Giselle.

"I'll call the police from the office, but I doubt if they'll do anything." He frowned. "Don't drive it until I've had a chance to go over it."

"I'd appreciate that."

He inclined his head, the skin around his eyes crinkling with his smile. "Still a whiz at engines, eh?"

Jessie shrugged, steeling herself against the temptation to laugh with him about an old joke. "I can change spark plugs."

"It's progress."

"We'd better hurry," she said pointedly. "Or we'll be late for our appointment."

"Right."

The police, harried with minor traffic accidents in the snow, took a report over the phone. That done, the three of them headed for Luke's truck, a utilitarian vehicle he no doubt used to transport lumber and finished carpentry goods. Jessie noted the fresh coat of paint and the immaculate trim, the cleanliness of the serviceable truck.

Giselle scrambled joyfully to the middle of the bench seat. Jessie more reluctantly climbed in behind her and closed the door. The scent of the cab caught her unprepared—it was a deeply masculine smell of wood smoke and forest greenery laced with a faint undertone of good tobacco. The essence of Luke.

A blue jay feather hung from the mirror, the quill end wrapped in a scrap of deerskin. The sight of it, shimmering in the gray light, gave Jessie a sharp jolt. She looked out the window.

Luke turned the ignition key and the tape player jolted into life, playing Van Morrison, "Almost Independence Day." One of her favorite road songs. Had he remembered that, or was it just coincidence?

A swift, sharp pain stabbed through her chest at the wave of memories. She felt dizzy with the melding of past and present, and a little panicky at the innocent assault on her defenses. She wanted to hold her breath, close her eyes and cover her ears. Shut him out completely.

Nostalgia, she told herself, forcing herself to breathe normally and focus on the landscape beyond the window. Soon the work on the weavers' project would be finished and she could get back to Albuquerque and her normal, ordinary life. Just for today, she had to endure these nostalgic signposts and the emotions they rekindled. Tomorrow, she could go home.

Unfortunately, she found fate aligned against her once again. In spite of the fact that they were only a few minutes behind schedule, the man they were supposed to meet at the gallery was not there. His secretary was convincing in her tale of a family emergency, and asked if they could come back the next morning at the same time.

Luke glanced at Jessie, raising his eyebrows in question.

She took a deep breath, weighing the continued strain of being in his company against her commitment to the project. "Fine," she said with a sigh. "I can stay one more day."

Back outside, he looked at Giselle. "Have you had breakfast?"

"Only a muffin."

"Do you have plans, Jessie?" he asked.

She wanted to say yes, but honor outweighed comfort. "No, not really."

"Why don't you come to my house and have some breakfast? I'll call someone to look at your car—we can take it from there."

The thought of being in his company for another several hours sent a fresh wave of panic through her middle. "Giselle, get in the truck."

Her daughter heard the tone of voice and obeyed instantly. As soon as Giselle slammed the door closed, Jessie said in a low voice, "Luke, this is just too weird for me. I don't know how to act or what to say, or anything." She looked at him with entreaty. "It's been eight years. I don't even know who you are now."

For a moment, his gaze was fixed over her head. A long muscle along his jaw tightened. He touched his chin, moved his foot, weighed his words. Through it all, she waited.

"You do know, Jessie," he said finally, as he looked at her. His dark eyes were sorrowful and beautiful and struck the chords of a thousand memories within her. "You'll always know me. Just like I know you."

That struck the wrong chord. "Right," she snapped and was about to push past him when he grabbed her arm just above the elbow.

"Jessie," he said in a low, harsh voice. "Give me a break, will you? We can't pretend we never knew each other, but we don't have to be enemies."

So close. Jessie stared up at him, snared by her own stupid nostalgic emotions, by the warm brown of his skin, the cut of his jaw and the gentleness of his mouth. With an almost physical need, she ached to bury her face in the shoulder of his jacket, to breathe that foresty smell of his skin in deeply....

She remembered how it felt, too, how perfectly her head nestled against his shoulder, how he rested his chin on the top of her head, how even their breathing seemed to synchronize when they were close.

Tears sprang to her eyes suddenly and she broke away. "Damn you, Luke," she swore. "I could have done without this."

His face hardened. "Me, too." He touched her back lightly, nudging her toward the door. "Giselle's waiting."

She entered his house, Luke thought, as if there were snakes hidden beneath the furniture. It was his own place, bought three years before, and he was proud of it. The simple bungalow had been stripped of its old plaster walls, and Luke had restored the original woodwork.

Once inside the front door, Jessie stopped in the middle of the living room and looked around. "This is nice," she said.

He couldn't prevent a chuckle. "I like it."

On the couch, curled around each other in a mass, were his cats. Nino opened one eye to see what the commotion was all about, then stretched luxuriously. Jessie made a soft, approving noise and went forward. "Oh, he's beautiful."

Luke smiled to himself as she gathered the huge black cat into her arms, stroking his silky fur. Nino butted his head against her chin and purred loudly.

"You're a sweetie," she murmured.

Giselle bent over Sylvester, but it was plain she was only doing it because she thought she ought to. "I have dogs in the backyard," he said.

"Can I go out, Mom?"

"Wouldn't you rather help me fix breakfast?" Luke asked, feinting a punch to her left arm. "I'm going to make French toast, if that's okay with you."

"I love French toast!"

Luke grinned. "Thought you might." He cocked his head in the direction of the kitchen. "Come on."

From the fridge he took a bowl of brown eggs and put them on the table, then took another bowl from a cupboard. "Break about six or seven," he told her.

"What's wrong with these eggs?" Giselle asked suspiciously.

"Nothing. They're just fresh. I get them from a farm out east." He stripped off his coat and draped it over a chair. Taking coffee and a filter out, he watched Jessie circling the living room, cat in her arms.

"What's wrong with plain old store-bought eggs?" Giselle asked.

Jessie looked up, and for the first time she smiled at him. No scowl or suspicion, just genuine amusement, an acknowledgment of his beliefs about food and the ways it should and should not come to the table. He lifted a rueful eyebrow and looked back to the child awaiting his answer. "Let's just say for now, these taste better."

Giselle's mouth pursed in doubt, but she dutifully broke a couple, then stared hard into the bowl. "They look the same on the inside."

"Yep." He measured coffee and ran cold water into the pot. "They taste good, too. You'll see."

In the living room, Jessie paused by an antique trunk, on which Luke had displayed a collection of photographs. Most of them were family pictures—his mother and father and Marcia. He watched as she picked out one of Marcia, shook her head with a smile and replaced it.

"Okay, what next?" Giselle asked.

"Vanilla, milk and salt," he instructed, crossing the linoleum to the table. "Then we're ready for the cooking."

"I hope you haven't made any for me," Jessie said from the doorway.

"Mom," Giselle scolded with severity, "you have to eat breakfast. You can't get your vitamins from coffee." With a saucy roll of her eyes, she confided to Luke, "I can never get her to eat enough breakfast."

He chuckled and glanced over his shoulder. "I never could, either."

"At least Giselle doesn't try to get me to eat rabbit stew in the morning," Jessie returned dryly.

"You loved it." He took a hefty stack of bread from the wrapper. "And we did make some for you, so you'll have to eat it."

"I'll do my best."

Which turned out, Luke noticed later, to be quite well. She ate easily as much as he did. "Pretty hungry after all, weren't you?"

"Unfortunately, yes." With a rueful smile, she patted her tummy. "I'm finding out all those people who told me your metabolism changes after you're thirty were right."

Luke followed her gesture and found himself admiring her round curves. Looked okay to him.

"Can I go see the dogs now?" Giselle piped up.

"Sure. Get your coat," Jessie replied.

She ran to fetch it, then bounced back through the kitchen. "I still can't believe you have dogs *and* cats," she said, buttoning her coat.

"Luke's home for wayward animals." With a self-mocking grin, he added, "I'm also running a home for abandoned console radios in the basement, if you hear of any strays."

Giselle gave him a perplexed little smile, but Jessie chuckled in her rich, husky voice. He glanced at her quickly, surprised how good her simple laughter felt in his hollow heart. "Watch the big one, honey," he told his daughter. "He'll lick you half to death."

She giggled. "Okay."

When he turned back to the table, Jessie's clear topaz eyes were fixed on him. The last of her smile lingered around her full lips and there was friendliness—maybe even a little more—in her expression. For a minute, the past didn't matter, and he was admiring a very attractive, sexy woman across the table. The rush of desire surprised him. He wanted to kiss her, to fit his palms to the swell of her round breasts....

He closed his eyes, clenching his teeth against the powerful vision. Too much time had passed to heal the wounds between them. Too much time and too many betrayals. Hers, by leaving him when he needed her and hiding his child. His, by leaving her in an entirely different way, the way he'd known even then would be most painful for her.

Shame at what he had become in those dark days sent a spiral of regret through him. He reached for the bag of tobacco in his pocket. "So, whoever is doing this harassment has targeted almost all the key players, except Marcia. You should be careful."

She frowned. "I guess so."

"It worries me." He quickly rolled a cigarette. "Did you see anybody at the hotel that you might have seen in Albuquerque?"

She shook her head.

"It's got to be an Indian." He took his time settling the cigarette just so in his mouth, then scratched a match with a thumbnail. He held the flame to the end of the cigarette, watched it flare softly orange. He shook out the match, exhaling. "An Anglo couldn't have gotten to Daniel's food or George's brakes without somebody noticing."

"Why does that tobacco smell so much better than regular cigarettes?" she asked with an edge of irritation.

"The way it's cured." He looked at the blue curls of smoke, remembering that Giselle told him Jessie quit smoking. With a grin, he asked, "You want one?"

She smiled, again reluctantly. "I gave up all my bad habits."

He exhaled sharply. "Yeah," he said in a voice rough with shame. "Me, too."

"How long has it been, Luke?"

"Seven years and four months."

Still, there was no change in her expression. What had he expected? A broad round of applause?

Bitterness swirled with his shame of moments before. As if the pair of emotions were an unstable chemical formula, he felt pressure build in his lungs and gut. Abruptly, he grabbed plates and silverware and carried them to the sink. They landed with a clatter in the old porcelain basin.

Behind him, he heard Jessie gather more dishes and bring them over. Luke felt her next to him, warm and smelling of shampoo. He stared rigidly through the window, watching Giselle dance with Tasha, his wolf mix. Quite a pair they made, both sable and cream, with their golden eyes. "Jessie, did you know you were pregnant when you left me?"

It was her turn to avoid his gaze. Long lashes swept down to hide her eyes. "Yes."

"Why didn't you tell me? At least give me a chance to pull my act together?"

She crossed her arms, head still bowed. "You were so damned set on destroying yourself, I didn't think it would make any difference." Defiantly she looked up, cocking her chin at that I-dare-you angle he remembered so well. "I didn't want to have to go through it all again."

"All what?"

"My mother quit drinking at least thirty times. She'd do okay for a while, then fall off the wagon again. And every time it was harder and harder to believe in her." She shook her head, glancing out the window toward Giselle. "I couldn't let my child go through what I did."

"She's mine, too!" A painful burst of anger swelled in his chest. "You could have given me a chance."

"Maybe somebody else could have," she said. "Not me."

He gave her a bitter smile. "Yeah, there was always that piece of you that you had to keep safe. Something nobody could ever touch. Not even me."

"I thought we agreed to leave the past alone."

"Maybe it's not that easy." He sighed and looked at her. Drawn by the wintry light washing over her face, he took a step closer. "Maybe it isn't really dead."

For a moment, she didn't move, just stared up at him like a deer frozen in the headlights of an oncoming car. Her body was only inches from his own, her lips a simple stoop away. Even through his regret and anger, he wanted to kiss her like he used to, hear the soft sigh of her breath as she released herself to him, taste the sweet velvet of her mouth....

As if he'd spoken his wish aloud, Jessie reacted. Her gaze flickered over his face and lit on his mouth, then flew back to his eyes, a little less afraid. Without thinking, he lifted his hand and brushed the translucent curve of her cheek with the tips of his fingers. Her lips quivered a little.

"God, Jessie," he whispered, "I can't believe you're still so beautiful."

With a small cry, she broke away. Slamming forks against stoneware as she stacked the dishes, she said harshly, "Don't." The word was almost strangled.

He closed his eyes in swift sorrow, then grabbed his coat from the chair and went outside with his daughter and his dogs, who offered what Jessie had never been able to give him—a whole heart.

Jessie cleaned up the kitchen automatically, pouring herself into the simple task in an effort to get a handle on her roaring emotions. It wasn't easy. The window over the sink faced the backyard, where Luke and Giselle scampered with three dogs and a Frisbee. With her hands sunk deep in hot, sudsy water, Jessie watched them. Under her breath, she was humming, something she did automatically when she washed dishes.

She shifted her attention to the suds, and the song in her throat became recognizable. "I'm On Fire," by Bruce Springsteen.

In spite of herself, she chuckled. The sound unknotted some of her tension. Ruefully, she had to admit to herself that there was something still smoldering on the hearth of the past. There was a restless, aching wish in her to feel Luke's burnished skin skimming hers, to feel his cool, heavy hair between her fingers, to feel him linked with her in the most ancient way.

And not just anyone. Luke.

Only Luke.

It had always been this way—and she knew from a moment ago that the chemistry hadn't changed for him, either. It didn't matter how much time had passed or what else had gone on between them, there would always be this thrumming, physical connection.

Even now her dreams were filled with Luke's laughing eyes as he kissed her by the orange light of a campfire; Luke's skillful hands coaxing a response from her body; Luke's long, brown body naked and warm next to hers beneath the covers in a cold, cold room.

She blew a lock of hair from her eyes. It had been so hard to leave all that behind. Only the wonder of the child growing within her had kept her from breaking down, going back to him. Then Giselle had been a baby, flesh and blood, with enormous needs that kept Jessie busier than she'd ever been in her life.

In time, Giselle grew older, and Jessie had begun to accept dates from a handful of men she thought she could trust. It never worked.

Over the past couple of years, she hadn't bothered, even though the dreams of Luke had finally faded. The success of her work and the network of friends she made

in Albuquerque gave her serenity. For male companion-
ship, she always had Daniel, who'd also filled the need
for a father in Giselle's life. It was enough. A part of her
had accepted the fact that she'd given the best part of her
heart away and would never find a replacement. She
learned to live with it.

But sometimes it was lonely. Lately, Jessie had begun
to think she might be stable and strong enough now to
find another man. Maybe not a great love or a wild passion, but a good and honorable kind of relationship, the
kind of relationship in which she could share her life and
old age. She wanted someone calm and easy to talk to,
someone she could trust.

Peace was what she wanted. Not passion.

Beyond the window, Luke raced over the winter-dry
grass and scooped a shrieking Giselle into his arms,
swinging her around like an airplane. Giselle, in complete trust, flung her small arms around her father's neck
and hugged him fiercely. For a moment, the two glossy
dark heads nestled together, and Jessie caught sight of
Luke's face. His eyes were closed, his expression joyous
and sorrowing all at once. Jessie, watching, felt tears well
in her eyes.

This was what had been meant to be. Only there should
have been a dozen children crowding around the legs of
this teasing and gentle man. Not just one, borne in secret far away.

"Oh, Luke," she said softly. "How did we ever let it
come to this?"

But she knew the answer. She also knew both of their
futures depended upon keeping the Pandora's box of the
past closed and locked. Luke was sober and she was

strong. Neither of them could survive another upheaval. Jessie knew it even if Luke didn't.

She'd see to it that the box stayed closed, desire or none. There was too much at stake now to risk everything.

Chapter Four

By the time Luke and Giselle came back into the house, Jessie had managed to pull her defenses more closely around herself.

"Mom!" Giselle said, leaning into Jessie's lap. "My dad says we can go to the mountains if you say it's okay. We can take Tasha with us, 'cuz she likes it up there."

"When?"

"Today," Giselle declared, as if it were the only possible choice. "Now."

Jessie glanced out the front window. "It's cloudy. Won't it be awfully cold?"

"Not really," Luke said. "We'll bundle up and put an extra pair of socks on. It's nice up there this time of year. Do you remember Cheyenne Canyon? Helen Hunt Falls?"

Jessie chuckled, thinking of her ragged copy of *Ramona,* Helen Hunt Jackson's famous novel of a California woman and the Indian, Alessandro, she loved. Jessie had discovered a dusty copy in the library when she was fourteen and read it three times—just that year. She'd lost count of how many more times she'd picked up the beloved book. "How could I forget?"

Luke grinned, and his face was suddenly ten years younger. He'd often teased her about falling in love with him because she had loved Alessandro first.

And in a small way, it was true. The first time she had seen Luke, hammering nails into the frame of her father's new study, she had been riveted. As he worked in the heat of a California afternoon, his long black hair braided and dark skin shimmering with sweat, he'd been the most singularly attractive man she'd ever seen. His back was bare and long and dark, his arms strong and hard-muscled. A red bandanna tied around his forehead kept the hair from his eyes. She stared at him through her bedroom window, her stomach tight, unable to believe he was real. He paused, wiping a forearm across his brow. And then he looked up.

Jessie, romantic and young, had thought with a painful pinch, *Oh, it's Alessandro!* Her heart flipped when he gave her a slow, mocking, sexy smile.

Much like the one he was giving her now. "What do you say?" he urged. "It's a little more touristy these days, but the falls are still the same."

"Please, Mom?" Giselle said, folding her fingers into a prayerlike petition.

Jessie realized that she had already decided in favor the idea, without giving much thought to the fact it would mean spending the day in Luke's company, in places they had been before, places where they had once been happy. She wavered, suddenly afraid.

Luke glanced up, sobering. "You don't have to go if you'd rather hang around town or something. I can take her myself."

Right. She trusted him with his child, but not that much. "I'll go," she said. "But I want to stop by the hotel and change my clothes. I know how cold it can be up there."

Then, thinking of the sweaters and shawls she wore in place of coats, she sighed. Coats were too heavy and bulky for anything but the coldest days. She had not brought one with her. "I don't suppose you have a spare jacket I could borrow?"

"Sure." He shook his head, smiling at Giselle. "You can't get her to remember her coat, either?"

Giselle rolled her eyes. "She's stubborn."

Luke laughed. "Yep."

As they left the city behind, Luke found the tensions of the past twenty-four hours begin to bleed away. They rode in his truck, Giselle between them, bundled with scarves and mittens and layers until she resembled a roly-poly little bear. Tasha, the wolf mix, rode in the back of the truck, over which Luke had put a simple camper shell. A narrow road took them into the canyon, past picnic spots and hiking paths he knew intimately.

Jessie pointed. "Look—chipmunk hill! Do they still live there?"

"No. A few years ago there was some kind of fight over the water in the creek, and sometimes it was dry for long periods at a stretch. The chipmunks moved on. Some of the trees started to die, and finally the officials or whoever agreed to let a certain amount of water out of the reservoir at all times."

"How sad," Jessie said.

Luke gave her a smile. "People need to learn to use water like the Navajo."

"Couldn't hurt."

Giselle lifted her head. "Daniel says everybody needs to learn how to live with the land like Indian people do."

"Is that right?" Luke nodded. "Does he still live on the reservation?"

Jessie chuckled. "No way. He'd be miserable."

A minor pluck of annoyance pricked Luke's chest at the fond intimacy of her tone. "Where does he live, then?"

"Albuquerque," Giselle offered. "Just a little ways from us. Sometimes I walk over there after school if Mom is busy."

Luke looked at her, wondering why he should be so bothered by that little tidbit of information. He hadn't seen Daniel in fifteen years—why should Luke care if he lived close to Jessie? Except—

Except he did care. He tucked the knowledge away to examine later, and pulled smoothly into a leveled spot and parked. "We're here."

Jessie leapt out of the truck eagerly. Luke climbed out from his side and helped Giselle down. Jessie, wearing jeans and one of his heavy, sheep-lined jean jackets, waited for them at the back of the truck.

A wind swept off the mountain and tangled in Jessie's hair, and Luke found himself mesmerized by the look of her against the trees and water. There was so much about her that hadn't changed—her thick, long hair and the wide oval of her face—but time had made her a woman. Her hips were sturdier, her thighs and belly not so slim. As a girl, she'd been pretty, with an elusive sorrow in her eyes, but there had been a lack of definition about her then. Newly forged strength of character underlying the still-winsome features gave her a vivid, clear beauty.

He went to stand beside her. In silence, they admired the view. Helen Hunt Falls poured in a rush of noisy silver over a wide shelf of rocks. Around the pool grew pines and aspens, and above rose the mountain, its summit buried in pearl gray mist.

"What an honor to have something so beautiful named for you," Jessie said, and he could tell by the quality of her voice that it still moved her deeply.

Luke glanced at her from the corner of his eye and saw she was close to tears. He smiled to himself. Nothing made Jessie cry—except beauty. Her acute sensitivity to it was what made her such an extraordinary painter—and one of the things he'd found irresistible, once upon a time.

To give her a chance to absorb and manage her reaction, he opened the truck bed and let Tasha out. The dog, excited beyond bearing at the plethora of new scents and the promise of adventure, moaned low in her throat and wiggled and bumped into Jessie's leg, licked her hand, and then licked Giselle's face.

Giselle giggled, pulling back and yet holding on to Tasha's fur.

"Tasha!" Luke said sharply. "Settle down." He managed to get her leash on, but again she wiggled and jumped and moaned in excitement, jumping up to put her enormous paws on Luke's chest and lick his face.

He laughed and scrubbed her neck. "Come on. We'll freeze if we don't keep moving."

At the edge of the pool, they paused to stare at the rush of water singing over the rocks. The falls moved too fast to freeze, but tiny silver icicles had grown on nearby rocks and trees.

"Wow!" Giselle cried. "It looks like a fairy place."

Jessie laughed in delight. "It does!"

A sharp wind gusted toward them from the road, cold as knives. "Let's get walking," Luke urged. "There won't be so much wind higher."

The snow wasn't deep, and the path was designed to accommodate the thousands of tourists who passed through the Pikes Peak Region every year. It climbed at a slow, steady rate, rising higher and higher above the creek. A streamer of cloud detached itself and dropped into the narrow valley, and Luke touched Giselle's shoulder, pointing with his chin to the sight.

"Oh!" she said in a breathy voice, and touched her chest in wonder. "We're above the clouds! Mom!" She grabbed Jessie's hand. "It *is* magic here!"

Jessie smiled, and Luke saw the scene reflected in a pearlescent wash over her face. "It makes me think of Brigadoon," she said to him. "As if some enchanted village will appear at any moment."

"Maybe an enchanted Indian village," he amended, chuckling. "Nobody else around here two hundred years ago."

That seemed to give her pause and she looked around her, as if seeing the scene with new eyes. "I wonder what it was like then."

"Yeah, me, too," Luke said, and grinning. "'Course, it would have been enemy territory in those days."

Tasha tugged hard at the leash, straining to sniff some invisible marker on the trail, and Luke let himself be pulled upward. Giselle skipped ahead.

"Stay close!" Jessie called. "Don't get out of my sight."

"And stay off the rocks," Luke added. They had rotted. The gift shop below had an entire bulletin board filled with newspaper clippings of unwary climbers who'd tackled the rocks in good fun, and fallen. A grim but cautionary testament to the harshness of the mountains.

Walking next to him, Jessie hummed as she looked toward the tops of trees and absorbed the scenery. It was a breathy little sound, some of the notes lost in the lower ranges of her throat, but it tugged Luke's memory. He struggled with it for a moment, but couldn't place the song.

They walked a ways in silence. Luke wanted to hear her talk. He cast about for a subject that would be safe. "Your work must be doing pretty well, if you can threaten gallery owners."

"Yes." She smiled a little shyly. "I'm still surprised every time someone buys something, isn't that silly?"

"Understandable."

She lifted a shoulder. "Maybe. A New York gallery called a few weeks ago—nothing's firm or anything, but they're exploring the possibilities."

"That's great," he said with a smile. "You know, you always had what it took. You just hadn't found your style yet."

"There's always a lot of luck and timing involved, though. I know artists far more talented than I am who aren't selling much."

"Did you stick with portraits?"

Oddly, she blushed, and he remembered Giselle telling him that there was a portrait of Luke in her house. "Some, but they aren't traditional." She blew on her fingers. "What seems to be selling are my paintings of women."

"Like what?"

"There's a series about a midwife that I really enjoyed doing. In fact—" she gave him an impish smile "—you know who I used as my model?"

He shook his head, pleased at the animation lighting her golden eyes. "Tell me."

"Mrs. O'Brien. Do you remember her?" She frowned. "Giselle, not so fast! Wait for us."

Mrs. O'Brien—an Oregon widow who lived nearby the Columbia River. They had worked for her the summer before they came to Colorado. "How could I forget? She made the best biscuits I've ever tasted. I've been trying for years to figure out how she did it."

"I know how," Jessie said teasingly, with a smug toss of her head.

"You cook?"

She rolled her eyes. "That or starve to death. Giselle couldn't grow up on fast food, now, could she?"

"Well, you gotta admit it wasn't one of your strong suits."

She shrugged. "No one ever taught me."

Luke inclined his head in acknowledgment of the subtle reference to her mother.

He cleared his throat, unwilling to delve into anything gloomy this afternoon, not when the ease between them was so sweet. "I like the idea of Mrs. O'Brien as a midwife."

"She was perfect, Luke." Unconsciously, he was sure, she touched his arm, leaning close in her eagerness. "There's one of her in an herb garden, with those gnarled hands and cornflower eyes." She flashed a mocking grin. "I haven't sold it yet, even though I've had several offers. Can't seem to let it go right now."

"I remember another one you didn't want to sell—that tiny one of the little girl we saw in Tijuana?" He eyed

Giselle's back and tipped sideways to keep her in sight as she disappeared around a curve. "Not so fast, Giselle!"

"I sold that when I went to Albuquerque. It tided me over."

That gave him a pang. Idly, he tapped the tobacco in his jacket pocket. "So what other kind of women do you paint?"

She gave him an uncertain look. "Are you really sure you want to hear this? Most people find descriptions of paintings pretty boring."

"You forget, Jessie, I was your number-one fan a long time before anybody else realized how good you were."

Her gaze didn't stray, but he saw a flicker of something oddly stricken cross her face. "I didn't forget." With a little shrug, not looking at him, she said quietly, "I'm pretty sure there would have been no paintings at all if it hadn't been for you."

He touched her hand on his arm. "So tell me about them."

She looked at him, then back toward the upsloping path. "Well, I just sold a group called 'Canning Time.' It's kind of a historical feeling, I guess—the thirties. Four women doing all kinds of things in a kitchen—getting the fruit, washing it, laughing."

"I'd really like to see them."

Suddenly she seemed to realize how intimate they'd become, walking close on the snowy path, enveloped by the silence of the winter day. She snatched her hand back and slipped it deep into the pocket of her coat. His coat.

Luke let her retreat. In a moment, he heard her breathy hum start up again. This time, the song clicked in. "I'm On Fire." Evidently, he wasn't alone in remembering how it had been between them.

Biting back a grin, he started humming along, loud enough for her to hear. A bright pink splash of color flooded her cheeks. He nudged her gently, chuckling.

She bent her head, but said nothing.

They walked for a long time in the soft gray day. Jessie finally protested that she needed to rest, and they paused at the edge of a wide, high field, blanketed with unbroken snow. Giselle and Tasha raced into the snow, kicking up sprays and tumbling each other into it.

Luke felt the cold air and the brisk walk in his blood as a tingling glow. Next to him, Jessie leaned against a pine, laughing as she watched Giselle. "I should get her a dog," she said. "I had no idea how much she liked them."

"Tasha's not just any dog. She's the greatest dog I've ever had."

"Really?" Jessie grinned up at him, cocking her head. A fall of hair rippled down her arms. "What about Boris?"

"Yeah, Boris was great, too." He rubbed his cold nose with cold fingers, thinking of the shepherd that had accompanied him on his wanderings for ten years. Every night for three weeks after Jessie left him, Boris had paced the house and howled mournfully.

"What happened to him?"

"He was so big, his hips started to go. I had to have him put to sleep. He couldn't walk anymore—I even had to carry him outside to do his business."

She regarded him steadily, a softness of sympathy in her eyes. It struck him all at once that it was *Jessie* standing here next to him. She was smiling gently, as if she wanted to tell him she knew how hard that had been for him, that she knew he'd wept privately when he buried his dog. She was the only one he'd ever let close enough to see that weakness in him. Embarrassed, he glanced away.

Overhead, an enormous blue jay—a camp robber—claimed a branch. With a flurry of wings and noisy straightening, he harangued the intruders, screeching at them like a fishwife to get out of his territory. Jessie laughed.

"You still like those evil creatures?" Luke asked.

"Yes, I do." She grinned. "They're sassy and strong."

Drawn by her grin, he stepped closer and then paused. All at once, the tumult of emotions that had risen at the surprises of the past day dropped away. Left in its place was a calm, sharp desire—a hunger that had never ceased, not in eight years; a need that still thrummed through him, like the eternal sound of drums in a heartbeat. He wanted her. Plain. Simple. Clear.

He licked his lip. "You're a blue jay," he said, touching the array of bracelets on her wrist and then the earrings winking through her hair.

"Am I?"

Earlier, she had kept up walls of fear between them when he stood this close. Now there was nothing, only Luke and Jessie the way they'd always been. Before she could protest, he bent and brushed a kiss over her cold lips.

The contact sent a zinging rush over his nerves. In the tiny second it took, he felt the slight dryness of her chapped lips and a hint of the warm moisture beyond. Her hair brushed his cheek, and her chin jutted up a little so she could meet him halfway.

He lifted his eyes to meet her surprised gaze. A snowflake caught on her cheek and he brushed at it, feeling his heart thump and his soul swell a little from the headiness of finding something lost. In her eyes he caught a flicker of pain and fierce desire. He winked.

Before she could protest, he quickly stepped away and joined his daughter in the snow.

The walk back took much less time. Jessie felt oddly free and calm as they hiked down. She and Luke didn't speak, but she felt his kiss lingering between them, not quite a promise, not fierce enough to be a threat. He seemed as content as she to simply be quiet.

Back at the truck, Giselle begged to be allowed to ride in the rear with Tasha. Jessie frowned, and Luke shook his head firmly. "Nope—there are tools and all kinds of other junk back there right now. Maybe another time."

Exhausted by the long walk and her romp with Tasha, Giselle looked mutinous. Jessie recognized the expression and stepped forward to gather her into a hug before she fell to pieces. "I think," she said to Luke over her daughter's head, "we have one very tired young lady here."

He returned her smile. "I've got some stew at the house. Some lunch and a nap and she'll be fine."

"I really think we need to go back to the hotel."

"Why would you want to pay good money to eat at a bad restaurant when you can eat my home cooking for nothing?" he said lightly, opening the bed to let Tasha into the truck. "If you want to go back to the hotel after lunch, I'll take you."

Holding her daughter close to her chest, Jessie looked at him. His black, glossy hair was tousled from his play in the snow, and the wind had stung dusky color into his high cheekbones. Tasha leapt into the truck and turned to give an adoring, thankful lick to her master's chin. Luke scrubbed her ruff, smiling fondly.

It was so easy for Luke, Jessie thought. He just opened up and loved things—dogs and cats and cloudy days and little girls. So easy. And they all loved him right back.

Just as Jessie had.

Her silence stretched a long time. Luke seemed to sense her gaze and he turned. Across the snowy ground, with a child of their making and a cold wind between them, they looked at each other. His strongly chiseled face was grave. She hoped hers showed nothing, but was afraid he could still read her all too well.

"Hotel or rabbit stew?" he asked at last.

Jessie couldn't repress the chuckle that rose in her throat. "You didn't tell me it was rabbit."

He slammed the doors closed on the back of the truck and winked. "Tastes just like chicken," he said, tongue-in-cheek.

Jessie inclined her head, thinking with relish of his fragrant stews. "It's been a long time."

"Is that a yes?"

She nodded. "I guess it is."

He grinned, and the expression gave his eyes a devilishly sexy tilt. "Will you show me how to make Mrs. O'Brien's biscuits?"

"I don't know," she said, pretending reluctance. "Maybe her biscuits are one of those things that just needs a woman's touch."

"Maybe. It's worth a try, eh?"

"Sure."

Giselle fell asleep before they had driven out of the canyon. She slumped against Jessie's shoulder. "I am definitely buying this child a dog," Jessie said quietly. "Tasha wore her out—and believe me, that's no small feat. She's like that battery—she just keeps going and going and going. . . ."

Luke glanced at the girl. "She's out cold now." He shook his head and signaled to join the main street out of the canyon. "She's so much like Marcia, it's almost eerie."

"I guess you'll want her to meet Giselle."

A strange expression flickered over his face. "Mmm."

"What?"

He touched his jaw, shifted the truck and glanced in the rearview mirror. "I, uh, already made arrangements. She'll be here this afternoon sometime."

"You had no right do that without my permission."

"I know." He sighed. "I'm sorry. I did it last night when I was feeling so blown away. If you want me to take you to the hotel now, I will. Marcia doesn't know it's you guys—I just told her there was somebody I wanted her to meet."

Jessie stared at him, holding the warm weight of her child against her, and suddenly realized it was not only Jessie who was upset by all this. Luke, too, had to grapple with the demons of the past. "No," she said. "It'll be all right."

He gave her a grateful smile and reached over to touch her hand. "Thanks, Jessie."

All at once she realized how much she had relaxed in his company. He was so damned easy to be around, so easy to talk to. He never seemed to expect anyone to be anything except just what they were.

Alarmed, she moved her hand gently from his and saw a ripple of hurt cross his features. Pressing her lips together, she resolutely turned her face to the window. "It's only fair."

His voice sounded tired as he said, "Fair doesn't have much to do with any of this."

"No," she agreed softly. "I guess it doesn't."

Chapter Five

At Luke's house, he gave Jessie the keys. "I'll get Giselle. Why don't you get the door open?"

"I don't mind, Luke. I carry her all the time."

He shrugged. "I don't."

Jessie moved out of his way, watching as he scooped the child into his arms, shifting so her head fell on his shoulder. In spite of herself, Jessie smiled. Giselle's mouth hung slack and her arms flopped around Luke's shoulders.

As they neared the porch, a small yellow car pulled in front of the house, and a woman got out. Wearing an ivory serape striped with orange, she had ribbons of black hair cloaking her small, slim body, and a face open and mischievous at once.

Marcia.

Jessie glanced at Luke, then back to Marcia, who crossed the yard eagerly.

Marcia caught sight of Luke, with the child draped over his shoulder, then glanced at Jessie. A tangle of emotions crossed her mobile face—surprise, dismay, joy, excitement.

In twenty years, Jessie thought in astonishment, Giselle would look exactly like this woman. Exactly. And Giselle had inherited that same buoyant energy.

"Oh, my God," Marcia cried at last, breaking the silent tableau on the lawn. "Jessie." She shook her head, coming forward to take Jessie's hands in hers. "Daniel didn't tell me it was *you*."

"I'm beginning to think Daniel had an agenda that had nothing to do with the project." Jessie clasped Marcia's small, cold hands in her own, tightly. "It's so good to see you."

"Ditto." She laughed and hugged Jessie fiercely, then moved toward Luke. "She's your daughter?"

Luke turned slightly, nodding. "She's sound asleep right now. I'm gonna lay her down and you can talk to her later."

Bustling forward, Jessie unlocked the door and stepped out of the way. Luke gave her a smile as he moved by, and somehow it lightened her heart a little. She smiled back, brushing the top of Giselle's head as she passed.

Marcia flung off her serape and dropped a big canvas bag on the couch. "I have to get a couple of things from the car," she said, pausing at the door. For a moment, she seemed at a loss for words. "I—Daniel didn't tell me—" She shook her head. "I didn't know you and Luke's old girlfriend were the same person."

Jessie raised an eyebrow. Obviously, Daniel had known all of it. If he knew Marcia and Luke, Jessie and Giselle, there was no way he had not put all the pieces together.

"I think Daniel was pretty careful to make sure none of us figured it out."

Marcia lifted her eyebrows and slipped out the door.

Then she popped back in and gave Jessie another quick, excited hug. "When I was eighteen, I had the most terrible crush on you. I wanted to grow up and be just like you. It broke my heart when you left."

From the archway between the kitchen and living room, Luke spoke in a calm, but very firm voice. "Marcia."

She rolled her eyes, but squeezed Jessie's hand. "Back in a flash."

Jessie turned toward Luke with a grin.

"'She keeps going and going and going,'" Luke said with a shake of his head. "See what I mean?"

Jessie laughed. "Yes."

He gestured toward the kitchen. "Come on. Let's make those biscuits. I'm starving!"

His kitchen seemed to be the heart of his house, Jessie noted as she shed her coat and followed him in. The rest, though warm enough, was rather neat and plain. On the counters in the kitchen were stacks of mail and magazines, a pile of paperback books, a basket of small woodworking tools. By the back door slumped a spare pair of boots. Magnets stuck notes to the fridge, notes scrawled in his large, bold hand—Meet Smith 9 am For Stairs. Buy Stamps!

Reading the notes, Jessie smiled to herself.

"What?" Luke asked, taking down bowls and a canister of flour.

She shifted her smile to include him. "Nothing. Do you have an apron? I can't do this without getting flour all over me."

"Maybe." He pulled open a drawer and dug below a stack of kitchen towels.

It struck Jessie that he was not, like many men, at a disadvantage without a woman to organize his household. "You know, it surprises me that you've never gotten married," she said suddenly.

He gave her the apron he'd found in the drawer and straightened to give her a rakish smile, tossing a thick lock of hair from his forehead. "I've been waitin' for you."

"Oh." She laughed, caught off guard by his teasing. Recovering, she added, "I seem to have that effect on men."

He chuckled as he put the stew on. Marcia came in, carrying a soft leather briefcase. She sat at the table. "Do you all want to talk for a minute? I had news from Daniel this morning."

Luke adjusted the flame under a pot of stew and turned. "Sure."

"What did he say?" Jessie measured flour into a bowl, unconcerned. Daniel treated everything as if it were an urgent issue. It was a method of getting things done, she supposed, but sometimes made him seem like the boy crying wolf.

Marcia opened the briefcase. "The other night, someone slaughtered some of the weavers' sheep."

Jessie looked at Luke. "The blood on my car?"

"My guess."

"They got your car?" Marcia asked with a frown as she riffled through the papers before her to pull out a single sheet. "That makes me uncomfortable. It means somebody knows what we're doing all the time."

"That's what I said this morning. It might be time to pull back a little. That's four or five incidents in just under a week."

Marcia shook her head. "We can't—not just yet. When Daniel called from Dallas this morning, he was worried about the weavers. Before he flew out yesterday, some of them talked to him. They're scared. There's a lot of talk of witches. He's worried everyone is going to pull out of the project."

Luke swore.

"I know. The trouble is, a lot of them were pretty wary of the project to begin with. They were afraid that if they got rich, they'd draw attention to themselves and get witched."

Jessie nodded, remembering some of the early meetings she had attended with Daniel when he'd set the whole thing up. "He seemed to convince most of them, though."

"Ah, hell," Luke groaned, drawing a hand over his face. "Witches?"

"You might not take it seriously, dear heart," Marcia said with raised brows, "but a lot of people still do. And whoever is behind the harassment knows that and is using it. Animals slaughtered and noises on the rooves of hogans—they're trying to scare the weavers off."

"And it's working," Jessie said.

Marcia nodded. "Unfortunately. But I think it's more than that, too. I talked with a grandmother early on and told her how much she could earn—" She shook her head with a rueful smile. "She laughed hysterically. No matter what I said, she didn't believe me. I think that's part of the problem now. They've never really earned what was possible for these rugs. Now they don't believe they can."

"So what now?" Jessie asked, folding her arms.

"Daniel wants to have another big meeting to reassure the weavers that no matter what, they aren't gonna lose. If the dealers won't pay what they should, we're prepared to open galleries of our own."

"That doesn't really address the witch problem, though."

"I know. We're going to lose some of the traditionals no matter what, but maybe if we find this 'witch,' some of the people on the fence will be reassured."

Jessie idly stirred the flour with a fork, pursing her lips as she tried to think of anyone she'd met who might be a likely culprit. She shook her head when no one came to mind. "When is Daniel planning to do this meeting?"

"I don't know. As soon as possible." Marcia glanced toward the window, frowning. "Trouble is, he's stuck in Dallas and doesn't know if he can get away. He's going to call me here tomorrow and let me know what's going on."

"So, in the meantime are we supposed to meet the gallery owner tomorrow?" Luke asked.

"Definitely. Word is, this guy is pretty sympathetic. He might be a big help."

Jessie nodded. "I've heard that, too." Turning toward the waiting bowl of flour, she measured baking powder and salt and stirred them together.

"Wait," Luke said. "You're supposed to be showing me how."

Marcia stood up. "How long till lunch is ready? I'd like to take a quick shower."

"You have time," Luke told her.

When she left, Luke stepped close to Jessie, close enough that she could smell the faintly foresty scent of his skin and feel his warmth along her side. A quiver rippled over her spine. Resolutely, she ignored it and stirred the flour. "The trick to making good biscuits," she advised, "is you can't bother the dough too much."

"Why don't you walk me through it?" he suggested, taking the fork from her hand. "'Teach a man to fish...'"

"And he'll teach his woman to clean it." She grinned. "Next step is the margarine. It has to be cut in, not worked in with your hands. That's what makes the biscuits flaky."

He gave her a quick glance, and Jessie felt the impact of his dark eyes all the way to her toes. Nostalgia again. Or was it? He was still so damned delectable. To avoid that sensual, beautiful face, she focused on his hands. Mistake number two. The long brown fingers were deft and graceful, and Jessie found herself admiring the lean strength of his wrists and the vein that ran down his forearm. In her mind's eye, she saw herself tracing the length of that vein, into the hollow of his palm, saw herself—

Stop it!

Once the margarine and flour had been cut into tiny nuggets, she led him through the stirring. "No more than twenty strokes." When the flour was moistened, she nodded. "Good. Now, the crucial part. You have to knead it, but only just a little."

She watched as he dipped his hand in the canister and scattered flour on the counter, then upturned the bowl with the slightly sticky dough. With the heel of his palm, he folded the ball over itself, kneading with sure, strong movements. "How do I know when to stop?" he asked.

"By feel, really." She reached out and pressed two fingers into the dough. "A little more. It should feel pliant, but firm."

"Ah—like a breast," he said with an evil grin.

Jessie's gaze flew to his hands, and an odd heat seeped through her. Dough made her think of skin anyway, and now, watching his beautiful, strong fingers curve around the plump roundness of the biscuits, the analogy was all too appropriate. Once more, she was assailed with awareness—the heat of his hip so close to hers, the movements of his skillful hands and the glossy fall of his hair around his neck.

Her body tingled and she found herself swaying ever so slightly toward him, awash with a deep, sensual hunger. More than anything—more than food or air—she wanted him, wanted to taste his mouth and touch his hair and feel her body pressed against the hard, long length of him.

"Is this enough?" he asked.

Jolted, she lifted her eyes and found him gazing down at her with a faintly amused expression around his lips. *Get real, Jessie,* she told herself, and taking a breath, tested the dough again. "I think so. Now roll it out about an inch thick, so you have fluffy biscuits."

His eyes crinkled. "Gotcha." Deftly, he cut the dough with a water glass and paused to admire the raw biscuits on their pan. "My mouth is watering already."

"Mine, too." The smell of the herbed stew filled the air. "That doesn't smell like rabbit, though."

He laughed. "It's beef."

"You're a terrible tease," she said, shaking her head.

"No, actually I'm good at it." He dodged to avoid her playful smack on his arm and slid the biscuits into the hot oven. Jessie found her eyes lingering on his long back, found herself remembering. . . .

With a deep breath, she turned away and began to sweep the flour leavings into the empty bowl. She started when Luke stood beside her. "I'll do that," he offered.

"I don't mind."

"Well, can I clean *you* up, then?"

Jessie looked down. Flour clung to her waist and breasts in a perfect intimation of the shapes below. "Honestly," she complained, brushing furiously at her front. "I can't even help without making a mess!"

"Hold on," he said, catching her chin with two floury fingers, "you have some on your face, too."

Jessie went still. Her gaze snagged in the gentle, persistent probe of his own, and she felt the flour dust on his fingers as they slid along her jaw, not at all businesslike. In his eyes was an expression she couldn't identify.

Yes, she could. Her mouth went dry.

In those impossibly dark eyes was a promise of lingering kisses and slow hands and all his opiate sensuality focused entirely upon her. As if to illustrate, his fingers floated higher, caressing the curve of her jaw and the edge of her earlobe. His thumb drifted to the edge of her lower lip and lingered there with a touch as light as a cat's whisker.

In memory and anticipation, Jessie's hips softened. Her breasts tingled and a slow pounding moved in her middle. Luke said nothing, but simply held her gaze for a long time, moving his fingers in whispery caresses over her face.

Then just as slowly, he moved away, leaving Jessie leaning against the counter for support, her heart thrumming with fear and disappointment in equal measures.

Her guard was slipping. If he'd bent to kiss her just then, she would not have had the strength or the will to resist him.

No. That wasn't even close to accurate. Not only would she not have resisted, she'd been dying for that kiss. Had been since this morning. She didn't want just a light, teasing brush of the lips of the sort he'd given in the mountains. She wanted the dark, deep kisses she remembered, the kind that made a woman forget everything she ever thought she knew about men and desire.

The drift of her thoughts hit her with the impact of a snowball in the face. Had she lost her mind already? It had literally taken her years to overcome the loss of Luke Bernali. She could not let it start again. It was too dangerous, too overwhelming for both of them.

Carefully, she untied her apron. "Luke."

He looked up, and all the teasing was gone from his face, leaving behind the raw, harsh planes and a tight mouth. "Don't, Jessie."

"I just think—"

"I already know what you're going to say." A muscle in his jaw tensed. "I don't want to hear it."

"What, are you a mind reader now?"

His eyes narrowed and he lifted a slightly sardonic brow. "You're going to tell me again how this whole thing is driving you crazy, how you can't handle it, how it would be better if we just keep things all smooth and even, right? Pretend nothing ever happened?"

"Luke, I don't want to fight—"

"Yes, you do." His voice was dangerously soft. "You could never just say what you were thinking, just tell me how you felt. It's easier to fight. Maybe you should just be honest with yourself for once."

"What makes you think you have all the answers?" Her hands shook with emotion and she folded them together across her breasts, feeling strangely bare under his sharp, dark gaze. "You always acted like you knew everything there was to know about everything and I was supposed to follow along in your wise footsteps—"

"No," he said, turning away. His eyes closed for an instant and he bent his head. When he spoke, there was deep weariness in his voice. "That was you, Jess. You made me some kind of hero." With a bitter twist of his lips, he looked at her. "Guess I showed you, huh? Made sure you saw my feet of clay."

Jessie stared at him, unwillingly hearing the truth of his words. The moment stretched between them, reverberating with a hundred things, a thousand things—betrayal and sorrow and love. So much love.

On his face was a fierceness—the fierceness he adopted to protect his gentle heart, a heart she had once known so well and had vowed to help protect. Instead, she'd learned the same old lesson over again. Not even love could save someone bent on destroying himself.

She backed away. "I don't think you'll ever know how much I loved you, Luke," she said in a bloodless voice. "I don't think you could."

Before she could completely humiliate herself, she fled the kitchen.

Luke didn't know where she went. The front door slammed, and he let her go, straightening the kitchen automatically. He set the table, struggling for his lost sense of balance. When there was no more busywork for his hands, he rolled a cigarette and leaned on the sink to look out the window. Another dark storm was rolling in over the mountains, and by the look of it, he thought there would be snow tonight. He welcomed it. Snow calmed things.

In his chest was a thick, pounding ache. Lower was an entirely different kind of ache, a desire so fierce he didn't know how he could keep it at bay for another twenty-four hours.

He liked women in general, and in general, they liked him. His ease with them was something he had grown up with, like his skill with carpentry and a love of science fiction. But with Jessie, it was always different—it had never been easy or simple or light with her.

No woman had ever affected him the way she did, slipped under his skin and moved there like she belonged in his blood. No woman made him feel like he was fourteen again, so hungry to lie down with her that he couldn't breathe or sleep without thinking of it.

I don't think you'll ever know how much I loved you.

From the door, Marcia spoke. "Did you know she was coming?" As always when they were alone, she spoke Navajo, believing it was her duty to keep her brother fluent in the language of their childhood.

He exhaled and stubbed out his cigarette, shaking his head. "No."

"Must have been quite a shock. Are you okay?"

He looked up. His sister's hair was damp at the edges from her shower, and her mischievous arrangement of features held a sober, concerned expression. "'You see, I am alive,'" he said, quoting an old Navajo blessing.

Marcia smiled in appreciation. "And how does it feel after all this time?"

He touched the knot of unsorted emotions in his chest. "I'll have to get back to you on that."

"Do you want me to leave?" She lifted her brows. "Let you two work all this out on your own?"

"There's no working it out, Marcia. Too much water under the bridge." Even he could hear the deep regret in his voice.

Marcia made a noncommittal noise.

"Don't get any ideas," he said in English. Once he'd been through detox and managed to stay sober for a while, Marcia had urged him repeatedly to see if he could find Jessie and make amends. Wounded and ashamed, he had resisted, accepting the loss of her as his punishment. Now he wondered what might have happened if he had.

Giselle wandered out of the bedroom then, her hair tangled and her eyes sleepy. "Where's my mom?" she asked, looking alarmed.

Luke brushed past Marcia and took Giselle's hand. "She just went out for a walk. She'll be right back, and then we can eat lunch."

The odd wariness in her eyes was so much like Jessie, Luke hugged her close. "Come here, honey. Remember I told you about your Aunt Marcia?" He drew her forward. "This is her."

Another adult might have handled the situation any number of ways, but Marcia instantly knelt and held out her arms. "I'm so happy to meet you!" she exclaimed. "You're my only niece—and do you see how alike we are? Look at your hair! And I bet you have a dimple in your cheek, don't you? Like me!"

Giselle laughed, emerging from her sleepy shyness to fling herself into Marcia's hug. Marcia moved side to side in exuberance. "We're going to have a wonderful time getting to know each other."

She pulled back, and in Navajo said, "Do you know about your grandmother?"

Giselle replied in the same tongue, halting but clear. "My mother didn't know much about her. But that's why she works with the weavers. For my grandmother."

Marcia smiled in satisfaction, smoothing Giselle's hair from her face. "Your mother has done well, sweetheart," she said. "Go wash your face and hands now. We're going to eat in a minute."

She ran off to comply. For a moment, Marcia didn't move as she stared after the girl. Finally she stood and looked at Luke, giving him a big smile. "Pretty neat."

"I agree." He suddenly remembered the biscuits and rushed into the kitchen, rescuing them just in time. "I guess we'll have to eat without Jessie."

"I'm here," she called from the back door.

Her voice, husky for a woman, rasped along Luke's nerves and pooled in his gut. He steeled himself before he turned. It didn't help. Her long hair rippled over her shoulders and arms and back, and her sweater clung sweetly to the curves of her breast and waist. He forced himself to look away.

He put the biscuits in a bowl. "Let's eat."

It was late for lunch. Until the edge had been taken from their appetites, no one had much to say. Once the worst of their hunger was appeased, the conversation turned to general small talk, spurred on by Marcia, who spread her cheerful good nature over the table like a fine cloth, easing the tension between Luke and Jessie with her usual skill. Luke had often thought she would be an outstanding diplomat.

Unlike Luke, she'd never felt an alien in any walk of life. She was adamantly proud of her Navajo roots, of her culture the way it had been taught by their parents, and so felt comfortable on the res. But she had been very small when they came to Colorado, and was equally at home among urban Indians and the various cultures she'd grown up with. He envied her that ease sometimes. At ten, he'd felt like an alien in the Anglo schools. By the time he felt at home there, he hadn't been sure he would ever fit in on the res again.

It wasn't that he was uncomfortable with himself or his roots, just that sometimes there was a schism between his childhood and his adult life, a separation that never quite seemed bridged.

Giselle finished her lunch, but still looked a little weary. "Can I go watch TV for a while?" she asked her mother.

"I don't mind if Luke doesn't," Jessie replied, looking at him for the first time since her walk.

"I don't mind at all. The channel changer is on the lamp table."

"Do you get Nickelodeon?"

He grinned. "Yep. Channel thirty-two, I think."

Giselle nodded. To Marcia, she said, "Would you like to watch with me?"

"I'd love to." With a wink toward the others, she stood up and took Giselle's hand.

Jessie began to clear plates. "Why don't you go in there with them? I'll clean up."

He touched her hand. "No. We can do that in a minute. I'd like to talk to you."

She sank into the chair, brushing the hair away from her face. He waited patiently until she looked at him with her pale topaz eyes, and it was nearly his undoing. Her mouth, so plump and sensual, was set in hard lines, but he could see the vulnerability there, the terror. It irritated him momentarily. "Relax, Jessie. I'm not gonna ravish you or anything."

The dart found home. A flicker of pain touched her eyes, but she simply pressed her lips together.

"Sorry," he said, shoving his bowl out of his way, "none of this is easy."

"I know."

He took a calming breath. "Look, I'm a little worried about the way your car was targeted. I'd feel a lot better if you and Giselle would stay here tonight."

"No."

"It's not for you," he said, and didn't regret the harshness in his voice this time. "I don't want Giselle hurt."

"I know who it's for," she retorted sharply. "That doesn't mean coming here would be any easier for me. Believe me, I can take care of my daughter. I've been doing it for years."

Embarrassed male pride rose in his throat and he felt his chin lift. "Marcia's here as chaperon if that's what you're worried about."

She made an exasperated noise and in a gesture he long remembered, shoved her fingers back through her hair, away from her face. "A little while ago, you asked me to be honest with myself and with you." She dropped her arms on the table, leaning forward to face him squarely. "This is as honest as it gets—I don't want to examine the past. I don't want it coming up at every turn. It's too painful and it was too long ago. If we can't find some way to be in each other's company without all those ghosts, I can't handle it."

"Pax, then," he said. "I don't think I can pretend like I never knew you. That's too hard. But I can promise I won't bring up any of the bad stuff, okay?"

"Nothing. Not good or bad." She swallowed, but her gaze didn't waver. "It isn't the bad stuff that's hard for me."

A swelter of mingled desire and pain rose in him at that. He wanted to reach across the table and grab her hand, press it to his mouth. Instead, he gave her a simple nod. "You'll stay here?"

She studied him, and he watched her thoughts play in kaleidoscopic whirls over the surface of her eyes. Finally she replied, "Yes. It's safer."

Luke fought the smile that threatened, fought the hope her acquiescence gave him. As long as she didn't run away, there was a chance....

He heard his thoughts and mentally swore. What the hell was he thinking? "I'll take you over to get your car."

Chapter Six

When Luke turned on the ignition, the sound of Van Morrison filled the cab, and Jessie couldn't bear the nostalgic emotions it aroused. "Do you mind if we don't listen to that?"

"I thought you liked him." He punched the button to eject the tape.

"I do. Just not right now, okay?"

"No problem."

So it was in silence they traveled. Luke didn't attempt to make small talk, and Jessie was grateful. In the quiet darkness, with thick, fat snowflakes drifting down from a sky made pink with reflected city lights, she felt herself relaxing. On the horizon loomed the mountains, great shadows. She shifted to look up at the sky through the window, watching tree branches pass in a blur. "The light here is so different than anywhere I've ever been," she said softly. "I still think about it—the way it comes through the canyon at Ute Pass on summer evenings and the way the dawn makes the mountains turn pink.''

"I like it when it's been raining." His voice, too, was hushed. One hand drew a sketch in the air as he spoke. "Late afternoon, when the clouds are starting to move on and the sun breaks through—it's the only time you can see there are valleys up there."

"I remember. And evenings last such a long time, soft and gray and forever."

"Yeah."

They pulled into the hotel parking lot. "I had a buddy of mine look the car over and check the engine. He took it to a car wash and got the sheep blood off, too. Should be okay."

"How much do I owe you?"

"Nothing." He pulled up alongside her car. "He owed me a favor."

Jessie put her hand on the door handle. "Thanks. I'll gather up our things and see you back at the house."

He turned off the engine. "I'll help you."

"I can manage, Luke, really." She desperately wanted a few moments alone, away from the lure of him, a few minutes in which she could think.

"I know you *can*," he said with a grin. "Why don't you let me be a gentleman?"

She opened her mouth to voice another protest, but he was already out on his side, slamming the door. So much for a few minutes to think.

A little annoyed, Jessie fell in step beside him. Snow fell around them, swirling in the still night, catching in his dark hair like jewels. As they climbed the steps to the second floor, she noticed their legs moved in perfect harmony, left, right, left. Their feet hit the stairs at the exact same instant, too, as if they were stepping in tune to some unheard rhythm. Deliberately, she double-stepped to break the harmony.

Foolishness. Even without their legs moving in step, she could smell the evocative scent of his skin, an aroma so fraught with associations it was nearly overpowering. And without his scent, she would have to contend with the almost magical beauty of snow in his hair and the perfect angles of his face and the faint quirk of humor on his lips.

She realized she was humming under her breath again. Same song. Flushing, she stopped instantly.

At the door, she dug the key out of her purse, but before she could fit it into the lock, Luke took her arm. Standing close, his body protecting her from the cold, he said, "You know, Jessie, if you really are on fire, all you have to do is say so." With a glitter of teasing in his eyes, he lifted her hand to his lips and pressed his mouth to her palm.

The press of that once-beloved mouth sent a wave of almost overwhelming need through her. Stunned, she stared at him, felt the heat and moisture of his tongue behind his lips, felt the smooth line of his jaw against her fingers.

Then he let her go, took the key from her and opened the door.

Much later, Jessie shifted irritably on the couch for the hundredth time, overheated and restless in the tangled blankets that made her bed. Around her, the house was silent with the sleep of the others. She had no idea how long they'd all been so silent, how long she'd been lying there, filled with memories. Hours.

No matter how she adjusted the pillows or shifted positions, the minute she closed her eyes, all she saw was

Luke against the screen of her imagination. Luke diving into a mountain lake, or dashing into the ocean, or working in the heat of a summer day, his skin gleaming. Luke laughing as he joined her in the shower, or made love to her under the stars in a meadow.

It was much more difficult than she had imagined to lie here in his living room and know, only yards away, he slept in a bed that smelled of him, his hair tousled and his mouth soft in sleep. It would be so easy to get up and go to him, to slip off the twisted gown she wore and crawl below the covers with him, touch him and kiss him gently until he awakened. She knew he would welcome her, that he would turn and pull her close to the heat and elegance of his skin. And then he would kiss her....

With an aggravated sigh, she threw off her blanket and put on her robe. She wasn't going to get any sleep tonight. She remembered there were books in the kitchen. She'd just make a cup of tea and read for a while—all night if necessary. Anything had to be better than this.

Creeping quietly through the sleeping house, she went to the kitchen. The overhead light was a harsh fluorescent, and she groaned as it flickered on. A fat candle sat on the table beside Luke's tobacco and cigarette papers. She reached for the candle, but found the tobacco in her hands instead. With a wave of longing, she lifted the bag to her nose and took a long, hungry whiff.

Alarmed, she put it back down and lit the candle, then flipped off the overhead light. Better.

Her restless sense of arousal began to fade as she heated water and found the mugs and tea. Amid the stacks of books and magazines, she found a promising thriller and settled at the table with the comfort of the very hot tea at her elbow. Her father, an Irish immigrant, had insisted tea could cure almost anything. While there were exceptions, Jessie had found it could come close.

She tried to read, even managed to turn a page or two without having the faintest idea what had transpired on the page. Disappointed, she put the book aside, and her attention fell on the pouch of tobacco again.

She bit her lip. Smoking was a stupid habit. She'd been free for two months. Well, seven weeks. Actually, only three if she counted the cigarette she sneaked at a friend's house.

Progress, though. She was making progress.

Her hand crept of its own accord over the table and caught the bag. She opened it and touched the tobacco inside, a familiar sense of irritation running along her nerves. They'd invented fat-free cream cheese, for heaven's sake—couldn't they come up with a safe cigarette? Like tea, cigarettes didn't disappoint a person. They were there when you needed them.

Too bad they killed you.

Biting her lip, she pulled the pouch open. Dieters were allowed to backslide sometimes. One slice of cheesecake didn't mean the diet had failed. One cigarette, particularly since she would never, ever smoke in front of Giselle again, wouldn't mean she'd failed, either. She took out a paper, trying to remember how Luke rolled them.

A little noise in the other room made her jump, and she dropped everything guiltily, pushing it all away from her. One of the cats raced into the kitchen, chasing a knitted ball, and started when he saw Jessie. She chuckled to herself and bent over to push the ball for the creature.

With a sigh, Jessie picked up the cigarette makings again, shaking her head even as she rolled it. The first one was a little lumpy and strange-looking, so she tore it apart and started over. At least this little quandary had taken

Luke out of her mind. Maybe if she smoked a cigarette, she'd feel more capable of handling the whole situation.

The second one she rolled turned out much better. She held it for a moment, her noble side trying to convince her weak side that she could still turn back. It wasn't too late. This cigarette could be torn apart just as the first one had been, and Jessie would be triumphant over her silly habit once again.

The weak side won. She put it in her mouth and bent over the candle, a kind of giddy excitement filling her. It was so evil—and so good—to smoke.

The cigarette caught and Jessie inhaled, slowly, savoring the sharp, acrid bite of the smoke in her lungs, and blew it out with a gusty sigh of enjoyment.

"Now there's a sound that would curl the Surgeon General's hair."

Jessie choked a little and, coughing, whirled to find Luke standing negligently in the doorway, one arm braced against the arch. His chest and feet were bare, his long legs clad in a pair of black sweats that rode low on his hips. His chest was burnished and brown, his stomach flat. A line of black hair ran down his belly. Dazzled, Jessie stared at him and felt a wave of longing so intense, it nearly made her ill. She told herself it was the cigarette.

The cigarette. She looked at it in her fingers, then back to Luke. "Are you going to scold me and make me put it out?"

"I'd rather take a bone from a pit bull."

"Good." Jessie took another drag, and a familiar wave of dizziness tingled in her veins. "Ah," she said, "now the poisons are kicking in."

He took a mug from the cupboard and made himself a cup of tea from the water still in the kettle. "Something tells me you weren't really ready to give up your bad habit."

She shook her head. "If I could smoke like you do, just a couple of cigarettes a day, I'd never give it up."

"'One man's pleasure is another man's poison,'" he recited, settling across from her.

The unfamiliar toxins made her stomach roll, and she stubbed it out. "That's enough. When I do it, I'm never sure why."

He pointed to the pouch. "Will it bother you if I smoke one?"

She smiled ruefully. "No."

"You couldn't sleep, either, huh?"

"Got tired of trying. Too many changes, too fast, I guess."

"Yeah." Deftly, he scratched his thumbnail over a kitchen match. "I was in there remembering all kinds of things I'd forgotten."

"Like?"

His gaze met hers, then shifted away as he sipped his tea. He inclined his head. "I don't know. Boris. That tent we had. Some of the places we saw...lots of things."

"Me, too," she admitted quietly. In this still, candlelit room, it was somehow natural to remember the good times.

"How's your dad, Jessie?"

She shrugged. "Fine. He got married four or five years ago—has a three-year-old child. I don't see him very much, though."

"Don't you want Giselle to know him?"

Jessie thought about it for a moment. "My father and I went through a lot together," she said. "Now we're like people who were thrown together in a war—we have this shared and painful history that's just easier not to remember. I remind him of my mother, and that's hard for him."

Luke studied her for a moment with that perceptive stillness she found so unnerving. Abruptly, he chuckled. "He sure wanted to kill me at one time, as I recall."

Jessie laughed in agreement. "It wasn't you, exactly. He couldn't believe I'd drop out of college and go wandering all over the country with a carpenter."

"I didn't understand it then," Luke said, "but looking at Giselle, I can see why he wanted you to finish college."

"I know. I understand, too." She frowned and glanced toward the window, where snow gathered in the corners of the little panes. "But it was the right choice for me to drop out. I wanted to paint, and that wasn't something he approved of, either. It wouldn't have happened if it hadn't been for our wandering." She looked at him and heard herself say, "Everything I am now somehow comes from that time."

The conversation was curiously peaceful, a recognition and honoring of the good her time with Luke had given her—but she was suddenly afraid it might lead them down paths she didn't wish to take.

Luke evidently had no wish to take those paths, either. "You know," he said, glancing around his cluttered kitchen, "I'm so settled now that I can't imagine wandering like that anymore. I couldn't do it."

"Me, either."

"We were so young," he mused, then roused himself, tapping the ash from his cigarette. "At least you settled someplace you'd never lived. I haven't left Colorado Springs for years." He lifted his eyebrows quickly, as if the admission embarrassed him. "I never used to be so set in my ways. Now I want my coffee just right in the morning, my newspaper unruffled, and work to start at eight."

Jessie shrugged and leaned her elbows comfortably on the table. "Humans are all creatures of habit. We have to develop routines so that we're free to manage the rest of our lives."

He grinned. "So maybe I'm not an old fuddy-duddy, eh?"

Jessie thought of his farm-fresh eggs and laughed. "Eccentric, maybe, fuddy-duddy, never."

"Eccentric?"

"I thought Giselle was going to get you on the eggs. You still don't buy them in the grocery store?"

Reluctant amusement hung around his mouth. "Hey, I've come a long way. Eggs and chickens, though—can't eat 'em if I think about the poor things all caged up in those factories."

He leaned back in his chair. Jessie found her gaze washing over his long brown torso, catching at that slim line of hair low below his navel. A thickness filled her belly, and she thought of her vision of going to him in his bed.

Alarmed, she stood up, nearly knocking over the chair in her haste. "Guess I'll make another stab at getting some rest. I have a long drive tomorrow."

He carelessly stubbed out his cigarette, watching her. Candlelight flickered yellow over the surface of his liquid eyes. Jessie couldn't move, couldn't even take her eyes from him. It seemed impossible that she had wanted to touch him again—just one more time—and now here he was. If she wanted to, she could reach out and stroke that long muscle in his arm.

He stood up and slowly rounded the table. Her breath caught, and she told herself she should slip away now, make some light excuse and go back to the couch. Her feet expressed the hesitancy, for she found herself backed into the counter as he moved toward her.

"You don't really want to go," he said, as he touched her hair, brushing it away from her face, "any more than I want you to." With one hand, he took her elbow and urged her closer to him. "In there, in my bed, all I could think of was touching you." He captured her hand and put it on his chest. "You want to touch me, too, Jessie. Touch me."

Jessie caught her breath as his thighs touched hers, and almost against her will, her hand splayed open on his chest. "Yes," she whispered, staring at the path her fingers made over his smooth skin. A familiar weakness struck her hips, and she swayed forward to press her forehead into the warmth of his bare torso.

He groaned, abruptly pulling her closer, locking their bodies into full contact. His hands roamed over her back and threaded through her hair, restless and gentle and urgent all at once. Against her cheek, she could hear his heart pounding and she clutched him, touching his back and ribs, renewing her long-stored knowledge. He bent his head and buried his face against her neck. "Oh, God, Jessie. If you knew how many times..."

With a low sound, he tipped up her chin and kissed her. Not gently. Not sweetly. It was the rough, deep kiss of a starved man, and Jessie heard a moan come from her throat as she met the thrust of his tongue, the raw embrace of his lips, the ungentle and ungraceful tangle of mouths too long unmet.

He pressed her against the counter, and through the sweats and her robe, she could feel his arousal, fiercely pressing into her. Something within her broke free in that instant, and she grasped his hips to pull him closer, opening her mouth to the full thrust of his tongue. She drank deeply of his exquisite mouth, feeling like she'd never believed she would feel again, vividly, vibrantly alive.

She found her hands in his hair, on his face, on his arms and back and waist—wherever she could reach him, touch him, *feel* him. As if he could not drink deeply enough, he caught her head in his hands and dipped again, suckling and plunging and tasting. His fingers stabbed through her hair and curled around her ears.

Once Jessie had believed that a single kiss from Luke could put to shame the entire course of another man's lovemaking. She found that hadn't changed. He used his lips and tongue and hands and focused so utterly upon a kiss it nearly—

Suddenly he lifted his head to take a ragged breath, still holding her head between his hands. His eyes blazed, liquid and nearly black in the low light. He stroked her neck and ears, almost roughly, and traced her cheek with the same urgent touch; then he placed another kiss upon her mouth, holding her gaze. "Damn, Jessie," he said in a ragged whisper. "Why did you leave me?"

For a minute, his words didn't sink in. She felt drugged with the feel of him, so long and hard and fierce. Blindly, she shoved him away from her. "You know why." She stumbled away, pushing her hair out of her face. Horrified at the way she'd lost it, she simply stared at him for a minute, trying to catch her breath.

She covered her face with hands that traitorously wanted to pull him back again, consequences be damned. "Luke...this is impossible!" she whispered, desperately. "This is what I was afraid of— We can't start again. We nearly destroyed each other."

He reached for her, taking her arm. "Jessie—"

"No, Luke." She broke away again. "We can't! Think about it. It's not about us anymore. This time we might destroy our child as well. I can't live with that. Can you?"

"Jessie, people grow, change—"

She set her mouth. "Not enough, Luke."

His chin lifted in a display of spurned male pride, but Jessie saw in his eyes the wound her words had delivered. Before she could weaken and make amends, she rushed from the kitchen for the second time that day.

For a stunned moment, Luke didn't move. His body ached with furious arousal. Caught in that chaotic heat, he briefly considered the notion of going after her. He'd follow her and cover her with himself and kiss her until she let go of the walls she erected. She wanted him as badly as he wanted her.

Instead, he blew out the candle with a furious breath and stalked into his room, closing the door firmly against temptation. He went to bed but didn't sleep. His hands burned with the lingering feel of her hair against his fingers. He could smell her perfume on him, taste the flavor of her on his mouth, feel the lingering impression of her unbound breasts against his ribs.

He shifted uncomfortably, wishing his anatomy would get the message—there wasn't going to be any relief tonight. The only thing that made him feel better was that he knew Jessie, too, was shifting and turning in her own thwarted desire. Fair was fair.

She had come undone in his arms, returning his kiss with fervor and hunger, her hands questing.

There were two Jessies, always had been. One was a cautious, careful survivor, wary of entanglements and anything remotely unpredictable. That Jessie was cool-headed, businesslike, no-nonsense.

But there was another Jessie, the one who had dropped out of college to wander with him, the one who crept out of her father's house to seduce him in his tent on the beach under a full moon, the one who had kissed him with such hunger a few moments ago.

He remembered once driving down the coast of California for a visit with her father. It was summertime, ungodly hot, and they'd both been exhausted. Luke suggested they take their lunch down to the ocean and cool off before going on.

They found a secluded spot, but it meant negotiating the rocky slope toward the beach. It was treacherous, steeper than it looked, and the cautious Jessie fretted a little over his safety. She came down behind him, carefully.

A sudden gust of wind swept upward, cool and invigorating. Luke whooped, standing up to feel it on his sweaty body. Behind him, he heard Jessie make the same kind of noise and he looked back.

She stood on a precarious outcropping, her toes curled around a rock. The wind blew so hard, her hair whipped out behind her in a nearly straight line.

"Jessie!" he shouted in warning, but the wind took his words. And as he watched, she suddenly reached down and tugged her blouse over her head and lifted it up in the wind like a flag, closing her eyes to the sun and wind, as if drinking them in. She hung on the ledge in a pair of jean shorts and a scrap of lace. He'd been struck with a sense of her power in that instant, as if the wind and the crashing sea were responding to her, this wildly beautiful woman hanging between sky and earth. On the beach below, they made love with untamed abandon, then laughed at themselves afterward with a sort of sheepish joy.

With a growl, Luke pulled the pillow over his head. He was never going to make it through the next day. She had to get out of his life, or get in it. Living on the edge like this would drive him—

To drink. The words crawled into his mind like a black snake, sinuous and unspeakably evil.

His arousal dissipated instantly. Maybe for once the cautious side of Jessie was right. Maybe she understood things he didn't. Maybe what was between them was so fierce and volatile, it would destroy both of them.

And in the process, it would destroy Giselle.

He couldn't let that happen. He would let it go, let her go. Better empty peace than the rage and pain that had once nearly consumed him—and Jessie, too.

Chapter Seven

In her dream, Jessie was painting a scene from the past—she and Luke in a field in Oregon. She filled her brush with greens and dabbed them on the enormous canvas, but they kept slipping off, falling into puddles on the floor. She looked down at the pools of green around her feet and realized she'd been trying to paint the same thing for a long time. In her dream, she frowned and wondered why she kept trying; she shouldn't be wasting so much time on one painting. There were other subjects she wanted to explore. But almost against her will, she dipped her brush again in the soft green on her palette and tried again.

"Jessie," came Luke's voice into her sleep world.

She stirred, realizing with relief that her dream was just that—only a dream. But just as she realized it, the paint on her brush stuck to the canvas. Eagerly she sketched a watercolor blur for the field, feeling jubilant.

"Jessie, it's time to wake up. We have to get to the meeting."

She opened her eyes. Luke bent over her, his hand warm on her shoulder. "I made you some coffee," he said. "It's right here."

"Okay. I'm awake." She blinked hard to make it true.

A hint of a smile crossed his mouth, and he rubbed her arm. "Coffee is right here," he repeated before he left her.

Groggily, she turned and struggled upright. Gray light fell through the window, and she glared at it with annoyance. Was the sun gone forever? The sun shone three hundred days a year in Colorado. Why was she getting three straight days of clouds?

She reached for the coffee, steaming and sweet and pale with milk. Excellent. She sipped it gingerly, hearing Luke and Giselle and Marcia chatter in the kitchen. A scent of food filled the air.

Jessie didn't want any. She looked at the clock and realized they'd let her sleep until the last possible minute. Grabbing her coffee, she rushed to the bathroom. "I'm going to take a quick shower," she called.

"Towels are in the cupboard," Luke answered.

There was no time for washing her hair. She showered and dug through her clothes, wishing for something stark and plain to wear. There was a tailored white blouse in her closet at home that would have suited her mood this morning. Unfortunately, she was stuck with her usuals— a flowing rayon skirt printed with paisleys and a poet's blouse with full sleeves and a romantic collar.

To compensate for the softness of the clothes, Jessie meticulously applied her makeup—foundation to cover the lines of strain and the dark circles under her eyes, blush to replace the color that had drained away, lipstick to hide her tense mouth. Her hair she pulled into a knot. The well-groomed and severe woman looking back at her from the mirror was not the Jessie Luke had known, was a long way from the instinctive, bohemian girl he'd fallen in love with.

Unfortunately Luke had not changed much at all from the man she'd fallen in love with. His hair gleamed like river water and his face was the perfect advertisement for the outdoor life, not too pretty, not too harsh, undeniably rugged and male. In deference to the meeting, he wore a crisp shirt paired with new jeans—about as dressed up as he ever got. His boots, as ever, were expensive and well-worn; he'd probably been wearing them for five or six years.

He got to his feet when she came into the room and put his coffee cup down on the lamp table. "Ready?"

She nodded. "Giselle, are you sure you're going to be okay?"

"Mom, she's my aunt."

Jessie glanced at Marcia, who gave her an impish smile. "We'll be fine. Don't worry."

Luke gathered the weavings, flung them over his shoulder and settled his hat with the beaded band on his head. "Let's go."

"Do you mind if I drive?" Jessie asked.

He shrugged. "No. I just don't want to be late."

It was a small thing, but it made Jessie feel more in control to drive. Her car didn't smell of forests and there was no blue jay feather on the mirror. The cassette tape was Enya and sounded of Ireland, not Van Morrison and lost days with Luke.

He didn't talk, didn't smoke, didn't move. When she asked for directions, he pointed out the turns, but otherwise just sat there. In the small car, his legs seemed too long, his shoulders too broad. He was tall for a Navajo. Once he'd told her he had a Spanish grandmother, a long way back in the family history, and that was where he'd gotten his size.

At the gallery, Luke took her arm impersonally, opening the door for her to go through first. Jessie murmured her thanks in the same matter-of-fact way.

When the secretary led them into the gallery owner's office, Jessie's heart sunk. Harlan Reeves sat behind a massive mahogany desk, a fit and elegant man in his early sixties. The silvered hair, the English suit, the discreet red tie, all signaled old money and interests. Not the best candidate for support.

But he stood up and rounded the desk, extending a hand. "Hello. You must be the representatives of the weavers' project. Come in. Sit down."

Jessie glanced sideways at Luke to see how he was reacting to the warmth in the man's tone. His face showed no expression.

"I'm glad you were able to come back today," Reeves said, sitting not behind the desk, but in another chair in the small grouping by a warmly curtained window that looked toward Cheyenne mountain. "My granddaughter broke her arm at school yesterday and she needed her grandpa there at the hospital before she'd let them set it."

Jessie smiled, warmed by the admission. "I hope she's all right."

"Oh, she's fine. Just a broken wrist. It happens." Spying the weavings, he reached out. "May I?"

Luke passed them over. "Mary Yazzi wove the first."

Reeves nodded. "I recognize her work at twenty paces. She's a great artist."

Luke unfolded from his stiffly erect position and leaned forward to point out design features he particularly liked. "These wefts are a unique trademark," he said. And to Jessie's surprise, he added, "They were my mother's invention."

Reeves peered over his glasses. "Your mother? Not Rose Bernali?"

Luke grinned. "Yeah."

"Well, I'll be damned. Do you have any of her work?" Reeves asked urgently, the rug in his lap forgotten. "I have a collector willing to pay almost anything you'd ask for them."

"Some, I guess," Luke said with a perplexed frown. "I don't know how I'd feel about selling them. Who is this guy?"

Reeves leaned forward and pressed a button on his desk. "Janet, bring me the Bernali file, will you please?" He leaned back in his chair and gave Luke an expansive smile. "I've been dealing in Indian goods most of my life, and there's probably not a weaver you could name I won't recognize. My grandfather started this business in 1902, when the rich were coming here in droves for the sanitariums." He leaned back and took off his glasses. "Every so often you see something special, a kind of magic or genius no one can ever pinpoint, but everyone agrees it's there. Your mother was one of them."

Luke leaned forward. "Who is the collector?"

"A Denver lawyer. Name's Garcia." Reeves flipped open the file. "He found the first ones at a flea market in Albuquerque, I believe, about ten years ago, and tracked down a few others through a reservation trader. He came to me four or five years ago, and I've helped him locate a couple of others. If I'd known she still had family here, I would have contacted you sooner. Would you be interested in talking with him?"

Luke glanced at Jessie. "I don't think so," he said. "I have a daughter now. That's her only legacy."

"I understand," Reeves replied. "Perhaps she'll inherit the gift." There was no rancor in his tone, and he took the rugs in his hands again. "Shall we discuss terms, then, for these?"

"Mr. Reeves, you need to understand why we're here," Luke said.

Reeves waved a hand. "I know. All the gallery owners know. You want a better price for the weavings or you'll open your own galleries. Am I correct?"

"Yes."

"I support the project," he told them. "I'm willing to do what I can to talk to some of the others around, as well, but you may not have much luck. They *will* call your bluff, so I'd advise following through on the leases for galleries of your own by summer."

"We're willing to deal with studios who will go along with our requests," Jessie said.

He smiled at her. "I'm counting on it. Why don't you leave an invoice with my secretary for these weavings, and I'll look it over."

Jessie felt a little nonplussed at the speed of his agreement, and she glanced at Luke for clues as to what should happen next. He seemed at ease as he got to his feet and held out a hand. "Thank you, Mr. Reeves. We appreciate your support."

"You let me know if you ever change your mind about letting some of your mother's work go, you hear?"

Luke smiled noncommittally.

Jessie added her thanks and collected her bag. As they turned to go, Reeves cleared his throat. "Let me offer a friendly warning, folks."

They both turned back.

"Most of the gallery owners are not taking kindly to this. There are some rumors—" he frowned "—that someone may have hired some thugs to harass members of the project."

Luke touched Jessie's shoulder, as if in protection. It surprised her. "Thanks," he said. "We guessed that might be the case."

"Take care then."

It was as they stepped into the cold from the gallery that Jessie was seized with a wisp of a vision. One moment, she was thinking of the very real danger she had now placed herself and her daughter in. The next moment, her eyes caught on the deep blue of the mountains below their adornment of gray cloud, and she was lost, seeing against that backdrop a clear, compelling picture of a woman.

She narrowed her eyes, still walking with Luke toward the car, but what she saw was Luke's mother bent over her loom. She had Luke's hair, that thick glossy mass, impossibly black and full of light. The face belonged to Marcia and Giselle.

Jessie had seen several pictures of Rose, always looking severely into the camera as if it were an ill-mannered and unfriendly intruder. In those pictures, Jessie always thought of Rose as a mother, then as Giselle's grandmother—a woman from such a different life-style as to be nearly alien.

What she saw against the mountains was Rose as a woman, an artist like Jessie herself, working in the strong Southwestern light of northern Arizona, uncovering a twist in a weft string that had become her trademark.

Absently, Jessie opened the car door, but paused to peer a little longer at the sudden painting in her mind. Half of her saw the brush strokes she would use, saw her hands mixing the oils to form a perfect sienna for the weaver's skin, a color like the wood of a living pine tree, pale brown with hints of warm red blood below.

Luke's voice, quiet as the forest she stared at so intently, swirled into the vision. "What do you see?"

Jessie answered without thinking. "A yellow fire and a baby sleeping . . ."

It was only then she realized she had allowed herself to drift so far. Before she could retreat, however, Luke smiled. "A painting."

She met his eyes. "Yes."

"Good," was all he said before he ducked into the car.

Jessie climbed in beside him, smiling to herself. As she settled into her seat, she bumped his arm and he playfully pushed back. "This car is too small for me."

She looked at him, only inches away in the cold car, and felt an odd thrill. It was *Luke* sitting next to her, her lost, beloved Luke, sober and calm and mature and still so achingly beautiful, he made her dizzy.

Without knowing she would, she leaned forward to kiss him, full on the mouth. She didn't close her eyes, and Luke didn't, either. For a full minute, she pressed her mouth to his and met the dark velvet of his eyes. Jessie felt all the scattered pieces of herself whirl together as she drifted there, lost in his eyes. Lightly, gently, their lips moved together.

His face was grave when she pulled away, and he caught her hand. "Jessie, you were right last night." He swallowed, touching her fingernails with his thumb. "We have to find a way to just be friends. There's too much between us."

She turned her face away, appalled and embarrassed that she'd kissed him so boldly, without any invitation on his part at all, and now he was rejecting the overture.

He tugged on her hand. "I've worked hard to keep things even in my life, Jessie. It's not always easy for me to stay on the wagon, you know?" He paused. "I don't want to lose Giselle the way I lost you."

"I understand," Jessie said, meeting his gaze with as much honesty as she could muster. She squeezed his fingers. "I really do."

He didn't let her go, and Jessie made no move to start the car. They simply sat there, holding hands in the cold. "I'm really glad to see you again, Jessie. I'm glad that through Giselle, there's always gonna be something strong between us, that you won't go away again." He smiled a little sadly. "You were the best friend I ever had."

The admission pierced her and she reached over to hug him. "Oh, me, too, Luke." He hugged her back, fiercely. She bent her head into the shoulder of his jacket. "I can't be sorry any of this has happened."

"No," he whispered, and tightened his arms almost painfully.

After a minute, they parted. Jessie started the car and drove back to Luke's house.

Marcia was on the phone when they came in. Spying Luke and Jessie, she spoke quickly in Navajo, too fast for Jessie to pick up what she said, then hung up.

Luke tossed his coat over a chair. "Was that Daniel?" he asked.

"Yeah." Marcia folded her arms. "How did it go with Reeves?"

"He was great," Jessie said. Shedding her shawl, she found her bag of art supplies and dug out a big sketch pad and a thick-tipped charcoal pencil. Settling on the couch, she added, "He's willing to do whatever it takes to get the project moving."

"Oh, that's great!" Marcia bustled in and sat next to Giselle, who strung beads from a multicolored jumble in a bowl. "That means four galleries that are willing to negotiate at the higher prices." From another shallow dish, Marcia carefully extracted a woven cluster of beads, probably an earring, Jessie thought.

Luke touched Giselle's necklace. "Pretty," he said.

"Marcia told me she has a little beading loom I can have." She lifted the strung beads and held them against her chest. "I like 'em all mixed up like this, don't you?"

His eyes tilted upward with his smile. "Yeah, I do. Will you make me a bracelet to wear?"

Jessie watched as Giselle looked at him a little warily, then wrapped the slender string around his brown wrist. The tiny beads looked fragile against the strong tendons. Jessie felt a deep tug at her heart. "It isn't long enough yet," Giselle said.

Marcia leaned forward. "You have to make sure you leave enough room for it to go over his hand, too. I'll show you how to tie it off when you're ready."

Jessie inclined her head and began to sketch the trio of them idly. Three dark heads and three pairs of graceful hands. Between Luke and Marcia, Giselle looked as if she belonged, the way she never quite belonged to Jessie. The knowledge didn't bring the jealousy she might have expected, but a kind of relief. Jessie had never been Indian, never would be, could never hope to give Giselle more than a cursory pride in being Indian herself.

"So what did Daniel have to say?" Luke asked, taking a chair.

Marcia bent over her shallow dish of beads. "He can't leave Dallas right now. He's been trying to set this meeting up for months, and the gallery owners there have finally agreed to talk to him." Carefully, she speared two beads on her needle and slid them into place. "He wants me to take the meeting in Shiprock, but I've got to go back to work tomorrow." She lifted her eyes. "He wants to know if one of you will go to Shiprock."

Jessie and Luke answered together. "I can't."

Luke gestured for Jessie to go first. She frowned. "Marcia, there's nothing I can say to those women. I don't have the right to say anything to them, and I also don't speak Navajo."

"Daniel told me you can, but you won't," Marcia answered with a grin. "Anyway, Luke does," she said, delicately shifting the earring in her hand.

"But I don't know a damned thing about the project," Luke protested with a scowl. "Surely not enough to lead any kind of meeting with the weavers."

Before the smile spread over Marcia's face, Jessie saw how neatly they'd been trapped. "So, you're going together, eh?"

"No." Luke stood and stalked into the kitchen.

"Marcia," Jessie said, glancing after him, "it would be too hard—there's too much between us."

"I'm open for suggestions," Marcia replied, putting down the beads. "If you have another idea, let's hear it. I just don't want all this work to go down the tubes. If someone doesn't get down there and address the fear of the weavers, there won't be a project left."

Luke spoke from the archway to the kitchen. "So why don't you go? Cancel your appointments and take a few days off?"

"Because I have three big recitals coming up this week and I can't run out on the children. You know that." Her voice was calm, but Jessie heard the annoyance low in her throat. "Sometimes that violin is the only thing of beauty those children have. I won't take it away from them."

Luke sipped his coffee, but Jessie could see the taut way he held his body, could see how the whole idea disturbed him. "I haven't been to the res since I was sixteen."

"You don't have to say anything you don't believe, Luke. You're the son of a weaver, you know the language, you know the way these people think. Jessie knows all the details of the project, she's been working on it since the beginning."

Giselle, looking from one adult to the next, suddenly stood up and looped the beads around Luke's wrist. "Can I go, too?"

Jessie saw how the gentle appeal weakened him, and she spoke up. "We aren't going, Giselle. In fact, we're going to have to get ready to get home or we'll be on the road all night."

"No!" Giselle whirled. "I don't want to go yet!"

"I know you don't," Jessie said, realizing she should have anticipated this resistance. "We'll work everything out, sweetie. I promise."

Giselle burst into tears and flung herself into Luke's lap. "It won't be the same!" she wailed.

Stung, Jessie stared at Luke, who looked back at her with a tight expression on his mouth. She saw her own guilt reflected in his eyes—they'd been so wrapped up in their own lingering emotions that they hadn't given enough consideration to the question about Giselle.

He touched the girl's hair. "You can call me tonight," he said. "Okay? And I'll come down and see you next weekend. I promise. Maybe your mom will let you come to my house on your Christmas break, eh? That's only a few weeks from now."

"I don't want to go home," Giselle whimpered softly. The words were doubly painful in such a mournful, quiet voice.

Marcia stood up and looked at Jessie, cocking her head in the direction of the kitchen. Jessie followed her. Marcia turned and put a hand on Jessie's arm. "I know this is hard for you. It's hard to be with Luke again."

"Marcia, you don't—"

She lifted a hand. "I do. What I want you to think about is how good it would be for Giselle to go there with you both. You've done so well with her, Jessie." Marcia touched Jessie's hair, stroked it softly. "She spoke to me in Dine this morning—that's so good."

"I didn't do that," Jessie said, shaking her head. "Daniel has been teaching her to speak Navajo since she was a baby."

"He told me that you moved to Albuquerque so Giselle would be close to Indian people."

A little thread of irritation passed through Jessie. "Daniel put you up to this, didn't he?" She narrowed her eyes. "He knows I don't like to get involved on this level."

Marcia evaded her gaze. "He does what's best. You know that."

"Best for who?" She flung up a hand. "I don't understand what game he's playing here. I usually talk to him at least once or twice when I'm on one of these trips. This time he's avoiding me."

"I don't know about that part, Jessie," Marcia answered with a shrug. "He seems a little restless when I talk to him, but I don't really know what's going on. Maybe he feels guilty for dabbling in your life like this."

"Maybe." She sighed.

"So what do you say, Jessie? Will you take the meeting if Luke does the talking?"

"Marcia . . ." Jessie could think of no protest, except for the fact that she couldn't bear to be in such close quarters with Luke for so many days. Not without a little breathing room in between. She needed some time to get things into perspective. She closed her eyes. "I can't think."

"Jessie, we need you. You're the only one available who has all the stats for the project. How many trips have you made over the past few months? How many people have you talked to? You can't just throw it all away." Marcia took her hands. "Please?"

Jessie looked at her for a long moment. Then she set her mouth and went to the living room. Giselle had curled onto Luke's lap, her hair spread around her like a silk cocoon. Luke bent his head close to hers and murmured something in a low voice. "Luke," Jessie said.

He looked up.

"If you'll come with me, and do the talking, I'll help you with the stats you need." She swallowed. "It'll give us some time to work things out for Giselle, too."

Luke looked at his daughter. "You want to go?"

"Yes."

He looked back to Jessie. "Okay."

Giselle leapt up and flew across the room. "Thank you, Mommy!" she cried, and burst into tears again as Jessie hugged her.

Holding Giselle close, Jessie met Luke's eyes. It had been hard on the pair of them to meet again, but their pain was nothing in comparison to the confusion Giselle felt. Firmly, Jessie picked up her daughter and crossed the room to Luke. Still holding Giselle, she bent and kissed Luke's glossy head, so Giselle would see her do it. "Thank you," she said.

Giselle bent from Jessie's arms and kissed his head in the same spot. "Thanks, Daddy."

He nodded. "I don't want to leave till morning. Give me some time to get things together."

"Fine with me," Jessie said, and let Giselle climb down.

Chapter Eight

Luke removed his tools and cleaned out the back of his truck, then loaded it with pillows, sleeping bags, extra food, cartons of cigarettes and cans of coffee for gifts. He would follow Jessie to Albuquerque, where they'd spend the night, then they'd drive to Shiprock in his truck. His aim was to make the bed of the truck a comfortable, safe place for Giselle to ride. At the last minute, he settled one of Tasha's favorite blankets in there, too, so Giselle would have some company. A friend had agreed to feed his other pets for a few days and bring in his mail.

He checked the fluids in the engine, the pressure in all four tires and the spare; stashed quarts of oil and transmission fluid under the seat and a five-gallon container of water in the back.

From the back steps, Jessie spoke. "Hey, General, looks as if we're set. Sure you don't want to load in some emergency flares and some snowshoes, just in case?"

Luke smiled reluctantly. "Never know what the weather will do this time of year. I don't want to take chances, especially with Giselle in the car. This way, we could get stranded anywhere and still be okay."

She lightly descended the steps and peered into the back of the truck, chuckling. "Some things never change," she teased, and he reveled in the genuine humor in her eyes. "I used to want to kill you for loading my pack so heavy."

"Made you strong."

"I guess it did. Are you planning to let Giselle ride back here?"

He nodded. "If you don't mind. I thought it would be more fun for her. She can take some books and a radio or something. If she needs anything, she can just tap on the window."

"Looks cozy."

"I used to like it. Marcia and I made up these really elaborate games and waved to everyone on the road when we were kids."

"Did you do it a lot?"

He lifted a shoulder. "About once a month or so, I guess, we drove into Farmington for supplies. Less in the winter."

"Don't you ever miss it?"

"Farmington?" He shook his head. "Not at all."

"I didn't mean Farmington, exactly—just living there, on the land like that. It's so different."

"Have you been there?"

"With Daniel to set up the project."

Daniel again. Luke shrugged. "Maybe I'm not as romantic as he is. I don't miss it."

"It didn't strike me as a particularly romantic place."
Unaccountably, she smiled. "Anyway, I came out to tell
you supper's ready."

"Okay, I think I'm done."

"Sure?" she asked, tongue-in-cheek. "Don't want to
add some parachutes in case we're stranded on a cliff and
have to make our way back to civilization?"

He grabbed her neck from behind. "Enough, woman.
You'll thank me if there's a blizzard."

She just laughed, dancing away from his grip to run
inside ahead of him.

Marcia had put herself in charge of the evening meal.
The scent of pork fat and green chilies and fry bread
filled the kitchen, and the windows were fogged over with
the cooking. The humid, scented air hit Luke's cold face
with a powerful feeling of welcome. As the sound of female voices rose and fell around him, he took off his coat
and muddy boots.

Giselle, wrapped in an apron that swallowed her and
dusted with flour from head to toe, set the table, gig-
gling at something Marcia said. Jessie reached for the
honey, and Marcia used a slotted spoon to take the last
of the fry bread from the skillet, piling it atop a big stack
already on a plate. Against the opposite wall, Nino and
Sylvester watched with deceptively sleepy eyes, tails
swishing.

All at once, an acute homesickness swept over Luke.
This was what his life had been missing, the chatter of
voices in warm supper kitchens and the smell of food
about to be shared with family. Jessie swung around to
deposit the honey bear on the table and caught his eye.
She grinned, unselfconsciously nibbling a piece of fry
bread, and touched Giselle's head, directing the girl to
put the spoons on the other side of the bowls.

To hide his feelings, Luke turned away for a moment, pretending to search his jacket pocket for something. He wanted this—a place to come home to, a woman he loved and children. Lots of children. He wanted four or five. Once upon a time, Jessie had wanted that many, too. Did she still? he wondered.

He glanced over his shoulder, trying to remember how old she was exactly. They were four years apart. He was thirty-six, so she was thirty-two. Plenty of time for more children. For an instant, he had a vision of her nursing a new little one in this warm kitchen. He would make her a rocking chair....

"Earth to Luke," Marcia called, settling at the table. "Come eat while it's hot."

Feeling oddly apart from them, he sat down, bowing his head as Marcia blessed the table. When he looked up, Jessie was looking at him with a piercing gaze. He met it for a brief moment, then reached for the food. Get a clue, he told himself. Get a clue.

She didn't even want to get close enough to kiss him, and he already had her bearing his children. But was it Jessie or Luke who didn't want to get close now? He found he'd lost track of who was moving forward, who was moving back—the scorecard was getting a little black from scratching it out so many times.

The image amused him, and he felt the tension slip from his shoulders as the chili hit his belly. "This is great, Marcia."

"I helped," Giselle asserted.

"So did I," Jessie said with a grin.

He chuckled. Maybe this little family scene wouldn't last. Maybe it wasn't all he wished it could be. But suddenly it didn't matter. He had one child, where a week before he'd had none. Around his table, arranged with gentle harmony, were people he cared about. Tonight, it was enough. "It's good," he said.

After supper, Marcia fetched her violin and played, mainly for Giselle, Luke knew. The violin—and the possibilities it unleashed in the lives of children—was her passion.

And it did seem to have a soothing effect on Giselle. Her sudden panic of this afternoon was gone, and Luke thought she seemed more at peace with the order of things.

He still worried about her, though. It was a pretty big change for such a little girl. Protectively, he held her in his lap for much of the evening, taking pleasure in the smell of her hair and the feel of her lean limbs. When it was time for her to go to bed, Luke volunteered to do the honors.

After a bath and a story, Luke tucked his daughter in and listened to her prayers, which she murmured in Navajo. It was touching, and he felt a new appreciation of the lengths to which Jessie had gone to make sure Giselle had contact with Navajo people.

As he straightened from hugging her, Giselle asked, "Do you think I might really be able to come here at Christmastime?"

"We have to talk about it, honey. Your mom might want to have you with her at Christmas."

Giselle, troubled, nodded. "Couldn't she come, too?"

Luke smiled. "She might have other things to do."

"Maybe you could just marry her and then she'd have to be here all the time."

Life looked so simple through the eyes of a child. He sighed. "I don't think so. But I'll tell you what—I promise I'll see you as often as I can. Okay?"

This was still not a completely satisfactory answer; Luke read the doubt in her eyes. But she was overtaken by a yawn that seemed to chase away any momentary concerns. "Do you think I can ride in the truck with you tomorrow?"

"That's up to your mom. We'll ask her in the morning. Go to sleep now. We have a busy day tomorrow."

When he returned to the kitchen, Marcia had spread papers all over the table—all material related to the project. It was the first time Luke had seen the actual statistics. There were lists of galleries all over Arizona, New Mexico, Colorado, Utah and Texas. A star marked each location at which a representative had appeared, and the response of each was highlighted different colors— green for positive, pink for negative. The pinks were predominant, but he was surprised at the numbers of greens. There was more support for the project than he would have imagined. All in all, he was impressed.

They drank a pot of coffee as they reviewed the paperwork. Luke asked questions, more of which Jessie was able to answer than Marcia. Jessie knew monetary figures, which weavers were more likely to hang tough and which were likely—due to financial pressures or fear of witches—to give up, and who was in charge of which portion of the project.

Daniel was the project's lifeblood. His computerized data bases and spreadsheets unified scattered bits of information and created an order from the chaos of people, issues and geographical distance. Marcia, whom Daniel knew from childhood, had become the main Colorado contact. And Jessie had been with the project from the beginning, when Daniel had come to her for information on the way galleries ran.

At one point, Luke felt his head spinning with the figures. He put the papers aside and rolled a cigarette. "I'm impressed," he said. "Daniel has done a hell of a job."

Jessie stacked various sheets into neat piles. "He's a genius, I swear. There's nothing he doesn't know."

A prick of jealousy stabbed Luke. "How do you know him, anyway?"

"We met at a powwow in Albuquerque— Actually, I mean, I sort of met him a few times before that, but—" She chuckled, and Luke's jealousy increased at the fondness in her tone. "I was very, very pregnant, and I slipped on some spilled pop on the floor." She shook her head with a smile. "Didn't really hurt myself, but once I was down, I was too pregnant to get up again. It was so embarrassing. A little boy tried to help me, but I was so huge and the floor was slippery so he just ended up beside me. We were both laughing our heads off by this time, and that's when Daniel came along."

Marcia hooted and slapped Jessie's arm. "That poor little boy."

"I know—poor thing. But I think he got a kick out of it." She lifted a shoulder. "Anyway, I guess the jolt brought on my labor, and Daniel is the one who drove me to the hospital and called my coach. He hung around until Giselle was born. After that, we just ended up being friends."

Luke glared at the end of his cigarette. About the same time another man had been rescuing his woman at a powwow, Luke had probably been drunk. The knowledge twisted his stomach.

With a stifled yawn, Jessie stood up. "If no one needs the bathroom right away, I'd like to wash my hair."

"Go ahead," Marcia said, glancing at the clock. "I have to be in Denver at eight in the morning. I'm going to turn in soon." She stood to give Jessie a hug. "Just call me if you need anything, okay?"

"I think it's going to work out just fine," Jessie assured her. "Don't worry." She bent down to embrace Marcia fiercely. "It was so good to see you. I'll give Luke my address and phone number. Don't be a stranger, okay?"

"Just try to keep me away from that girl," Marcia said. "Take care."

Jessie left the room, and Luke watched Marcia settle everything back into her soft-sided briefcase. He heard the water whoosh through the pipes as Jessie started her shower, and he had a brief, heated vision of her stepping into the spray, free of the shield of her clothes.

With an annoyed grunt he stubbed out his cigarette.

"You don't have to be jealous of Daniel, Luke," Marcia began.

"I'm not jealous."

"They've had plenty of time to get together, if they were going to."

Luke narrowed his eyes. "You're seeing ghosts, little sister. I'm not the jealous type."

"Whatever you say." She shook her head, smiling, and dropped a kiss to the top of his head. "Good night. Take care of them."

Luke got up to feed the dogs. Outside, the clouds had cleared, leaving behind a sky cold and bright with stars. With a sense of relief, Luke breathed in the crisp air. The dogs crowded around him, licking his hands and making small noises of anticipation. "Sorry it's late, guys. I got sidetracked." He scrubbed Tasha's ears, rubbed Tiny's belly and let Misha kiss his chin. He filled their dishes with food and made sure there was no ice in the water bowl.

When he turned back toward the house, his gaze snagged on the bathroom window. The light was still on. He'd never given much thought to what a neighbor might see through this window at night. It was plain there was no curtain over the frosted glass, and a blurry but undeniably female shadow figure moved against the light.

Jessie.

He told himself to go inside and leave her to her privacy, but his legs made no move. Cloaked by the darkness and silence, he was riveted to the spot, watching her shadow against the glass as she leaned backward to put her head under the light gray shadow of spray. She lifted her arms to thread her hands through her hair. Luke found his gaze fixed on the long, curved line of her throat, and followed it downward to the blurred, rounded shape of her breasts, uptilted with the arch of her back.

Damn.

He shifted uncomfortably, suddenly and urgently aroused. It wasn't that he could see so much—in her clothes her figure was more visible than this. It was the thought that beyond that glass, she was gloriously naked and streaming with water. He wanted to be in there with her, wanted his mouth on those uplifted breasts and the curve of her neck. He wanted to fill his hands with her flesh and fill her up with himself.

Abruptly, she disappeared and Luke frowned, staring intently at the vacant, unbroken span of frosted glass. After a moment, he suddenly realized what had happened—she was finished with her shower.

Appalled, Luke vaulted into motion. He rushed for the back door, tore off his coat and skidded into a chair, breathing heavily. With shaking hands, he rolled a cigarette and had just scratched the match to life when she came into the kitchen.

He'd had no time in his guilty rush to steel himself for the look of her. Without speaking, she took a mug from the cupboard and put a tea bag into it and busied herself with the task before she looked at him.

Her hair, wet and neatly combed away from her freshly scrubbed face, trailed over her tightly belted robe. The robe itself was a plain white terry cloth that effectively hid every inch of her body, and she wore no makeup.

She shouldn't have been so damned sexy.

But his mouth was dry. When she crossed the room to sit at the chair next to him, the scent of soap and her moist skin added to the pressure in his loins. He realized his cigarette burned in his hand unnoticed, and distractedly flicked ashes from the end.

"Luke, I think we should talk about what we're going to do about Giselle."

A hard thudding in his chest made it impossible for him to smoke. He stubbed the cigarette out, trying to keep his eyes from Jessie. "All right," he managed.

He looked at her. It was a mistake. A big mistake. Her robe gaped a little at the neck, and below, her thin cotton gown had stuck to the damp flesh of her breast. Through the fabric he could see a hint of the dark edge of her nipple, a far more vivid detail than he wished to notice.

Without knowing he would do it, he reached for her hand on the table, dragging his gaze from the temptation of her almost bare breast.

"I don't think I can really talk right now, Jessie," he said. Slowly, he moved closer and touched his lips to the smooth edge of her chin.

"Luke," she protested.

He kissed her jaw, tasting the moist freshness of the shower on her skin, and when he found himself teetering unsteadily at the very edge of the chair, he swiftly left it to kneel in front of Jessie, putting his hands on her thighs. The scent of her body enveloped him.

"Luke," she whispered, "I don't think—"

To halt the words, he kissed her. Her mouth was deep and sweet and all too willing, and he groaned at the enfolding softness. He deftly untied the knot of her robe. She made a small, husky sound when the heavy terry cloth parted, and he knew she was as aware as he of the transparency of her gown. Lace in an open weave edged the neck and ran down the front. Luke traced the line of it with one finger and realized she wore nothing at all below.

"God, Jessie, I don't know how you expected me to resist you when you're dressed like this." He stroked her thighs and kissed her neck. "Maybe you didn't want me to."

"Maybe not," she agreed in a whisper, and shifted to touch him. Her mouth fell on his temple, and her fingers restlessly laced through his hair.

Every inch of him thrummed with a passion so vivid he could barely breathe. In an agony of desire, he touched the soft shape of her breast. Unsure of how far she was willing to go, Luke gave her time to pull away if she wanted to, if she wasn't ready. Her nipple pearled against his thumb.

With a deep groan, he pulled her from the chair onto his lap, and Jessie made a sharp, surprised noise at the sudden, intimate contact between them. She cupped his face in her palms, settling closer, letting him pull her tightly against him, not protesting when his hands slipped below her gown to caress the length of her thighs.

She kissed him deeply, with no holds barred, nibbling his lips and suckling his tongue and opening herself to him completely. Luke explored the satiny length of her thighs and—

The awkwardness of the position defeated them both suddenly. Luke fell to one side, catching himself painfully on one elbow, and Jessie tumbled with him, bumping her head on the chair as they went down.

Luke nearly surfaced then, aware that they were not alone in the house, that they were sprawled on the kitchen floor on a cold winter night, that the linoleum was not the most comfortable thing in the world. "Are you all right?" he asked, reaching for her.

"No," she whispered, and touched his lips with the tips of her fingers.

Luke swallowed. Her long white robe protected them from the cold of the floor. Jessie gazed at him with her wide topaz eyes, her lips soft and gently parted, her gown demure and covering nothing. A wave of need stole his reason once more and he found himself bending to kiss her again, to taste that mouth so long lost and so deeply missed.

His hand fell upon her belly, and it was a new shape to him. Surprised, he lifted his head to examine with his eyes as well as his fingers the new, gently rounded shape.

She caught his hands. "Don't—I've never really gotten it back in shape."

Back in shape. Once her flat belly had been a source of pride for her. His child had changed her forever.

The knowledge caught in his throat. Against his will, a vision of another man picking her up when she was too pregnant to stand alone slipped into his mind.

He closed his eyes and thought of that same man driving her to an Albuquerque hospital late at night while hundreds of miles away Luke had no doubt been in some bar, telling lies as he tipped back another shot of tequila.

Shame knifed through him. He eased away from her. "I'm sorry." He shifted and wrapped the edges of her robe around her body, covering her. "I was wrong to start that."

She sat up, clutching the terry around her like a shield. In her eyes, he saw a sharp pain, the same confused and vulnerable expression he'd glimpsed this afternoon, and he cursed himself for his weakness.

Gently, he helped her to her feet, letting go when she stood beside him. "It's not you, Jessie," he said tightly. "I'm an ass and I know it. I'm sorry."

Before he could weaken, he stalked out of the kitchen, taking his conscience and his struggle with him.

Jessie slumped in her chair, stunned and confused. Against her belly and the side of her breast, she could feel the imprint of his fingers, hot places on her cold body. There was a slurry feeling in her legs and a thwarted congestion in her breasts and loins.

She felt like she was going crazy, wanting him and not wanting him, trying to balance the past against the present and the love she still felt for him against the fear that his sobriety would not last. How could she spend the next three or four days with him and pretend to be just his friend? How could she pretend to make room for him in her life as Giselle's father when all she could think about was making love with him?

Suddenly he was back in the doorway.

Jessie spoke from her frustration. "So much for the dramatic exit, huh?"

His jaw tightened. "I forgot that I'm supposed to ask you if Giselle can ride with me to Albuquerque."

She laughed harshly. "That couldn't wait until morning?"

"Jessie—"

"You can't keep doing this to me. I don't know what to think from one minute to the next."

He glared at her. "I already told you I'm sorry. I made a mistake."

"We have to work something out about Giselle, and I don't see how we can if we keep going back and forth like this."

"There's nothing to work out." His voice and face were drained of all expression, but Jessie could feel his agitation, saw him swallow. "We just need some time—" he cleared his throat "—to learn to be friends."

"Time?" She made a noise of derision, and stood up. "Friends? Do you know how much time it took me to get over you? Now here you are again, and I'm supposed to know how to be your friend?" She heard her voice rising and swallowed to calm it. In a fierce near-whisper, she said, "You were more than my best friend, Luke. You were my whole world."

He winced, as if she'd hit him, and for a long time, he stood there without speaking. When he finally spoke, his voice was rough. "There are things you can never pay for, as long as you live. I think of you all alone and so pregnant and—" He bowed his head. "All my life, my father told me not to drink. He showed us the Indians who were drunk in Farmington, so it would scare us, so we'd be ashamed." His face was rigid with the effort of holding back some powerful emotion. Jessie wanted to reach out, but was afraid he would shatter if she did.

He shook his head. "I don't have any words for this. I can't make it right and I can't go back in time. I just have to live with it."

His shame struck her with terrible poignancy. "I didn't want to leave you, Luke. I just didn't know what else to do." She crossed her arms to hide their trembling. "I loved my mother so much, and no matter what I did I couldn't keep her from drinking. I kept thinking if I'd just be really good, maybe she wouldn't have to drink."

"Jessie, you don't have to—"

"Yes, I do." Tears streamed unchecked down her cheeks. It seemed so important to make him understand. "When I found out I was pregnant, I just couldn't bear the thought that Giselle would grow up doing the same thing."

Luke moved abruptly and took her into his arms. "Shh," he whispered into her hair. "I know, Jessie. I never blamed you." In the fine trembling in his body, she felt his emotion. "I missed you and I wanted you, but I never blamed you."

She buried her head in his shoulder and let go of a sorrowful moan. "This is crazy. I feel like I'm on a roller coaster."

"It's the roller coaster that scares me. We've both been through a lot. I'm getting too old for this. I need things to be balanced."

She nodded, wiping ineffectively at her tears.

"Time, Jessie. That's all we really need. A year from now, I'll show up to get Giselle for the weekend and you'll wave as you go out with your new boyfriend."

That scenario struck her as more than a little unlikely, but she grinned at his attempt at humor, anyway. "Good night."

"Good night, Jessie." He hesitated at the door, then turned away again. Jessie wasn't sure whether she was relieved or disappointed.

The feeling was still with her the next morning as she loaded her suitcase into her car.

For one thing, it was damned hard to let Giselle crawl into the truck with Luke, instead of Jessie's car. Everything seemed out of control, out of her reach. A part of her wanted to throw a screaming fit, grab her daughter and run away, far away, from all that had happened. Instead, she gritted her teeth and vowed to find some way to take control of her life once they were back in Albuquerque.

The last thing Luke carried from the house was a box of cassette tapes. Spying it, Jessie came forward. "Let me see what you have."

He popped open the lid, and Jessie riffled through the tapes, reading the labels—some factory-generated, but most in his own hand. She shook her head over the collection. Santana and Bob Seger and Tom Waits mixed with Van Morrison and the Doors. "You have anything at all from, say, the new century?" she asked.

"Are you trying to tell me something?"

Jessie grinned, grabbing the Santana and a Crosby, Stills and Nash she hadn't heard in ages. "Don't try and play any old-fogy music to your daughter."

"What does she like?"

"Michael Jackson and any rap I allow her access to."

"Rap?"

"Rap." Jessie picked out a Jackson Browne, too. "You should see her dance."

He looked pained. "I'm old."

Jessie grinned and took the tapes. "Me, too." She waved. "I'm sure I'll make better time than you will, so I guess I'll just see you in Albuquerque."

"Okay." He snapped the tape box closed. "Drive carefully."

Once she got out on the open road, with the tape player blasting old rock and roll, Jessie found herself taking a long breath of relief. It was the first time in well over a week that she'd been alone in any real sense of the word. The clouds had cleared off, leaving behind a sky the color of a blue jay's feathers. It was something she loved about the Southwest—all that clear, open sky and the sunshine somehow made her feel more cheerful.

Luke rode behind her for some way, but she lost him in the traffic through Pueblo and didn't worry about it. Once she stopped glancing in the rearview mirror for his truck, she was well and truly alone.

She liked the open road, always had. Those days on the road with Luke still counted among the most precious of her life. They'd gone everywhere together, up and down the West coast, into Canada, across the Great Plains and through the South.

It struck her as odd that the one place they never went was Indian country. Not north or south, not anywhere close. They skidded by Montana and the Dakotas, somehow missed Oklahoma, New Mexico and Arizona. And he'd said something about not being on the res for a long time when Marcia originally asked if he'd go down there with Jessie.

She flipped the Santana tape and turned it up a little, nodding in time to "Oy como va" as she tried to remember what he'd told her. She knew the family had returned to the reservation for a year or two after Luke's mother died. He'd been sixteen then. Why hadn't he ever gone back?

With a frown, she remembered with an uncomfortable sense of guilt that once he *had* wanted to go back, just after his father died. It had been a terrible time for him, and he kept pressing Jessie to go with him to the reservation to live for a while. Even now, she had trouble understanding why she had been so adamantly against it. She'd been afraid, afraid that she'd lose him there, lose him to people she didn't know and who wouldn't accept her. Their relationship had been just the two of them for so long....

Jessie blew out a deep breath and wished for a cigarette. In retrospect it was easy to see how lost Luke had been after the death of his father. She had just kept telling herself he'd get through it.

And he had, more or less, by simply drinking it all away.

She didn't kid herself about the drinking. It had lurked for years between them, a sleeping bear in the background, never really dangerous but always waiting. At first, it had made Jessie paranoid—not everyone was like her mother, but that had been, after all, her major experience with alcohol. She tried to be reasonable, to explain away Luke's fondness for beer as part of his trade—he was a construction worker. Wasn't drinking a part of that culture?

But even early in their relationship there had been times, at a party or when he fell prey to the odd dark mood, that he'd seem to lose control, wouldn't quit drinking until she dragged him incoherent to bed. The next day, he would be desperately ill and depressed.

For weeks afterward, he was always so ashamed and contrite that Jessie found herself soothing him, trying to ease the bleakness in his heart. Trying to make it all go away. By reassuring him, she reassured herself. He was just a social drinker who sometimes lost control.

A hundred times since leaving him, she'd berated herself for not reacting to the signs sooner. Maybe if she'd been a little more alert, a little more aware, she might have been able to help him, instead of waiting until it was too late and walking out.

Now they were traveling toward the past in more ways than one. In his truck, they would be together on the road, the way they had been once upon a time before disaster struck. And their journey would take them to Luke's childhood and whatever it was that he thought he'd lost.

What would happen to him then?

And what would happen to Jessie?

Chapter Nine

The trip from Colorado Springs to Albuquerque took a good seven hours under the best of circumstances. Luke figured Jessie, in her small car, would make it in about eight, including a couple of stops for food. In his truck, stable but far from powerful, it was going to take closer to nine, ten if he counted breaks for meals, to let Giselle and Tasha attend to nature and run off some of their restlessness.

Luke thought it was one of the best days of his life so far. He and Giselle talked and talked about everything and nothing. Giselle wanted to know about Luke's parents, and he told her little snippets he remembered, things that would make her laugh and make her think and be proud she had been born to them.

He found himself thinking of his father, as he had been so often the past few days. Jack would have been ashamed at Luke's drinking, but maybe Luke could make up for it by being a good father to this child.

By seven, Giselle was drooping visibly and Luke took pity on her, pulling into a diner outside Sante Fe. "How 'bout some supper, little bit?"

"Yeah!"

He called Jessie to let her know they'd be there soon and ordered hamburgers and soup, coffee for himself and milk for Giselle.

She made a face. "I'd rather have pop."

"Pop will rot your teeth."

"So I'll brush 'em when I get home. We're not far away now."

He raised his eyebrows. "Nice try, but no dice."

She shrugged and fell back against the booth. "I'm gonna be so glad to sleep in my own bed tonight. Do you think Tasha could sleep with me?"

"She's not really used to being in the house at night." He pulled the tobacco from his pocket. "She probably wouldn't like it."

To his surprise, tears welled in Giselle's eyes. "I think she would. Why have a dog if you aren't gonna let her come inside and sleep with you?"

He studied her as he rolled the cigarette. "To love and play with outside."

"I think you're being mean."

Their burgers arrived at that moment, and Luke was glad for the diversion. "Why don't you eat your supper and we'll talk about it later."

With a sigh, she tossed her hair over her shoulders and looked at her plate. "Oh, great," she said with annoyance.

"What?"

"Pickles!" she grumbled with disdain and fastidiously flipped them off with one finger. "I hate pickles. They make everything stink." She gave him a level look. "My mother knows that."

Luke bit back a smile, seeing the telltale signs of exhaustion in her manner. "Is that right?"

Slapping her bun on top of the hamburger, Giselle took an experimental bite. She chewed it with an expression of disgust and swallowed. "Tastes like pickles."

He chuckled.

"Are you laughing at me?" she asked.

"Yes I am, Your Majesty."

"I'm not Your Majesty." She frowned and slumped back against the booth. Below her eyes were circles of exhaustion. "Whatever that means."

Luke signaled for the waitress. "Bring me something to take these out in," he said, indicating their meals. "We're going to have to go."

He bundled up the burgers and bought a couple of small bottles of juice on the way out. As he suspected, Giselle ate and fell promptly asleep.

The working-class neighborhood in Albuquerque was easy enough to find, and Luke parked in front of a small, simple adobe with a courtyard in front. Leaving Giselle in the truck, Luke rang the doorbell. When Jessie answered, he said, "She's out cold. Turn back her bed and I'll carry her in."

The child barely stirred as he lifted her in his arms, just slumped against his chest and sighed deeply. In her room, a little-girl place full of dolls and stuffed animals, he tugged off her shoes and dress and covered her with a heavy quilt.

"Come on in the kitchen," Jessie said to Luke, kissing Giselle's forehead. "I made some cookies and tea."

Luke glanced over his shoulder as he turned out the light. A canopy of stars painted on the ceiling glowed in the dark above Giselle's bed. He grinned at Jessie.

She lifted a shoulder. "It was fun."

The rest of the house was small and open, with soft ledges and cutouts in the walls. He liked it. On the worn couch were piles of pillows in jewel tones, and a multitude of plants crowded the big front window. She gestured him through to the kitchen.

"Wow!" Luke whistled softly at the tangles of flowers growing in the room. Big windows lined one wall, and scarlet and white and peach flowers bloomed in pots of every description. The only flowers he recognized were the geraniums and begonias, but there were dozens of others in a splashy palette of colors. From the ceiling hung vines and coleus, and from the tops of every available surface were strings and tangles of plants. He touched a papery pink flower. "You really have a green thumb."

"This is nothing," she said with a smile. "You should see my studio. It's really out of control." She gestured, oddly formal, for him to sit down at the simple oak table by the window.

"I'd like to," he said. "See your studio, I mean. I'd like to see your paintings."

She shifted her head, neither a yes nor a no. He decided not to push it. He sat down, and an awkward little silence fell between them. The table was set with blue placemats and stoneware mugs and a plate of cookies.

"Tea?" Jessie said.

"Sure." He cleared his throat and looked around.

"I didn't have any herb teas or anything," she said. "I don't drink them."

"This'll be fine."

A blue point Siamese wandered out from below the table to plainly bump Luke's knee. "Hey, there," he said, relieved at the diversion, and scooped him up. The cat purred loudly and instantly.

"That's Blue," Jessie told him, and she smiled a little more naturally. "He's a glutton for affection and he's annoyed with me for going away."

The cat slumped, delirious with joy, and closed his eyes to lean into the fingers on his head. Luke scratched under his chin.

"Is Tasha okay?"

"Yeah. She's in the courtyard." He grinned to himself, thinking of Giselle's collapse at the truck stop. "Giselle wanted Tasha to sleep with her."

"I wouldn't have minded."

He shook his head. "Ah, she was just having a little breakdown. I had the audacity not to know she didn't like pickles."

Jessie laughed, and he found himself letting go of a breath at the natural sound of it. "She's a monster when she's tired. She has two speeds, fast forward and stop. When she hits the collapse point, she's awful."

"I just gathered her up and put her back in the truck. She was asleep in about five seconds flat." He let the cat down and sipped his tea. It was hot and sweet. "Mmm. If I'd known she was that tired, I wouldn't even have bothered to stop."

Jessie shifted, reaching toward another chair, and Luke was struck with the beauty of her hair spilling over her arms and torso. The natural waves were deepened from the braid she'd worn all day, and it struck him that she'd let it down and brushed it out carefully before he got there. A single barrette caught some of it away from her face. When she straightened, a stack of photo albums in her hands, her hair moved with her, as sensual as silk over flesh. He swallowed and sipped his tea.

"I thought you might want to see these," she said and glanced away a little shyly. "They're pictures of Giselle."

He didn't reach for them right away. He wasn't sure he wanted to see them, if he was ready to understand just exactly how much he'd missed. He didn't know if he could manage any more emotion today.

Jessie, sensing his hesitation, looked up with her enormous golden eyes. "Please, Luke. I can't make up for you losing the time, but maybe I can fill some of it in for you."

He studied her and felt his gaze slipping over her face to the tenderness of her lips. A stirring heated his loins. "Tell you what," he said. "Come sit over here and look at them with me, and it's a deal."

She smiled and scooted around, until he could feel her warmth, smell her perfume. Just right. He opened the first book. "Ah, baby pictures."

It wasn't as painful as he thought. In fact, it was somehow cozy to sit next to Jessie in her flower-strewn kitchen, feeling her arm brush his every so often, and see how Giselle had grown. More often he found his attention on the curve of Jessie's cheek than on the photos of a time long gone. His gaze snagged over and over on the delicate silver earring she wore, on the simple curve of her neck, on her hands with their long fingers.

He began to feel restless, smelling her warmth and seeing all the details of her again, so close.

There was only one bad moment. Luke turned a page and found himself face-to-face with a picture of a two-year-old Giselle, laughingly embracing a similarly laughing Daniel. "Damn, he hasn't changed at all," Luke said, thinking the picture made Giselle look like Daniel's child.

"Neither have you, Luke. Not really."

Next to the first picture was another, this one showing Jessie in a pair of shorts, her long legs tanned and gleaming, as she held up a string of trout. Luke wanted to touch the open expression on her face, the trusting smile she was giving the camera, and wondered who'd snapped the shot.

There were a lot more pictures like that in the second book, pictures of the life Luke had missed out on, pictures of Jessie and Giselle on Christmas morning, pictures of Daniel place-holding where Luke might have been.

And yet, not even the jealousy and regret could blunt the growing wish he felt to have her close to him. As she closed the album, her hair brushed his hand and he turned his hand to let it flow over his palm, silky and heavy. A lock caught on his fingers and he hastily withdrew to let it free.

Before she could pick up the third book in the stack, he asked, "Will you show me your studio, Jessie? I'd really like to see the work you've done."

She bent her head and plucked nervously at the edge of a photo album. After a long moment, she said, "All right."

"Is it wrong to ask?"

"No." She seemed about to say something else, but just shook her head as she stood. "This way."

She led him to a room off the kitchen, probably used as a sun porch in other homes. The first thing that struck him was the smell—oil paint and thinner mixed with the moist notes of potted plants. It was peculiarly evocative and piercing—a smell he remembered and had stowed away in some forgotten place in his mind.

Plants crowded the benches along the windows, big and small, flowering and not, hanging from the ceiling and filling little jars lined up on the sills. He chuckled. "You're right about the plants."

She stepped aside, primly folding her hands in front of her. "The paintings are over there, against the wall."

But he didn't move right away. Instead, he stayed where he was, letting her get used to him inside her private sanctuary, giving himself time to absorb the intimacy of the smells and sights in the room. There was a futon against one wall, with a Navajo blanket flung over the back, and he saw by the artlessness of it that the blanket was used more for comfort than decoration. He imagined her sitting here late at night, the blanket around her shoulders, a cup of tea in hand.

A nearly completed painting rested on an easel, one of a woman nursing a child. He stepped forward, drawn by the warmth of the brown flesh tones, the curve of the baby's cheek, the almost audible peace emanating from the painting. "Ah, Jessie," he said quietly and reached out, not touching the work, but brushing his fingers in the air over it.

He saw a soft, pleased smile touch her lips, and a little of the tension left her shoulders. Encouraged, he moved toward the stack of canvases leaning against the wall and knelt before them. Here was the midwife she'd spoken of, and another of a gaggle of young Spanish women, laughing together in a little knot. Emotion filled his throat as he looked at them. There was exquisite detail and mood in the works, a maturing of the raw style he had so admired when she was younger.

Beside him, she gestured with a fluttery movement, sending the bracelets on her arms into a soft clatter. "I seem to always be painting women," she said. "Don't really know why."

"Jessie...oh, honey." He shook his head. "These are beautiful. Even better than I expected." He looked up at her and straightened, intending to tell her more, to tell her exactly what he liked.

But behind her on the wall was the reason she'd been reluctant to bring him here, and it stole the words from him. A painful, sharp pinch touched his chest and he closed his eyes for a minute.

It was a portrait of himself, the painting Giselle must have meant when she told him there was a picture of him in her house. Like all of Jessie's portraits, it had been rendered on a large canvas. It portrayed Luke ten years before, his hair long and caught back in a single braid that slipped over his shoulder as he bent to ruffle the fur of his dog, Boris. So simple. Luke, shirtless and barefoot beneath a pine, playing with a dog he still missed.

But as with all her work, the details and the mood made it powerful. In the paintings of the midwife, he felt the sturdy strength of a woman who'd spent her life tending expertly to the needs of others. In the mother and child, he felt the peace.

In this simple painting of himself was...love. It was in his face, in his hands, in the eyes of the dog—the love of the painter for the man in her work. It wasn't blind love, for there was arrogance on his brow and too much pride in the tilt of his jaw, but it was clear and true and powerful.

I don't think you'll ever know how much I loved you, Luke.

He closed his eyes again, struggling to keep some semblance of control. Until this moment, until he saw her vision of him, Luke had not grasped how much leaving him had cost her. Thick emotion crowded his throat, pressed into his mouth, and he reached for her hand blindly. He pressed her fingers to his lips. "I'm so sorry, Jessie," he whispered.

"I thought painting it would help," she said in a small voice. "But it didn't."

There was only one thing he could do. He tugged her hand and pulled her beloved body close to him, folding her into his arms so he could press his lips to her hair. He held her tight, clinging for the strength she gave him, trying to find some way to breathe again. He tried to speak and could only say her name, over and over, like a prayer.

Jessie wept into his chest, curling her fingers into the flesh of his back with painful force. Luke embraced her, kissing her temple and stroking her hair, aching for all the things that could never be undone, all the days they had lost, all the broken dreams they'd shared. "Jessie," he whispered, touching her chin.

She lifted her face. "You can't imagine how many times I wished you'd just step out of that painting," she said. Her slim fingers traced his jaw. "So many times, Luke. And here you are."

"Here I am." He bent to kiss her, gently brushing her lips, then the tracks of her tears. He kissed the side of her jaw and her eyelids and the end of her nose, asking forgiveness, offering the only healing he knew how to give. She leaned into him, her body ceasing to shudder and tremble, her spine softening under his hands. Her breasts and belly warmed him.

A thundering pounded in his blood, slow and deep. All he had ever really wanted was Jessie, and wood for his hands, and children to love. Once more he drank of her mouth, tasting the lingering sweetness of her tea and a hint of vanilla from the cookies. He curled his hand around the slender column of her neck, sliding his hand below her collar to touch the heat of her shoulder. Their tongues danced and swirled, making him dizzy. Her hands restlessly moved on his back. His knee bumped her thigh and he used the small awkwardness to pull her closer, lacing his legs between hers.

There was thick silence around them, the stillness of deep night and winter. But as Luke began to open the buttons of her blouse, he heard music all through him, the music of the wild ocean that was Jessie mingling with the deep, pounding drums of his blood. Her flesh was soft as doeskin, and he opened his palm over the upper swell of her breast. She swayed a little and clutched his arms, making a soft, warm sound.

Without hurry, he pushed the blouse from her and she let it fall to the floor. Luke found the clasp of her bra and tugged it open, and then her breasts were against his palms, warm and infinitely soft. "Oh, Jessie," he whispered, stroking her. He stopped kissing her for a moment to see her, to give his eyes something to savor.

In the low yellow lamplight, her pale skin took on a sheen of warmth and her hair glittered around her like a shawl. He touched a length of the warm brown mass of it, caught it in his hand and lifted it to his face. "I love your hair," he said. "I worried sometimes that you would have cut it off."

She shook her head. "No."

He raised a hand to curl it around her breast, stroking the rosy aroused tip with his thumb, gauging the fit against his palm. A smoky expression darkened her eyes, and she reached for the buttons on his shirt. "I want you," she whispered.

He didn't want to end up on the floor again, and glanced over her shoulder toward the futon in the corner. A part of him was afraid if he paused, she would have time to think, and would stop and push him away. Another part of him wanted to make sure this was something they did with their heads as well as their hearts.

He took her hand and led her to the futon. "Help me with this," he said, tugging at the foot of it.

But she didn't move. Luke yanked the futon into a bed. Then he straightened, meeting her eyes across the vastness of the mattress. With calm, deliberate movements, he unfastened the buttons of his shirt, then carelessly tossed it aside. He waited, wanting her with a wildness he kept hidden.

In the quiet of the night, she paused, staring at him with an unreadable expression in her eyes. Standing there dressed only in her skirt, her hair only barely cloaking her breasts, she was as powerfully sexy as she'd been that day on the rocks.

Her gaze flickered, straying from his face to lick at his body, and Luke knew that her hunger was as deep as his own. She met his eyes and ceremoniously lifted her arms to remove her bracelets, turning to carefully place them on the windowsill. She turned back and knelt on her side of the bed. She lifted her hand. "Luke."

He dove toward her, snagging her close against his chest. "Touch me, Jessie," he groaned, aching with long dampened hunger.

"Oh, yes," she whispered, as she lifted her hands to stroke his chest and belly, his hips and the outside of his thighs. He cupped the sides of her breasts and suckled her neck.

He gave a hoarse cry when her hands at last circled and freed the buttons on his jeans, setting him free, and he heard a sharp sound of pleasure escape her as he kissed her hard, feeling their teeth click and lips bruise. She stroked him restlessly until there was a fever he could not contain, no more.

Luke made a small, victorious sound as he pressed his face into the velvety texture of her skin—ah, the warmth and silk and shivery tremblings. His passion, leashed for endless days, exploded.

He kissed the hollow of her throat and her chin, suckled the rosy, eager tips of her breasts, tugged up her skirt to stroke the quivering flesh of her inner thighs. A dampness met his questing fingers and impatiently he tugged away her panties to touch her, to make sure she was as impatient as he. At his caress, her breath caught high in her throat and she grabbed his shoulders to pull him up to her.

He went willingly, groaning over the erotic brush of her breasts against his chest, and the eager work of her hands, which freed him from the prison of his jeans. He found the buttons to her skirt and nearly tore it in his haste to get it out of his way.

But then, ah, then they were flesh to flesh. Thighs and bellies and chests, arms and lips and tongues. He kissed her, reckless and uncontrolled and unafraid. Jessie met him with eagerness, making small pleased and hungry noises as her hands moved on his back, on his arms, in his hair. Each time he heard her voice or touched her breast or felt her hair tangling in his fingers, he felt a small explosion of disbelief and joy—it was *Jessie* moving sinuously against him, Jessie who fiercely kissed him and stroked him and urged him to touch her.

He could wait no longer, nor could she. With one fierce thrust, they were joined and cried out in unison at the brilliant shock of it. They went utterly still, as if stunned.

Then together they began to move, and within Luke there was a sense of wholeness and perfection that had little to do with lust and everything to do with spirit. As completion neared, he gathered her as tightly as he was able, tangled them close and prayed wordlessly for things he couldn't name.

Jessie clutched Luke close to her, the rippling aftermath shuddering between them. The polished sleekness of his shoulders rested against the underside of her arms, and his black hair fell over her hands. His lips moved on her neck, against her shoulder, and as their breathing slowed, he began to shift his weight.

"Don't go," she whispered, tightening her hold. "Not yet."

He lifted his head and there was a gleam of amusement in the darkness of his eyes. "I liked that," he said in a low, sexy voice, moving his hips against her. "Let's do it again."

Jessie smiled at the old password. "And again."

"And again." He kissed her quickly, then shifted, holding her close as he rolled to his side. "I'm not going anywhere," he said, "I just don't want to crush you."

He reached for the blanket and tossed it over them. Jessie closed her eyes, absorbing the feel of him so close, so dear after such a long time, and breathed deeply the scent of him. Then, afraid somehow it was an illusion, she opened her eyes.

His face was only inches from her own, harsh and beautiful. "A woman saw the painting of you," she said. "She told me there was no way you were real." With her fingers, she touched the sweep of his intelligent brow, the high brown angle of his cheekbone. "She thought I made you up." He didn't move, just watched her with those rich, dark eyes.

Unwilling to think, wanting only to feel, she moved closer and pressed her mouth to the same path her fingers had taken, feeling the fragility of skin over sharp bone and the brush of his lashes and the strength of his unstubbled jaw.

She had dreamed this so many times, dreamed of just touching his beloved face as she looked at it. He held her loosely, and she bent to kiss his shoulder and the column of his throat and the hard, flat nipples, her hands eagerly absorbing the plane of his belly and the curve of his ribs.

He caught her arms and pulled her up the length of him. She lay on top of him, their legs tangled. With a deeply serious expression, he stroked her face. "Don't hide, Jessie. There's nothing we have to do or say, not about the past or the future." His voice roughened. "I've been waiting too long to let you hide now."

He pulled her face down to his and she kissed him, her lost Luke. If she did not have to think of another time or place, she was free to love him now. Just for tonight.

Chapter Ten

Jessie had no idea how long they stayed there, curled together, not sleeping but speaking little. A long time. His body felt right next to hers, dipping where hers swelled, swelling where hers dipped, so no matter how they moved, their bodies settled into a comfortable fit.

Words were too dangerous. Their hands spoke for them. Jessie wanted to touch him everywhere, wanted to explore his chest and the crook of his elbow and the edge of his ear. She touched his hair and his thighs and his mouth, sometimes using a palm, sometimes her mouth or simply her eyes.

And he spoke in return, learning again the circumference of her wrists and the new shape of her belly, the curve of her hip and the length of her hair.

They kissed, over and over, and Jessie wondered that she never tired of his mouth, his tongue, the click of his teeth against hers, the tickling spray of his hair as it fell forward to brush her cheek.

And at last she again grew aware of the pointed, growing weight of him against her thigh, and his hands began to linger on her breasts. His kiss grew more urgent, and Jessie felt the answering rise of desire in her belly. She moved against him, letting her fingers walk the length of his arousal to let him know she would not mind a second round.

This time, they made love very gently, as if it were the most sacred of rituals. Luke moved with reverence and skill, his mouth and hands plying her most secret places, all the places he had learned in his years with her.

He moved to enter her slowly. When they were joined once again, he paused and grasped her hair in his hands. "Look at me, Jessie," he said in a raw voice.

She opened her eyes to find his dark gaze fixed upon her face. Slowly, he dipped to kiss her and lifted his head again, his hands almost painfully tight in her hair. As he began to move, his gaze did not waver, and Jessie trembled with the intimacy of him moving and staring together. She blinked, and he tightened his hands. "Look at me," he said again.

Her body quivered in warning around him, but his expression didn't change as he paused to kiss her, drawing out the moment as long as he could. She clutched his shoulders, struggling to look at him, and then both of them were out of control, their gazes locked in fierce acknowledgment of the power this joining wrought. Jessie gripped his shoulders and cried out a little, but she rose to his challenge.

She tumbled over the edge, coming apart in his arms. Time and breath paused as he let himself go. Sweaty and exhausted, Luke dropped his head to her shoulder. Jessie held him close, feeling his heart pound against hers, heard their breath tangling.

He kissed her again deeply, so hungrily and desperately Jessie wanted to weep with it, weep for all the beautiful days now lost forever. She gasped, her heart breaking, and touched his hair and his face and found herself trying to draw him closer and closer.

Abruptly, he broke away. Jessie cried out in surprise, feeling suddenly bereft as he grabbed his jeans from the floor and tugged them on in haste.

"Luke," she whispered.

He didn't look at her. "I can't do this."

Jessie clutched the rough wool blanket to her breasts and sat up, shoving her tousled hair away from her face with one hand. "You said till dawn." She gestured toward the window. "It's a long time till then."

He winced, as if some insult had been uttered. "No. It's not me you want." He stabbed a finger toward the painting. "That's the man you want, over there. Alessandro. Some romantic Indian to sweep you away." He lifted a bare, brown shoulder. "You want me now, tonight, but in the morning, you'll push me away because you can't deal with the real McCoy. I thought I could handle it. I can't."

"That's not fair."

"I don't give a damn about fair, Jessie. You've blown a hole the size of the Grand Canyon in my life." His eyes narrowed, his mouth set. "I can't pretend with you. I never could."

"I didn't start this tonight, Luke. You did."

He nodded slowly, hands on his hips, staring at the painting.

Jessie stared at him, aching in every cell in her body. It would probably be best for both of them if this ended here and now, with no lingering tenderness tomorrow. But the truth was, she didn't want him to go. Tugging the blanket around herself, she stood and reached out to touch his face. "Please don't go, Luke."

He stared at her for a long moment. All at once, a low cry came from his throat and he grabbed her roughly. "This is gonna kill me, Jessie," he whispered in her ear. "I can't be in some middle place with you."

She embraced him. Her body trembled with the two prongs of knowledge flooding through her. No man would ever take his place. And yet, she knew she would wish in the morning that this night had never happened. "Just hold me," she whispered, and her trembling grew. She buried her face against his neck. "Please, Luke, just hold me."

He swore, but she felt his resistance give way, felt his arms circle her, felt his hands pull her into the heart of him. Together they curled on the mattress. Only then, held tight against the heat and center of him, did Jessie stop trembling. Tucked into Luke's embrace, she fell asleep.

Dawn crept into the room, still and pale. Luke had not slept, not all night, and he felt the lack in his weary shoulders and grainy eyes.

Against his chest was Jessie, soundly sleeping. He bent his head to the nape of her neck and pressed a kiss to a sliver of bare skin he could find through her hair. It was a light kiss, not meant to disturb, but she shifted ever so slightly, nestling closer. An ache of hunger rose in him, and he found he could not resist combing a handful of hair away from her neck to kiss the vulnerable place below her ear. Again she stirred, just a little.

There wasn't a woman on earth harder to awaken than Jessie. She clung to sleep in the mornings like a baby with a blanket. And he'd always loved the challenge.

This morning, his need to touch her was more than the playful challenge of stirring her awake to her passion, to the sleepy smile she would wear when she finally realized his hands were not her dream. This morning, as dawn crept ever brighter into the room, his touching her was a prayer.

As a child, filled with the stories told beside winter fires, Luke had been terrified of nighttime, when Sun and Changing Woman were out of touch, and the world was no longer in balance.

And so he had welcomed dawn as harmony restored. Sun and earth joined once more, as man and woman were joined, creating balance.

This dawn, he touched the soft breast of his woman. He kissed her shoulder and stroked her long thighs until she moved and turned toward him, open and vulnerable the way she would not be in an hour. He joined with her and felt them blend and balance as Sun crept into the embrace of Changing Woman, the mother from which they'd all sprung.

When they were finished, he held her close, not speaking, then slowly released her and left her in the bed alone, hoping she would feel the chill of his absence.

In the quiet of the flower-bright kitchen, Luke made coffee. As it brewed, he fed Tasha, checked the fluids in the truck and examined the sky. Clouds to the west, which was the direction they were traveling. He checked the store of matches.

By the time he went back inside, Giselle was up, making herself a bowl of cereal. "How come my mom is sleeping in her study?"

"Maybe she wanted to." He got a bowl out for himself and sat down. "Feeling better this morning?"

"I was very tired last night. Sometimes it makes me grouchy."

He chuckled and touched her hair. "Me, too."

From the other room, Luke heard the shower rattle to life. "There's your mom. Good. We need to leave pretty soon."

"Hmm." Giselle stared at her cornflakes for a minute, then looked at Luke. "You know, my mom doesn't usually sleep without any clothes on."

Luke struggled with his expression, wondering what in the world Jessie would want him to say. "Is that right?" he said at last.

"Yeah. She likes to wear these very pretty gowns with lace all over them, which she says I can wear when I get bigger. But she doesn't sleep without them."

Luke concentrated on his food, hoping this line of conversation would just burn itself out.

"You know what I think?" Giselle asked with a coy smile playing around her mischievous mouth.

"What do you think, my little elf?"

"I think you and my mommy were kissing like they do on TV. Without any clothes."

"What are you doing watching stuff like that on TV?"

She widened her eyes. "It's not my fault. It's on commercials all the time."

"I guess it is."

"So, were you?"

"Was I what?"

She sighed. "Kissing my mommy like they do on TV?"

"Giselle," he said, putting down his spoon. "Some things adults do are private."

A grin, filled with teeth of mismatched sizes, blazed across her face. "You were! I knew it."

Jessie came into the kitchen, dressed in jeans and a heavy cotton sweater. "Were what?" she asked.

Luke gave her a warning glance and held up a hand. "Don't ask. This child is a bit too precocious for my taste, if you know what I mean."

"Are you asking about kisses again?" Jessie said, sipping her coffee. "Didn't I tell you it isn't polite to ask people about personal things?"

Giselle looked at her bowl. "Not even my own dad?"

"Nope," Jessie returned. "If people want you to know personal things, they'll tell you."

"Grown-ups are so weird," Giselle said with a sigh. She carried her bowl to the sink. "How are kids supposed to learn anything if nobody tells them anything?"

Jessie chuckled and smacked her daughter's rear with a playful hand. "Nobody said you can't ask questions, just that you can't ask people personal questions about themselves. Go brush your teeth and get ready to go."

Giselle tossed her head. "Okay, but I'm going to have some questions for you later."

"Great. If you do as you're told, you can ask me a million questions."

As Giselle obeyed, Luke chuckled. "What a kid."

"Yeah." Jessie shook her head, then stiffly poured another cup of coffee, her ease gone. "Luke—"

He held up a hand. "I don't want to talk, Jessie. It doesn't help anything." A stab of disappointment sliced through his chest. "Last night never was."

She took a deep breath. Relief, he thought. Looking at her coffee cup, she nodded. "It's best that way."

He ignored that. "Come eat some breakfast. We have a long drive ahead of us."

"Ugh. I hate cereal." She glared at the boxes. "I hate breakfast."

"You can't get your vitamins from coffee," he said with a grin, imitating Giselle, and kicked out a chair. "You have to eat."

She slumped at the table and rubbed her face. "I'm also not fond of all you cheery morning people."

"Poor little owl," he said.

With a roll of her eyes, she pulled the cereal over and poured some into a clean bowl.

"You did pretty well with that line of questioning," he said. "I didn't know what to say."

Jessie glanced over her shoulder, lowering her voice. "I don't know why she's so curious lately, but every time she sees kissing on TV, she wants to know how people get babies."

"She seems so young."

"No, not really. Not to start being curious." She glanced at him. "You can smoke if you want to. There's an ashtray in the drawer by the sink."

"I had one outside already." He leaned forward. "So what do you tell her?"

"The truth. Just depends on the day and how much she's asking. Seems like the easiest way."

He nodded and watched her as she ate. With her hair braided away from her face and no makeup, Jessie looked oddly vulnerable. Her skin, so tender and easily bruised, showed tiny marks from his loving. The sight made him want her all over again. Resolutely, he looked away.

Giselle returned carrying a brush. "I need my hair braided."

"I'll do it," Luke said. "Come here."

"You know how to braid hair?"

He chuckled. "Sure. I used to braid my own all the time."

"I forgot. How come you don't have long hair anymore?"

"For a man it's easier to get work if you don't have long hair." He divided Giselle's hair. "It's easier shorter."

"I like the picture of you with it long," she said, bouncing a little.

"Be still," he said, tugging the hair into a tight weave. "I have to work with people who don't like it, though. You don't want me to starve to death, do you?"

She giggled. "No."

Jessie gave him a small, creaky smile, the first of the morning. In spite of everything, they were so familiar with each other it was hard to maintain distance or walls. He was thankful for that.

He finished Giselle's hair. "We oughta get going."

Jessie washed the bowls and sent Giselle to get her things from her room—a stack of tapes and a radio, a box of crayons and coloring books. In a jar were the beads Marcia had given her, along with a small spool of thread and three slender beading needles. "Okay," she chirped, donning her heavy parka. "Me and Tasha are ready."

In the kitchen, Jessie filled a tall thermos with coffee, bent to give the cat a quick cuddle and joined them. "Me, too."

"Let's do it."

Just that quickly, they were on the road again. Jessie sipped coffee from a plastic cup and stuck her feet under the blast of heat from the vent. That was one good thing about these older trucks, she thought vaguely. Always enough heat. Almost against her will she felt a rush of anticipation—she loved to be on the road in the morning, traveling toward the unknown and unexplored. The open highway held promises of adventure and excitement.

She glanced at Luke, so handsome and rugged in the early morning. If not for Giselle in the back, it would be all too easy to imagine nothing had ever gone wrong between them, that the past eight years had never taken place.

As if he read her mind, he glanced over. "Just like old times, eh?"

"Yes," she admitted. "More or less."

"I'd forgotten how it feels to be on the road." He glanced at the side mirror. "I think I've missed it."

"I've been doing it a lot lately, with all these trips to galleries."

"Do you always take Giselle?"

"No. She'd miss too much school." Uncomfortably, she glanced toward the Zuni mountains and the high gray clouds above them. "I took her to Colorado Springs for sentimental reasons."

He gave her a piercing look and reached across the space between them to brush his fingers over her cheek. "I'm glad."

The tender gesture and the warmth of his fingers brought last night back to her, lush and sensual and overpowering. Throat tight, she shifted away.

Abruptly, he dropped his hand. Shoving the box of tapes toward her over the seat, he said, "Find some music to put on. There are some other tapes in the glove box if you don't find anything you like in this box."

Thankful for the distraction, Jessie riffled through the case. No Van Morrison, thank you very much. Nor Jackson Browne, nor Crosby, Stills, Nash and Young. None of this music would do. It all sounded like the past. "You're hopeless," she said with a sigh.

"I told you I was. Coffee and newspaper at six, work at eight." His smile was rueful. "I'm in a rut."

Shaking her head, Jessie opened the glove box. A spill of papers, tools and cassette tapes, even a couple of paperback books, exploded out, spilling into her lap. It surprised her into laughter, for this, too, was something she'd once teased him about—his tendency to load glove boxes with all kinds of emergency paraphernalia. "Ah, I think I found the parachute, General," she said, shaking her head.

"At least there's a reason for everything in there. I saw the mess in the back seat of your car."

"Touché," Jessie replied without apology. "There are only so many hours in a day. If I get around to cleaning something, it seems silly to waste it on a car."

She dug through the pile of things in her lap, sheaving paper into a stack she slipped back into the glove box.

"Wait," Luke said. "There should be a bag of tobacco under all that stuff. Drag it out for me, will you?"

She dipped her hand into the dark hole again, chuckling to herself. Her fingers encountered something heavy and cold and she drew out a man's heavy silver cuff inlaid with turquoise and coral and abalone. Her heart pinched. Gingerly, she settled it around her wrist. "I can't believe you still have this."

"Well, I do." He pulled a package of cigarette papers from his shirt pocket. "Roll me a cigarette."

"Why is it in your glove box?"

"The tobacco? That's where I keep it."

"No." She lifted her arm, feeling the cool weight of silver against her skin. "The bracelet."

He shrugged. "I wore it one day and took it off to work. How 'bout that cigarette. Please?"

Jessie dropped the subject, but she didn't take the bracelet off as she attempted to roll the cigarette. In her mind's eye, she saw the Oregon meadow of her dream, the meadow she had tried to paint. It was a day torn from the past, a soft summer dawn by the Columbia River. A mist had clung to the firs and dotted Luke's long black braid with silvery beads of moisture. In the woods, blue jays scolded, squirrels chattered and a single deer danced to the edge of the river to drink, until it caught sight of the humans and bounded away again, leaping with exquisite grace over a low fence. Jessie, taking the magical morning to be a sign, gave Luke the bracelet she had purchased at a Seattle street fair. It was a token of the vow she had given him that morning, a vow to love him always.

In her mind, it had been as binding a vow as anything uttered before a priest or clergyman in a church. In her mind, she had married Luke Bernali that day. She knew he'd viewed it the same way.

Now she rolled a cigarette for that same man, in a truck much like the one he had been driving then, the weight of his bracelet on her arm. In agitation, she rolled the paper too tightly around the tobacco and it tore. "I can't do this."

"It's all right," he said quietly. "Don't worry about it."

The gentleness in his tone unnerved her. It told her he, too, remembered that cool morning and the vow she had spoken. She took off the bracelet and threw it into the glove box. "I'll do it."

And, as if rolling a perfect cigarette were all that mattered, Jessie concentrated on doing just that. The paper smooth between her fingers, a pinch of moist tobacco...

"That's right," Luke said. "Now just shake it out so it's even."

She did and managed to smooth the paper around right, too. With a toss of her head, she handed it over. He grinned as he took it, then devilishly offered it back to her. "Maybe you need it worse than I do."

"Don't tempt me," she said darkly. "I'll throw every scrap of tobacco you've got right out the window."

He laughed and scratched a match with his thumbnail, rolling down the window so the smoke would go outside. "Now dig that bracelet out and give it to me."

"I'd rather not."

"I know." His mouth was firm in profile. "But it's mine, and I want to wear it."

"I don't want you to."

"Too bad." Abruptly, he stuck the cigarette in the corner of his mouth and leaned over, snagging the bracelet from the glove box before she could stop him. With a lift of his chin, he cut her a glance and slapped the silver cuff on his wrist. "You've got your painting. I've got my bracelet."

Jessie didn't respond. The mess from the glove box still sat in her lap, and with annoyance, she grabbed a tape without checking to see what it was. She stuffed it in the tape player, then shoved everything back into the glove box the same willy-nilly way she'd found it. Just as she slammed the box closed, music poured into the cab.

"I'm on Fire," by Bruce Springsteen.

Luke roared with laughter. Jessie slumped in her seat and glared out the window. "One of these days, I'm going to strangle you."

"No, you won't." He grabbed her hand and kissed it. "You love me and you know it."

Chapter Eleven

Luke teased her to keep from slipping away, but it was a lost cause. She curled up against the window and pretended to sleep, and he knew it was her way of escaping him. He tried not to mind, tried to tell himself he'd known it was coming and ought to have been prepared. He tried to tell himself—

Yeah, right. He'd been trying to tell himself since she dropped into his life again that it was dangerous to get close. But as usual, his heart overrode his reason. Now he would pay the consequences.

Jessie was simply incapable of letting down her guard completely, of giving her whole self to another person. The damage of her childhood made it so, and all the wishing in the world wouldn't change it.

Irritably, he passed a slow-moving car. Once, he'd been willing to settle for that portion of her heart that she could give, but it had nearly drained him dry. No way he'd do it again.

If she wanted him this time, it had to be on his terms. All or nothing.

As she shifted back and forth, pretending to sleep, he set his jaw and focused on the dry high plains through which they passed, the jutting buttes and carved arroyos, the grayish green clumps of sage and clusters of yucca. There was no essential difference in the landscape itself; from southern Colorado onward, they had passed through the same country.

But slowly, the feeling of the land and the people changed. Not so many ranchers in hats and boots. Not so many crisp, square towns with a single stoplight at the center. More little villages centerpieced with an adobe garage and filling station, often with a rangy-looking dog guarding the step, places where the language spoken would as likely be Spanish as English.

There weren't so many people out, bustling here and there on morning rounds, but Luke knew in the hills there were women cooking and men tinkering and children laughing. Somewhere, music was pouring from a radio up there and the song would be a Spanish ballad.

As they passed through one of the little villages, Luke gave a slow wave to a man crossing the highway and the man waved back, just a raised hand. It gave Luke a curious rush of pleasure. Here, he knew how things were. He knew what to expect.

Giselle banged on the window. Luke glanced in the rearview mirror, and she exaggeratedly rubbed her stomach. Beside her, Tasha popped up, tongue out as she panted.

Luke gave Giselle a nod of acknowledgment and looked at Jessie, reaching over to tap her arm lightly with the backs of his fingers. "Hey, Jess. Time to wake up."

She straightened, blinking, and Luke wondered when she'd passed from pretending to sleep to the real thing. "I think we'll stop in Gallup and get some lunch. Okay with you?"

"Sure." She yawned.

Luke had never spent any time in the reservation border town of Gallup, but it wasn't much different from Farmington, to the north. Neither were large towns, but the streets were thronged on the weekends with Indians come to shop.

This was Saturday. An odd dissonance—equal parts nostalgia, fear and delight—rose in Luke at the familiar sight of bruised pickup trucks and old cars crowded into the parking lots of small shopping centers and restaurants. It was this he'd been half dreading, half anticipating since Marcia suggested he and Jessie come down to lead the meeting. Everywhere were Indian faces, young and old and in-between, keenly familiar in shape and color and arrangement of expression.

As with the little villages on the road, he knew what these people were doing. He saw a youth carrying a toddler wrapped into a round bundle against the chilly wind, and chuckled, thinking of himself and Marcia. A mother strode along the street, dragging a two-wheeled basket half filled with purchases, and behind her trailed a gaggle of stair-stepped sons with new haircuts. Luke recognized the tan marks on the back of their necks.

He smiled to himself, pleased at the warmth it aroused in him, the feeling of belonging. He glanced at Jessie but could read nothing in her face.

Spying a sign for a family restaurant above several blocks of low-slung buildings, Luke made a left turn in the direction of the sign.

And here was another familiar sight. At the doors of bars hung men and women, laughing. Music spilled through the windows. It was not too early to see an older man stumbling with measured concentration toward a truck, his keys in his hand.

Luke saw them and felt a sound go off in his head, a little roar. Throat tight, he forced himself to look only at the road, driving slowly to make sure he saw what was in front of him.

He took a breath and blew it out as they reached the parking lot of the restaurant.

"Are you okay?" Jessie asked.

"Fine," he said and grabbed his jean jacket from the seat. For a minute he didn't know if he wanted the hat or not, but the dithering irritated him and he grabbed it defiantly. He wasn't going to start second-guessing himself here. He'd be himself and let everybody else—Indian and Anglo alike—draw what conclusions they would.

Giselle and Tasha both leapt from the back of the truck, and Luke looked around for a field where he could let Tasha relieve herself. To the side of the building was a waste area, and he leashed the dog. "You two go in and get a seat," he said. "I'll take Tasha to do her business."

Jessie glanced toward the restaurant and turned back, shaking a loose strand of hair from her face. "We'll wait for you."

Surprised, Luke took in the stiffness of her back, the restless swing of her earrings against her neck—and almost teased her about her shyness. Instead, since he'd felt a similar clutch of the feeling over whether to wear his hat, he only nodded. "It will only take a second."

So it was together they went inside, with Giselle between them. The lunchtime crowd was thick. A smell of sizzling meat and onions scented the air, and a small cloud of smoke hung near the back.

As they walked through the room, Luke felt a sense of pride over his beautiful daughter and the woman everyone would assume was his wife, walking so straight with her long braid gleaming in the low light. The deep pleasure he felt at being with them, among these faces that echoed the faces of his childhood, gave him a small shock.

They were seated in a booth near a window. "I'd like coffee," Luke told the hostess as he slid in. "Cream and sugar, please."

"Your waitress will take your order when she has a chance."

"That's fine. Would you tell her I'd like some coffee as soon as she can get it?" He glanced at Jessie with raised eyebrows. She nodded, and he said, "Make it two."

The hostess, a girl not more than twenty, dressed up way too much for such a place, rolled her eyes as if he were a bit thick. "I said she'll take your order when she gets a chance."

He opened his mouth to insist she could relay the message, but Jessie touched his hand. He sighed. "Fine."

When the waitress came, bearing two cups of steaming coffee, they settled on hamburgers all around. "No pickles for the little one," Luke said. Giselle leaned against him with a smile.

Jessie stirred sugar into her coffee. "So, kiddo, are you having a good time back there? Are you bored yet?"

"No, it's fun. Like having my own little house, just me and my dog."

"*Your* dog?" Luke teased, bumping her with his elbow. "You aren't going to steal her away from me, are you?"

Giselle lifted her eyebrows with a grin. "I might. You better be careful. She already loves me. I can tell."

"Oh, yeah?" Luke winked at Jessie. "What makes you think so?"

"She likes to lay on me and lean on my leg and she licks my hand all the time."

"Pretty good signs." More seriously he added, "If you get tired of riding back there, just say the word and you can ride up front with us."

"I would, just to keep you company, but I think Tasha would miss me."

Jessie chuckled. "It's perfectly all right if you want to stay in the back."

In the booth behind Jessie, a chubby toddler suddenly popped over the top of the seat and grabbed Jessie's braid with a gleeful noise. Giselle giggled as her mother turned around, smiling, to loosen the clutch of fierce fingers. "Ow," she said playfully.

The toddler laughed and reached out again, this time for the dangling earrings at her neck. Jessie caught his hand. "Gotcha."

A young teenager caught hold of the baby. "You getting in trouble, Eli?" he said, giving Jessie a flirtatious little smile. "Sorry."

"He's cute."

"Mom," Giselle said, as the baby was lured with a french fry into sitting back down, "I think you should have more babies. They like you."

"Oh, really?" Jessie replied with a grin. "And I think if she's anything like you, one child is enough."

"But I'd like to have a brother. It would be fun."

"Glad you think so."

Listening to this, Luke was assailed with his recurrent vision of Jessie holding Luke's son at her breast, sitting in a rocking chair he made for her. The wish to make it true gave him a pang in his stomach.

To his relief, the food came. As they ate, Luke listened to the rise and fall of the voices around him. It was not the same growling undernote of murmuring voices in the Springs, but a lilting mingling of English and Navajo, a comforting rhythm that fell like music in his ears.

And yet, he didn't know these people. He didn't really belong to them anymore.

Jessie jolted him out of his downward spiral of thoughts. "How do you know Daniel, Luke?"

"We were friends as children. His mother's land was close to ours, sometimes we took the sheep out together." He lifted a shoulder. "I wasn't supposed to hang out with him, though, because he was bad."

"Bad?"

"He was always doing something to start trouble. My dad didn't want me to get a bad reputation."

Jessie gave him a quizzical smile. The light struck her eyes exactly right, setting the pale color ablaze with such beauty, he caught his breath. It annoyed him that Daniel had been Jessie's friend all these years, that Daniel had known of Luke as Giselle's father and had done nothing. "He wasn't always as perfect as he is now."

"Perfect?" She wiped a smear of mustard from her lip. "Are we talking about the same person?"

"You're the one who said he's a genius, not me."

"Oh, there's no doubt about that part. He's smarter than anybody I've ever met." Her pale eyes twinkled. "He's also impatient and wants everything done yesterday, and he has a hard time understanding that the rest of the world has to sleep and eat and doesn't compute figures at warp speed."

Luke lifted his coffee cup, appalled that his emotions were so evident, that Jessie was grinning at him now because she knew he was jealous. But her assessment was surprisingly acute. He found himself returning her smile. "He hasn't changed much then."

"He drives me crazy if I spend too much time with him."

Luke looked at her. Now her face was open, her eyes unshuttered. "I drive you crazy, too," he said deliberately.

"No comment."

All at once, surrounded with the lilt of Indian voices in a city not unlike Farmington, with his lost love sitting calmly across the table from him, Luke felt as if he'd fallen into the twilight zone—into some alternate version of how his life might have been if only he'd made some different choices.

It scared him. He'd been struggling to keep his life on a perfectly even keel for so long that the new influx of emotions stimulated by this place, on top of everything else that had happened the past week, made him want to explode.

Abruptly, he stood up, tossing his napkin down beside his empty plate. "I need to take a walk."

Giselle looked up at him. "Can I go with you?"

He had envisioned himself alone, but the appeal in her sweet face was irresistible. "Ask your mom."

"Go ahead," Jessie said. By the strain around her mouth, Luke could see she didn't want Giselle to go, but in the straightness of her spine, he saw the stubborn pride that would not allow her to admit it. "I'll pay the bill and wait at the truck."

For a moment, he hesitated, thinking he should urge Giselle to stay and keep her mother company. But Jessie wouldn't meet his eyes, and he spun on his heels. Nothing he said would change her mind.

Damn, he thought, rubbing his chest restlessly with the flat of his palm. It was going to be a long three or four days.

Jessie paid the bill, thinking it had been a mistake to agree to this trip. She walked out to the truck, hearing Luke's words to her earlier—*you love me*. The phrase had haunted her for hours.

Now she flung open the truck door and settled on the passenger side, leaving the door open to dangle her feet out and look around her. *You love me*.

She had curled into her corner of the cab and pretended to sleep while they drove, but even with her eyes closed, it was impossible to escape Luke. He hummed along with the music, sometimes breaking into actual words in a tuneless tenor made sweet with his enjoyment. It was one of the little things she had forgotten and now seemed doubly dear—how much he loved to sing along with all his old rock and roll and just how awful he sounded.

Last night he had slipped through all of her defenses, had filled her with himself in ways that went far beyond physical. The essence of him had wafted through her pores and stained her heart once again.

Now she sat in the cab of his truck, enveloped by the scent of him, and looked toward the side street down which they'd traveled—that road to ruin littered with Indians drinking, even so early in the day—and thought of his tuneless hum.

Yes, she loved him.

But loving him was never the question, never had been. Even as she had loaded her meager possessions into her car and disappeared from his life, she had loved him. Even when he was drunk and unbeautiful and unintelligent and all the gentle funniness of his personality disintegrated in drink, she had loved him.

But loving someone didn't mean it would work. No matter how hard she tried to forget it, overcome it, come to terms with it, the fact remained Luke was an alcoholic. It was a permanent condition. He had reformed, or recovered or whatever the current term was, but at any moment, he could fall again.

At any moment.

Living with her mother had shown Jessie just how grueling it could be to wait for that fall. She couldn't face the daily doubt again. Not even for the love of Luke.

But, oh, how she wanted him!

Panic rose in her chest, jolting her heart out of rhythm. She wanted to run. Far away. The only way she had managed to rebuild her life before was by removing herself from Luke's physical presence. This time, because of Giselle, there was no place to go. Forevermore, her life was linked with his because of the child they had borne.

She stared down the side street and watched a steady stream of people move in and out of a corner bar. With a deep sense of sorrow, she thought of the people in there who would be in jail by evening, intoxicated beyond coherence of any sort. She thought of the ones who would be sleeping in alleys and on the streets out of town. She thought of the ones who had died.

And she thought of Luke, who was free now. Who had somehow survived, all on his own. Without her.

She hated this town. Each time she passed through it, it brought out the worst of her co-dependency, her need to keep people from dying. She wanted to station herself on the streets and take car keys away from everyone who had too much to drink, to organize squads of people to find the ones who were going to freeze to death and get them someplace inside.

But most of all, she wanted to be there in the morning, when they weren't drunk anymore, wanted to be there with a kind word to staunch the bleeding wounds to pride and self-respect that were the very worst part of an alcoholic's life. Jessie had understood that even at seven years old. It had been more painful to see how much her mother regretted her actions than it had been to see her drunk.

With a small noise of pain, Jessie buried her face in her hands. She thought she'd made so much progress the past few years, and yet, here she was again, as co-dependent as she'd ever been, aching with a need to fix everything.

And it was this flaw in her personality that made her so terribly, terribly wrong for Luke, who was strong and sober and clean now. He'd fixed himself. And Jessie would likely only lead him back the other way.

Somehow she had to keep him at arm's length, for his sake as much as her own. She had to find new defenses, new ways to keep herself aloof, safe against the assault that Luke brought simply by being.

If she didn't, all the fragile beauty she'd built in her life would be destroyed—and perhaps the fragile balance in

Luke's life would also be destroyed. Neither of them could take the chance.

A blast of wind struck Luke and Giselle as they stepped out the doors, dry and cold. "Button up, kiddo."

"Hey," she said with a giggle, "my mom calls me kiddo."

He took her hand. "You don't want me to call you that?"

"No, it's okay." Her wide, pale eyes were sober. "I like it."

They got Tasha from the back of the truck and started walking. "Is Daniel going to be there, where we're going?"

"No. He's doing something else. That's why we're all going."

"Oh." She pursed her mouth, then looked at him. "You know, him and my mom never kiss like they do on TV."

Luke chuckled. "Is that right?"

Tasha found some wildly fascinating scent and they paused to let her examine it closely. "Really," Giselle said. "My mom never kisses anybody like that."

Luke squeezed her hand gently. "Daniel has been pretty important to you, hasn't he? You like him a lot."

Giselle shrugged once. Her face grew quite still. "Not as much as you," she said.

The simple words told him a lot. Daniel Lynch, his childhood rabble-rousing friend, had been there for both Jessie and Giselle. For a minute, he struggled with the feelings of guilt and sorrow the knowledge aroused, looking around him to get a handle on his emotions.

In a battered grayish truck parked at the side of the road sat a woman in traditional dress, a velveteen blouse and a three-tiered skirt patterned with stars. Her great mass of hair was held in a chignon at the nape of her neck with a child's rubber band, and strings of turquoise weighted her earlobes.

This could be his mother. And that man, standing by the gas pump in his good boots, with a round belly pushing against the buttons of his cheery calico shirt, could be his father.

He looked at Giselle. This, now, was his daughter. All he could do was move forward with her—there was no time or room for regrets or the jealousy so obvious even a seven-year-old wanted to reassure him.

"Daniel was my good friend once. We rode horses together sometimes, and slept outside. Has he taken you camping?"

"Yeah. Taught me to fish, too."

"Good." He squeezed her fingers. "I hope we get a chance to see Daniel while we're in Shiprock. It's been a long time."

"Me, too. My mom said maybe he'll get done with his work and come there when he's finished."

"Maybe he will." Luke whistled quickly to get Tasha's attention as he turned around. "Your mom will wonder where we are. Let's get back."

When they returned, Jessie sat in the front seat of the truck, her feet hanging out the side of the open passenger door. Before he joined her, Luke opened the back to let Giselle and Tasha in, saw them settled and fastened the gate tightly. Then he rounded the truck to Jessie's side. He smelled tobacco and bit back a smile. "Hey."

She looked up, and Luke saw the evidence of recent tears in her eyes. It pierced him—the smell of tobacco and the dampness of her lashes, combined with the stoic set of her lips—and without thinking, he tugged her close, pressing her face into his shoulder.

She tumbled into him, her fingers clutching his arms almost painfully. Luke bent his face to her hair, reveling in the new and yet familiar texture on his cheek. Ah, she was so vulnerable! A swelter of protectiveness and sorrow and hunger rose through him once again. If only he could keep her safe, shield her from anything else ever wounding that fragile and generous soul. He closed his eyes and held her close, his chest so full he could barely breathe.

It was too much. Too many feelings, too many new things to deal with. This was what got him in trouble before. His emotions—too big for his heart—all the sorrow for his father and the full measure of love Jessie could never completely accept had overwhelmed him. He hadn't known what to do with such big feelings. He still didn't know. If Jessie could accept what he offered, there would be a circle, a flow back and forth that was healthy and strong. Without the circle—

Without that give-and-take, his feelings filled him much too full, like now, with her head cradled in his shoulder and her soft hair in his hands and the child they'd made waiting behind them. It made him short of breath.

When he could let her go without sharpness, he eased away. "It's going to be all right, Jessie. Things will work out."

She raised her eyes, and he saw his doubt reflected there.

"We better get back on the road," he said. "Looks like it might snow."

Jessie nodded, not meeting his eyes. He rounded the truck to his side, restlessly rubbing at his chest with the flat of his palm. Yep, it was going to be a long three or four days.

Chapter Twelve

Snow was flying loosely in the gray afternoon by the time they reached Shiprock, hiding the tip of the monolithic stone the Navajos called "the rock with wings."

"Do you know where we're going?" Luke asked.

Jessie directed him through town to a plot of land on the outskirts. It was the home of Mary Yazzie, a middle-aged weaver who had made countless trips over the immense reservation the past few months, trying to gather support for the project. The ranch-style house sat alone and vulnerable-looking in the middle of a wide, empty stretch of desert. A small hogan squatted on one side, facing east. Sheep huddled together in a large pen and a black goat bleated at them from his post atop an overturned washtub.

Parked in front of the house were three trucks and a fairly new-looking Jeep. Around to the side was a faded gold Buick without tires. Luke tapped the horn to announce their arrival as he slid in next to the Jeep, then took a breath. "Well, kid," he said with a wry twist of his lips, "it's showtime."

"You're more nervous about this than I am."

"Nervous isn't the right word." He tapped his hat down on his head. "It's been a long time."

Three dogs, lean and rangy, raced around the house, barking and wagging their tails. Inside the cab, Tasha howled in return. Jessie cast a glance toward the window. "Will she be okay with them?"

"Tasha has never met a dog she didn't like or couldn't bully."

Behind the dogs came a spill of children, mostly girls. From the back of the truck, Giselle said, "Mom, let me out!"

Jessie chuckled. "There's her howl."

"And I don't have to ask if she'll be okay."

"Giselle is always okay."

And she was. Within moments of her emergence from the bed of the truck with Tasha—over whom the children oohed and ahhed, then skittered from in delight— she was enveloped in the bevy of girls. The three boys ran off separately, to no doubt plan some ambush.

A woman came out of the house, wearing jeans and an oversized T-shirt, her long, dark hair caught back in a beaded barrette. She waited on the concrete steps for them to approach, nodding as Jessie greeted her. "This must be Luke Bernali," she said. "I haven't seen him since he was a child, but I would know that face anywhere."

"Yes." Jessie indicated Luke with a wave of her hand. "Luke, this is Mary Yazzie, the one who made the rugs we showed in the Springs."

Luke nodded. "It's good work."

"You have many relatives in this country," Mary said. Her long eyes sparkled. "And you grew to be even more handsome than we said you would."

To Jessie's great astonishment, Luke lowered his head as if embarrassed. Dusky color stained his cheeks.

Mary laughed, making a low sound in her throat, a teasing, "Ahh!"

Jessie nudged him. "You can dish it out, but you can't take it, huh?"

He gave her a rueful grin, then looked back at Mary. "We brought you some things. I'll get them."

Mary waved Jessie in front of her, into the sparsely furnished living room. "Eeeh," Mary said against Jessie's ear, "he's like morning! No wonder Giselle is so pretty."

Jessie chuckled. "And what about me?"

"You know what I mean," Mary said with a laugh. "They don't make too many like him."

The room was filled with women and children, and Jessie nodded to another woman she knew, suddenly feeling her old awkwardness descend. Oh, why couldn't Daniel have been here to do this himself? He was outgoing and he knew everyone. Jessie was shy and out of place no matter where she went, but especially here. She sat down in a place someone made for her, feeling all her words dry in her throat, not knowing where to put her eyes.

When Luke came in, bearing the bags of cigarettes and coffee, a little murmur went up. Two of the older women stood to greet him, talking in Navajo. Jessie only picked up a handful of words in the excited chatter, enough to know they remembered him and were exclaiming in wonder over him. The Navajo didn't speak a dead person's name, but it was evident his mother was well-remembered and respected.

Luke caught her eye across the room and winked, tilting his head to indicate she should come to him. Gladly Jessie joined him. He put a hand on her shoulder and spoke to the women, saying something along the lines of Jessie being the mother of his daughter. The rest was lost in the rising, lilting sound of the words, the clicks and stops Jessie had tried to master and knew she never would. Even saying something as simple as hello could be massacred by Anglo tongues into a completely different meaning. It was no surprise to her that the language had proved to be an unbreakable American code in World War II.

Detaching herself from the knot of grandmothers, Mary touched Jessie's arm. "Let's make coffee."

In the kitchen, Mary nudged her. "Now I know why you've been working so hard."

Jessie smiled, shaking her head. "It's not like that. I didn't even know he was working with the project until I got to the Springs."

Mary gave her the coffeepot. "I'm glad to see you both here. Daniel sent word things are going good for him in Dallas. He thinks maybe he can get away by late tomorrow night, but you should go ahead with the meeting in case he can't. Luke will talk?"

Jessie nodded, watching Luke through the open doorway to the other room. His apprehension seemed to be fading as he laughed with the grandmothers and smoked with one of the younger men. He looked exactly right in the group, and she saw, now that he was among them, how his gestures were Indian, that little lift of his chin and the circles he made in the air with his hands. It was strange to hear the Navajo pouring from his mouth instead of English, and yet oddly right, too, for his every-day talking held the same musical lilt.

Mary touched her arm. "He was one who shouldn't have left us, I think," she said quietly. "Not like Daniel, who can come and go. This one—" she lifted her lips toward him "—he didn't like the world outside. He took a pony and ran to the mountains when they told him they were going to the city."

"He never told me that."

"It's good he's here. You'll see."

A sound of splintering glass rang into the kitchen from the yard. Mary bolted toward the back door, and Jessie ran to the window, thinking of Giselle.

The smaller children weren't there. Mary shouted at a knot of young men, probably in their late teens, clumped around two other boys locked in combat. A shattered glass sat in shards by the bottom step.

"Stop that!" Mary cried, clapping her hands sharply. "Take your fight somewhere else!"

At the sound of Mary's voice, three of them ran off toward town, including one of the two who had been fighting. His opponent picked up a rock and threw it after him, furiously, hurling insults about manhood after him. When the boys didn't stop, the youth yanked his jacket into place and, with a black look toward Mary, stalked off toward the tireless Buick. He flung himself over the hood to stare at the sky.

Mary came back, shaking her head. "My son. He's always fighting."

Jessie watched as the one remaining youth crossed the yard, obviously to offer sympathy. Both wore high-top tennis shoes and black athletic jackets, their long hair loose. "He's young," she said, "maybe he'll outgrow it."

"He's angry with everything, that one." A worried expression crossed her face. "Already he gets drunk and arrested. I don't know what to do with him."

"How old is he?"

"Just now twenty. He has no work, nothing to do. He should find something." Then, as if she had said more than she wished, she turned away, busying herself with a plate of doughnuts she gave to Jessie to take to the others.

Jessie took the plate, glad she was spared the need to comment. What was there to say?

At dusk, Luke took a walk. The air was cold and dry, and the spitting snow had begun to stick to the grass in the fields. On the horizon, the rock with wings stood against the light. He admired the graceful carving that gave it its name and wondered how rocks like this always took names of ships and castles in English. It didn't look like a ship to him. He narrowed his eyes—maybe an old clipper ship. Yeah, there was the sail.

A wing and a sail—not so different. Flying away.

Being here made him feel split, as if he had two minds. At ten, he'd been desperate not to leave, had imagined living alone on the land to be a better choice than leaving it entirely. Now that he'd been away so long, he felt like an alien or maybe an expatriate, worn and weary from a nearly endless sojourn.

A goat trailed behind him, nuzzling his hand sometimes to see if there was any food in his palm yet, if some carrot or other juicy morsel had materialized. "I'm telling you," Luke said, "there's nothing here." He paused to hold out both hands, palms up, to illustrate. The goat sniffed curiously, then gave up.

Two youths sat on the hood of a car not far from the house. Luke caught a swift, furtive movement as he approached. He nodded toward them. They stared back rudely, with flat, surly expressions. Hiding something. Luke acted as if he were going to pass them, feeling their alertness, and cut his eyes back in time to see the bottle they had hidden in a paper bag.

He turned. "Keep it away from the little ones," he said.

"We're not stupid," one of them said with narrowed eyes. Mary's son Joaquin, Luke thought. He wore a bandanna around his head and thick strands of turquoise around his neck. If it weren't for the curl of his lip, he might have been a good-looking youth. The other was milder, looking away when Luke warned them.

For a minute, Luke paused, wondering if it would make any difference if he said something—something like, "Hey, that's no good for you, you know." Or even more. "I've been there, drinking like this, and it doesn't help."

It would do no good, but he said it anyway. "You oughta leave it alone yourself."

Joaquin pointedly ignored the advice, asking instead, "Is that woman with you?"

"Yeah," he answered. Clearly.

"Too bad," he said and nudged his friend to mutter something vaguely lecherous under his breath. Wise, Luke thought, not to say it so loud he had to do something.

Shaking his head, Luke left them, glancing at the sky to gauge what was left of daylight. The old habit made him smile. He was no longer afraid of the night, but the boy he'd been wanted to make sure he didn't stray too far from the safety of the house with darkness coming on.

An outcropping of sand-colored boulders sat by the road. Luke climbed to the top and rolled a cigarette. The house looked cheery, light spilling from the windows in welcome, the hogan alive now with a fire inside it. Sheep bleated into the quiet, and the children's voices echoed faintly from some hidden spot. From the direction of town came the sound of engines and tinny music from a radio.

He smoked and gazed at it all. How could he ever have thought this place hostile to him? It felt as welcoming now as a mother's arms, like the happiness of the grandmothers who had greeted him, touching his face and laughing and teasing him. He remembered some of them. That was really something. He liked it.

From where he sat, he could see people drifting in and out of the hogan, more staying now as the night grew thicker. Children particularly gathered there, and he saw Giselle with another little girl ducking to look inside, curious but reluctant. The other child tugged Giselle's hand, but she hung back. Luke saw from her posture she wanted to go in, but wasn't sure about it.

Again he saw Jessie in his daughter, in that edge of wariness. It plucked at him and he jumped down from the rock, crushing his cigarette beneath his boot heel. With Jessie it was too late—he couldn't protect her and keep her safe and teach her to trust. The damage done to her by her mother was too great to overcome.

But it wasn't too late for Giselle. He strode across the brush to her side and took her hand, speaking in Navajo. "Let's go in. There will be stories tonight."

Still she hung back. "What about my mother?"

He inclined his head and glanced toward the house. "We can see if she wants to come, if you like."

"Okay."

Together they went inside the house. Some of the grandmothers sat at the kitchen table, not talking, sharing a plate of brownies as they watched TV on a small black-and-white set on the counter.

Jessie was curled up in a corner of the living room couch, her stockinged feet tucked beneath her. She was reading the paperback novel from his glove box. For an instant, he was struck with a strong sense of her beauty, as impossible to catch as the elusive mist in the mountains.

"Hey," he said. "We're going out to the hogan. Do you want to come with us?"

She took a long breath and let it out on a yawn. "I don't think so. I'm tired tonight—maybe I'll just stay here and read."

He nodded and cleared his throat, aware of the women on the other side of the room. "We'll be sleeping in the truck. In a little while, I'll get that together."

Giselle frowned. "I want to sleep with the kids, in there." She lifted her chin toward a bedroom at the back of the house. "Nikki said I could if it was okay with you."

"Sure." He spoke without thinking, then looked to Jessie for confirmation. Her gaze was lowered, showing nothing.

Suddenly she looked up and her topaz eyes were ablaze with emotion she didn't try to hide. "Maybe I'll just camp in here on the floor with everyone else."

Luke lifted his chin, thinking of the youth who had made comments about her. Nothing could happen in a roomful of people, and the youth was obviously full of a swaggering bluster of the kind that was more noise than action, but he didn't want even a ripple of discomfort while they were here. "It would be better for us to be in the truck. We'll talk about it later."

Without waiting for her answer, he turned on his heel and took Giselle outside.

Together, he and his daughter entered the hogan and took a place at the edge of the gathered number. Mary Yazzie made room for him, smiling at Giselle as they sat down together, Giselle in front of him, leaning against his chest.

The man talking told a story of the Holy People to his grandchildren, who sat nearby his feet, their faces washed orange by the fire. Luke felt everything flow away from him as he sat there. This, too, he knew, someplace deep inside of him. The smell of the fire and the earthen walls of the hogan and the flickering light, all enhanced with the sound of a voice telling an ancient story.

Giselle listened, rapt. Against his chin, her thick hair was cool and smelled of the outdoors. Her long, slim hands rested on his knees and a single strand of beads circled the brown wrist. He touched it; she looked up and gave him a smile, then went back to listening.

At the sudden deep wonder of her presence, Luke wanted to hug her very tightly. He resisted, smiling a little to himself. She was everything he had dreamed a child would be. Everything he'd hoped, and just as precious as he had imagined. Without children, a man was rootless.

Awash with gratitude, he whispered to Giselle that he would be back and went to find Jessie. Just once he had to tell her how he felt, how glad he was. All the rest— well, all the rest could be worked through or not. This thing, though, this gift of his child, was powerful beyond expression. Luke wanted her to know that.

* * *

Jessie was bone weary. The long night coupled with the day's driving had left her almost breathlessly tired. All she wanted was to find a corner to sleep in.

Instead, she held the book stubbornly in her hands, trying to read. Once she dozed off and drifted for a time on the quiet sounds around her, the television in the other room with canned laughter, the snorting comment of one of the grandmothers over the behavior of the characters and the murmuring agreement of the others.

In this room rolled a soft conversation in Navajo about horses and, she thought, rodeo. It was hard to be sure. Sometimes she understood more when she was not trying too hard. Sometimes even a whole sentence would be clear in a strange way, not as if she were taking the time to translate each word into English, but as if she heard it in context in the original. Something silly usually, like, "the horse with gray spots ran fast."

Outside, a wind began to blow in gusts, rattling the windows. This sound, too, was incorporated to her drifting doze, until one particularly violent blast slammed hard into the house and startled her. She sat up, blinking, hearing the surprised laughter of one of the middle-aged women sitting on the other side of the room.

It struck her that she was by herself once again, in a way she hadn't been for a long time, alone in a place she didn't know, with few people she knew at all.

She blamed Daniel. Daniel had set her up with a man she had never wanted to see again, bullied her into taking this meeting, and left her alone to deal with everything he'd dredged up.

And she knew he'd done it all on purpose. He didn't like her to be afraid. From the beginning of their friendship, he had pushed her in little ways, all the time. He dragged her to galleries with her portfolio and made sure she followed up on the calls. He taught Giselle to speak Navajo from the time she was a baby girl, then sometimes refused to speak English at all because he thought Jessie should learn to speak the language, too.

He brought her to the reservation for the early meetings with the weavers, pushed her to talk to gallery owners, and finally insisted she take on the Colorado Springs galleries, knowing she had reasons she didn't want to go.

Some days she could cheerfully kill Daniel Lynch.

The truth was, most of what he'd done, Jessie had needed, and when her humor was a little lighter, she was able to laugh at it. But he wasn't always right, even if he thought so. He didn't really understand the stakes between Luke and Jessie. It bothered her that he'd known of Luke all these years and never let on, then thrust her into a situation where she'd meet him again. She didn't understand what had made him do all that.

And for all of it, she wished he were here. She felt lonely. She felt like an outsider, even with Luke and Giselle close by. Giselle was wrapped up in the wonder of all the children. And Luke—well, she knew she couldn't let her guard down with him. It was just too dangerous.

Deeply thirsty, Jessie headed for the kitchen. The old women around the table peeled the skin from roasted chilies as they watched TV. Only one of them even glanced up as she came into the room. Feeling self-conscious, Jessie took a glass from the cupboard and poured some water. She drank it, then retreated to the doorway to watch the grandmothers at their task.

If Daniel had been here, he would have been outside now, talking with Mary's son, or listening to the stories the elders told in the hogan, or joining in the conversation about horses in the other room. Daniel didn't know what it was like to be the odd man out all the time. He simply couldn't grasp the idea of having no place to go home. His home was here, forever, no matter how far he strayed. For Jessie, there was no place like that. She was eternally the outsider.

It had been a protective habit, at first. As a child, there had been secrets she was desperate to keep hidden. She couldn't have friends over because she never knew what her mother might do. Once, her mother had shown up at a parent-teacher conference in fourth grade, drunk and much too loud, her lipstick smeared uncertainly over her mouth. Jessie had wanted to die of embarrassment, and isolated herself even more firmly the next day against the careful sympathy of the teachers and the snickers of the other children.

Only Luke had seemed to understand her isolation. Their shared loss of mothers, coupled with that sense of being set apart from the rest of society, had drawn them together more powerfully than anything else.

When Luke had wanted to return to the reservation upon the death of his father, Jessie had been deeply jealous of the link he had to the land, to a place he could call his own, a place that was home. It shamed her now to realize that she'd wanted him to remain as isolated as she, home only with her, as she was home only with him.

She hadn't realized the price she would pay for that. The price he would pay.

Suddenly she felt a presence behind her, and Luke's long fingers fell on her shoulders. She turned, yearning once more for the feeling of wholeness she had known with him—only with him.

"I came in to see how you were doing," he said quietly, squeezing her shoulder.

"I'm all right," she replied, and now that he was here with her, she meant it. Where loneliness had been a moment before, there was relief and a hunger as vast as the canyons riddling the desert. She stared at him and thought his face seemed to reflect the very land to which he'd been born....

Just like Daniel. Both of them belonged here. She didn't. She didn't belong anywhere, not even with Luke. She wasn't whole like they were. She was rootless and cowardly and afraid to take chances, to be vulnerable enough to belong anywhere.

Through all the pushing Daniel had done, and through the week in Colorado Springs, Jessie had tried to be brave, to do what was required without whining or crying that she was afraid. All at once she saw herself as the fourth grader with her defenses shattered by the gentleness of teachers. She saw herself, too, much later, pulling to the side of the road to release the agonizing sorrow she felt driving away from Colorado Springs—and Luke—with a child in her belly.

If you never let people in, they could never hurt you. If they didn't know you, they couldn't wound you, couldn't reach you.

Luke, after all these years, knew far, far too much.

"What is it, Jessie?" he asked, reaching for her.

Unable to speak, she whirled, grabbed her coat from the couch and bolted out the front door. The wind slammed into her, and Jessie welcomed the ferocity of it—the roaring drowned her thoughts. She tumbled into it, running face first into the violence that so reflected the tumult in her mind. Overhead, thick clouds obscured the stars, as her past overshadowed her present.

Icy snowflakes pelted her cheeks and ears, and still she ran. Ran away from Luke and memories of her mother, ran from the isolation that had dogged her all of her life and seemed as real as any witch or beast that roamed this land.

She heard Luke behind her, his voice a thin cry in the noise of the wind. In panic, she ran harder, stumbling once on a rock and righting herself before she fell.

Abruptly he overtook her, grabbing her shoulders and spinning her around. "You can't run this time, Jessie!" he cried above the noise of the wind.

With a violent gesture, Jessie flung his hands from her shoulders. "Leave me alone!"

Fury crossed his face. "I can't believe you lie to yourself this way."

"It's my life and my lie."

"No, it isn't. Not anymore. The minute I walked into that gallery, it wasn't all you anymore."

She stepped backward, breath coming hard, ready to run again at the first chance. He wouldn't follow her twice.

He grabbed her. "Stop it, Jessie!" He dragged her into his arms, the wind whipping her hair into a wild animal all around them. "I've been trying to respect your limits," he said, and his hands formed an unbreakable vise on her arms, "trying to do what's best for you, but I'm not going to let you lie to yourself."

Jessie saw the kiss coming and tried to duck, but he caught her face in his hand. His lips claimed hers and he was kissing her—kissing her mouth and chin and nose, her cheekbones and eyes and forehead, kissing her and kissing her and kissing her until Jessie couldn't breathe for the fierce gentleness of it.

"Tell me this isn't the way it's supposed to be," he said raggedly, pushing her hair from her face. "Tell me this isn't the way it always was between us." His mouth touched hers again, and Jessie grabbed his shirtfront, drinking in the taste of him, the feel of his mouth, the smell of his skin, the hard lines of his body.

As if he felt her weakening, his touch gentled and there was now only the sound of the wind and Luke's arms close around her, his strong, lean body pressed against the length of hers and the taste of his beloved mouth on hers.

Tears flowed from her at the tenderness in him. His honest heart was so open to loving her even when he saw all her flaws, all her warts and insecurities.

She kissed him, tasting the salt of her tears, drinking him in as if enough would fill her. When he lifted his head and smoothed down the windblown mass of her hair, she looked at him, wishing she could love him back the same way, that she could forget the lessons of her childhood. As if in cooperation, the wind suddenly died for a moment.

"It's not over," he said into the quiet.

With a cry, Jessie wrenched herself from him. "It has to be, Luke." Tears tightened her throat. "I'm not strong enough. Not strong enough to face down the past or face up to the future. I can't."

"Jessie—" He swore violently and kicked a good-size rock in his frustration. Jessie watched it tumble over and over until it came to a halt a few feet away.

He turned back, his hands in his pockets. "You know, Jessie, you aren't the only one who's afraid. I'm afraid, too—afraid that one morning I'm going to wake up again in a park and won't remember how I got there." He stepped forward, intense. "It made me sick to be that man, but I have to face my life one day at a time."

Her throat felt as if it had closed completely. She couldn't seem to get any air through it, much less the words Luke seemed to be waiting for.

For a moment longer, he stood there, staring at her intently. Then with a sudden, abrupt shake of his head, he said, "Go off and hide then. I'm tired of fighting."

He strode off into the darkness. Jessie heard his boots crunching against the rocks until the wind blew to life again and stole the sound away.

Chapter Thirteen

As she walked back toward the house, Jessie tried to keep her mind blank, tried to concentrate upon the way the house looked against the vast night, how the wavering orange light of the fire spilled through the doorway of the hogan, looking warm and friendly. The wind quieted a little, though it still gusted in capricious bursts.

In Albuquerque, she had come to know Indians of many nations—Lakota and Yaqui and Pima, Cheyenne and Comanche. She had come to understand a little of each of their cultures, had learned to paint the differences in their faces. Each face, each culture, was different from the others, linked only by being the original nations of the continent.

But of all of them, she loved the Navajo, and not only because she had first loved Luke. There was something about the nation as a whole that somehow reflected her own nature, something essentially private and reserved—almost shy. And yet they were strong, relentless survivors, as she herself was. There was great beauty in the things that came from them, in the silver and the beads, and above all the weavings.

As she walked back in the wide, open darkness, she thought of the beauty prayer, made famous by writers. *Beauty all around me.* Yes. And here it was, the beauty. It was in the sheep and the women bent over the stove tonight at supper and the wavering light falling from the door to the hogan; it was in the lilting words she would never speak but would one day understand well. It was in the sky and the rocks around her, and in the sharp song of the wind.

Beauty all around me.

She found Luke sitting on the end of the truck gate, smoking. He glanced up when she approached, then turned his face away again without speaking. Jessie took a breath and sat down beside him, feeling the truck sink a little under the extra weight.

She didn't speak, but when he passed his cigarette toward her, she took it and inhaled a breathful of the smoke, blowing it out into the cold night.

"I tucked Giselle in," he said.

"Oh, maybe I ought to—"

"She said she'll see you in the morning."

Jessie gave him back the cigarette. "She loves it here."

He inhaled the night air, nodding. "Listen," he said, inclining his head. "How quiet it is."

From a distance, a coyote howled. "He must be hungry."

"Or lonely," Luke said.

Jessie thought about that, then looked at him. "Mary told me you ran away when you found out you were going to move to Colorado."

"Yeah." The word was soft, self-mocking. "I took my horse and some food and rode to the mountains. I stayed there four days before they came to get me."

"Wasn't it lonely? You were so young."

He shook his head and passed the cigarette back to her. "No. It seemed worse to leave completely. The city seemed so far away. So different."

Jessie nodded, looking at the glowing ember of the cigarette for a minute before she lifted it to her mouth. The first hit had made her a little dizzy; this one seemed to shoot straight to her brain with a whirl. "That's enough," she said.

He gave her a cockeyed grin. "See? You're learning."

"Maybe." She swung her feet back and forth. "Was it because your mother was sick that you left?"

"My father heard of the sanitarium in Colorado. They were just starting to give people the medicine they use now. Mom was pretty sick, and the doctors wanted her to go to the sanitarium." He shrugged. "It worked. I can't complain. She lived longer there."

"Seeing Marcia and Giselle makes me wish I'd known her."

He chuckled. "Do you know what your daughter told me this afternoon?"

"No telling. What?"

"That you never kiss Daniel like they kiss on TV."

Jessie felt the heat of embarrassment spread through her cheeks and was grateful for the darkness. "He's my friend."

"He was my friend for a long time, too. It was Daniel who helped me run away that time."

"Really?" She grinned, trying to imagine the two of them as children, plotting a doomed expedition. "I can see that."

"Giselle thinks a lot of him."

Jessie pressed her lips together for a minute, knowing this was a sensitive area. "He's like her uncle, you know? He—" She almost said, "takes the time to be with her," but knew it would wound Luke.

"I know." He dropped the cigarette and stood up to crush it beneath the heel of his boot. "I guess we should hit the hay."

A ripple of awareness spread through Jessie at his words, a slight, quivering heaviness in her breasts and belly. "I guess so," she agreed, but made no immediate move.

He was very close, close enough for her to smell the scent of him, that foresty note of his skin. "Do you want me to sleep in the cab?" he asked.

Jessie hesitated. "I don't know."

"That might be the most honest thing you've said to me." His gaze, dark and liquid, met hers. Against the night, the harsh planes of his face were shadowed, like the mesas all around them, and Jessie caught her breath at the wave of longing she felt. She had to consciously restrain herself from reaching up to touch his jaw.

Beauty all around me.

He took a step closer, and now his body was just barely between her knees. With one hand, he reached out to shift a lock of her hair over her shoulder. "We don't have to make love." His voice, quiet with the night, seemed more accented than usual, giving his English a hypnotically musical sound. "Let me hold you. Just for tonight."

Jessie found she had no will to resist when he swayed forward, his fingers tightening on her shoulder, to kiss the side of her neck. She knew she should tell him to go to the cab, or volunteer to go herself. And yet... and yet....

"Oh, Luke," she whispered with a hint of despair, her body betraying her. "I can't stop needing you."

"Maybe you aren't supposed to," he said. Swiftly he gathered her close, wrapping his arms around her, lowering his face to her hair with a sigh. His hair brushed her mouth, coarse and cool.

Even just being next to him made her feel better, made the weariness slip from her shoulders and the anxiety of the past week seem far away. She lifted her arms and wrapped them around his back, hugging him close, unable to turn away from the one thing that would make her feel whole and right. It was only for tonight. One more time she could take what he wanted to give. One more time, she could love him.

Easing away, she scooted back into the truck. Luke waited at the tailgate, and she saw from the hard line of his jaw that he thought she was going to make him go to the cab. She held out her hand.

He stood there a split second longer, as if he regretted his choice; then he jumped into the truck, slamming the barriers closed behind him. An involuntary rush of pure need rippled through Jessie as he bent his head, and the light from beyond caught his hair. She reached for him, putting her hand on his thigh.

He smiled and lifted her hand to his mouth. "Kick off your shoes, honey. It's gonna be a long day tomorrow."

Jessie yanked off her boots and unbuttoned the heavy jacket, then zipped open one of the sleeping bags laid out on the pallet. He stopped her. "Let's put them together."

She nodded, lifting her end up so Luke could join it to his. It was a deeply intimate act, especially in the pure, unbroken silence of the desert. They crawled in together, one from each side. Jessie felt deeply shy and didn't know quite what to do next.

"Come here," Luke said, lifting the bag to make room for her to ease up next to him. From long habit, she nestled her head in the hollow of his shoulder, and once again all the tension flowed out of her.

He held her close. "That's it."

Jessie sighed, letting go. Only with Luke had she ever felt this sense of perfect ease, this perfect safety. Only with him had she ever been able to let down her guard and allow another human being to see her.

It had been so shattering to lose it.

Against her temple she felt a warm triangle of flesh at the opening of his shirt. One of her hands rested on his waist and the other was curled close to her. Idly, he moved his stockinged feet against hers.

But it wasn't as easy as she had imagined to just lie there. His hands moved on her back, up and down. She found her own hand moving, too, over his ribs and back, to his upper arm below the cloth. The sound of his breath in her ear was intensely personal.

Slowly, he began to massage her scalp, a luxurious experience Jessie had missed. She let her head fall against his palm and smiled at the soft sound of amusement that rumbled from his chest. "Putty in my hands, woman."

She made no reply.

After a time, he shifted a little until he could touch her face, and applied the same exquisite pressure over her forehead and temples and along her jaw. The deft fingers were gentle and powerful at once. With her eyes closed, Jessie reached for the opening of his shirt, where the tantalizing warmth of his skin waited.

He caught her hand. "No. I have some discipline, but not that much."

Jessie opened her eyes. "What about mine?"

He leaned closer, fingers brushing down her neck. "What about it?"

With one hand, she reached up and touched his mouth, brushing her fingers over the well-cut lines, feeling the firmness soften. "Kissing doesn't count as making love," she whispered and strained upward a little.

"No," he said as he came closer. "No, it doesn't." He wrapped his hands around her and pulled her tightly against him. Their hips nestled together. Slowly he bent over her and brushed the lightest possible kiss over her mouth. "Like that?"

A pulse began to thump in her groin, in her breasts, in the lips he'd just teased. "No," she said, and swallowed. "Try again."

"Mmm." This time, he hovered close for an instant, his lips bare millimeters away from her own, then his tongue brushed the edge of her lower lip and the corner and the bow.

He didn't move away, but hovered again, close yet not touching her. Against her belly, she could feel Luke's arousal pressing against his jeans, ready to burst the fabric to touch her, and she smiled at the way his teasing her aroused *him*. "Try again," she repeated in a throaty voice.

"Hard to please, aren't you?"

"Very."

This time, he really kissed her, but with the same slow savoring he'd used a moment before. First his lips and hers, sliding and playing, then the slight opening and the barest brush of tongues. Jessie lifted her hand to his hip, unable to avoid touching him, and she arched a little against his erection. His hands clutched her shoulders tighter and his tongue unexpectedly plunged.

And suddenly, Jessie didn't care anymore about the past or the future. Only now mattered. Only Luke and his hands and his mouth. "If we take off our shirts, it doesn't count as making love, does it?" she asked breathlessly.

In the darkness, his eyes held a rich shine of light. He shook his head and reached for the hem of her sweater. Jessie lifted her arms and let him pull the fabric over her head. "Better," she said.

Luke's hands fell on the front clasp of her bra. "Wouldn't you like to get rid of this, too?"

"Of course."

He smiled as he released the clasp, then slipped it from her body. "Much, much better," he said, touching her with both hands.

"Now you," Jessie said.

"Well, if you insist." He shed his shirt quickly and then he was against her, sleek and warm, his torso against her bared breasts. He held her that way, trapped between his legs and wrapped in his arms, skin to skin, their heads cradled side by side on the pillows.

"So now," Luke said, his voice husky with a need he was trying to hide, "we have kissing. And bared breasts." His hands cupped her lazily. "I suppose kissing breasts is out of the question?"

Jessie closed her eyes, knowing she was lost when he spoke like that, when he touched her like this.... "I don't know," she managed to whisper over the clamor in her blood.

"Maybe I should try it, just to see." His thumbs teased her almost irresistibly, and she felt him slip closer, felt his hair brush her chin.

And at last, at last, his mouth swept over the swell of her breast, edging close to the aroused tip. Wickedly, he barely kissed the aching point. "Like that?" he murmured, and his breath was as tantalizing as his touch.

Jessie could manage no more than a sigh.

"Or this?" As he had done with her mouth, he just tasted her nipple with small licks, tiny flickers of his tongue. But after a moment, it was as if he forgot to tease her, for he made a long, low sound deep in his chest and his mouth opened full and hot over her, took her inside.

She cried out softly and clutched his head, dragging him up to kiss him. "I think," she said, reaching for the buttons of his jeans, "it's getting too hot for any of our clothes."

"Oh, yeah." He groaned as she teased him, stroking his erection through the straining fabric of his jeans. "But I'm afraid that's going to qualify—"

She didn't let him finish. She kissed the words from his mouth, her hunger so deep she could not bear to think that it was anything but exactly right, exactly what she should do.

They knew each other so well, knew how to shift this way or that, to ease from the clothes in ways ungraceful but efficient. Socks and jeans and underwear were shed in haste, until there were only limbs entwined, and lips, and hands.

All at once Jessie felt the sleek warmth of his thighs against hers, and then he plunged with a single, sharp thrust, joining them. Jessie cried out, grasping him as he moved inside of her, fiercely, roughly, their bodies rocking against each other with bruising intensity. She felt his hands on her shoulders, his fingers digging into her flesh. His face was dark with hunger when she looked at him.

They roared into the height of the moment, crying out, clutching each other closer, closer. It was like the windstorm, endless and violent and clearing. When together they rolled to their sides, neither had the breath to speak. They kissed, hands still roving, bodies still pulsing, hearts pounding. Jessie put her palm on his chest to hear the racing beat of his heart and grinned. "That definitely qualifies as making love."

He laughed softly, curling his fingers in her hair. "And that's only the beginning, honey." He brushed her cheek. "Only the beginning."

Luke didn't question her sudden change of heart. In the darkness and the cold, on the hard metal bed of the truck, he was happier than he had been in many years, holding her warm body next to his in the sleeping bags they'd zipped together.

Tonight, she was different. Almost insatiably hungry for him, almost unbearably giving. He gave as clearly as he was able, trying not to think of tomorrow or tomorrow or tomorrow, or anything past. Just now, for them, for what had been.

When they lay together, sated at last, he thought there had been a healing. The resistance had gone from her, and the fear. She nestled her face in his chest, her hand draped around his waist, and made a soft sighing sound of contentment.

He closed his eyes, just holding her. In the morning, she might not remember why she had done this, why she had decided it would be all right to make love with him, one more time. He was prepared for her to be cold and distant once again.

But surely she would not be able to remember this night, and last night, and not want to work to overcome what lay between them. Surely there was some answer. His fingers tightened involuntarily against her ribs. "I love you," he whispered, his face in her hair.

He thought she was asleep, but at his words, she pressed close, her forehead to his chest, her fingers almost painfully fierce on his side. Abruptly, she lifted her face and kissed him hard on the mouth, and he tasted her tears once more. He chuckled gently. "I have seen you cry more in the past few days than I did in the whole time we were together."

Unabashedly, she wiped at them. "I feel so emotional. Like everything is too big for me, too much for me." She touched his mouth. "When I doze off and wake up and you're still here, it seems like a miracle."

"I'm here," he said. "Yours for the asking."

A wicked grin spread over her face. "Oh, really?" Her hand slipped down and cupped him boldly. In seconds, he was half-ready again. "Are you Superman?"

"Looks like I just might be, under the right circumstances," he said, and groaned as she moved her hand deliciously. "Ah, Jess," he moaned, his hands in her hair.

She laughed, the sound throaty and warm. "You think there's a record for the most times in a single night?"

He could not reply, not with words. He reached for her, touching the silk of her breast as her hands worked their magic, awash in the wildness, the passion, the power that was Jessie.

He must have slept finally, rubber-boned with lovemaking, for Tasha's bark startled him awake. He blinked, disoriented for a minute, then heard an odd scrape on the outside of the truck. In the cab, Tasha growled low in her throat.

Stealthily, he eased free of Jessie's embrace and slipped into his jeans, hearing again an unidentifiable noise on the body of the truck. Quietly as he was able, he turned the handle of the window on the back of the cab, lifted it and eased his body through the opening.

Outside the night was freezing and his feet were unaccustomed to the rough terrain. He had to pause to pick a burr from his big toe before he rounded the side, cautiously.

Crouched by the passenger door was a man, smearing something dark over the door. "Hey," Luke said, "what the hell are you doing?"

The man looked up and dropped the jar in his hand, bolting away from the house, through the dirt of the driveway toward a short bluff across the road. Luke ran after him.

Given the advantage of shoes, Luke might have caught him faster. As it was, he found himself leaping over yucca and praying he wouldn't land in a patch of prickly pear. He couldn't avoid the goat heads, though. One stabbed the ball of his foot. Cursing, he kicked it out with the other foot and kept running. Wind chilled his chest and arms. A stitch caught in his side.

All at once, the man tripped and went down with a strangled cry. Luke sprinted and tackled him before he could recover, feeling the air whoosh from both of them.

The light was eerie and cold, pale with the clouds overhead. Luke dragged the man to his feet, smelling whiskey as the youth—for he was no more than twenty—staggered uncertainly against the clutch of Luke's fist on the back of his jacket.

Luke recognized him. It was the boy who'd been drinking with Mary's son earlier in the evening. As he stumbled, he laughed, a high, whinnying sound that shouted of rabid drunkenness.

For a moment, Luke froze, staring into that face—that drunken Indian face. Revulsion swept him, deep and nauseating. It stole his breath. With a violent gesture, he shoved the youth away. The boy stumbled and fell in the brush.

Luke sucked air into his lungs, trying to calm himself. On the ground, the young man laughed and muttered something unintelligible, ending with, "Eh, Tonto?"

"Who are you working for?" Luke asked.

"The Meeker Galleries, man. They paid me and my boys big money to harass all you earnest Injuns." He let go of a cackling laugh.

With a head-splitting sense of rage, Luke grabbed the youth's coat front and hauled him to his feet. He smelled sour alcohol and a long stretch of no bathing. "Why?" he demanded, shaking him. "Why would you betray us that way?" He shook him again. "Don't you know they just used you?"

The laughter had fled the young man's eyes, leaving behind only a sullen, flat expression. He didn't resist the shaking, but didn't answer, either.

Jessie appeared from nowhere, wearing her jeans and sweater but no shoes. She grabbed Luke's arm. "Leave him alone," she said.

Abruptly, Luke dropped the youth and spun on his heel, almost physically ill with revulsion and disgust and other emotions he couldn't even name.

At the road, he paused to look back, reason telling him he should not leave her alone with the drunken youth. From where he stood, he couldn't hear what she said, but the tone of her voice was instantly, painfully familiar. It was gentle, quiet, reasonable—infinitely patient.

As she knelt to help the youth to his feet, Luke felt his nausea grow. Memories crowded in, memories of Jessie so gently helping him at moments like this; Jessie making coffee in the morning, giving him tomato juice and aspirin without a single word of censure.

He saw she would manage the youth without help—as she had managed himself, managed her mother—and limped toward the truck, remembering himself awakening in a park on a brilliant Sunday morning.

The youth slumped on the ground, making no move to run. In the dim, cloudy night, Jessie could see little about him except that he was very drunk. His hair was long, tied back from his face in a ponytail, and an earring shone silver in the night. He looked up at her dully, swaying a little even in the sitting position. She knelt beside him. "Can you walk?"

"I can do anything, lady," he said, the words slurry, and laughed like a hyena before he tumbled over sideways.

There was probably nothing Jessie hadn't learned about drunks at one time or another. This one was a long way gone, maybe even dangerously so. Gently, she took his arm. "You can't stay out here. And I can't carry you. Let me help you up."

He swayed upright and managed to find his feet. Up close, he smelled bad. Jessie caught her breath as she steadied him. "Okay. Let's go."

"Hey, baby," he said, reaching for her, "mebbe—"

Jessie shook her head, intersecting the grasping hand before it did any damage. "It's cold," she said, urging him along.

He wasn't tall and that made it easier. She flung his arm around her neck and walked him toward the house, feeling a moment of doubt as she saw the darkness all around. Finally she opted to go in the back door. They were less likely to awaken anyone that way.

Once she rounded the house, the youth mumbling incoherently beside her, she saw the kitchen light was on, and Mary Yazzie was visible through the window. Good—she would have some help.

"Come on," Jessie said. "There's stairs here. Careful."

But in spite of her warning, the boy went down, cracking his head against the concrete. He made a sharp noise of pain. Jessie swore, realizing she should have seen it coming.

The back porch light came on, and Mary came outside. In the yellow light, Jessie could see blood gushing from the wound on the youth's forehead. She also realized who it was—the quiet friend of Mary's fighting son.

In a harsh voice, Mary said, "Let's bring him inside."

"What's his name?" Jessie asked as they propped him in a chair.

Mary's lips were tight. "Rudy Salazar. He's one of my son's friends."

"I remember seeing him this afternoon."

Jessie wet a dishcloth with cold water and pressed it to the bleeding cut. Rudy knocked her hand away with a profane curse.

She lifted her hand and bent close. In a dangerous voice, she said, "If you do that again, I'll drag you back outside and let you freeze to death."

He glared at her, but didn't move when she pressed the cloth to the cut again. Jessie looked at Mary. "We need to keep him here. He may not be acting alone, but he's one of the ones disrupting the project."

Mary nodded. Her gaze slipped away, and Jessie guessed her thoughts. If this was one of her son's friends, was Joaquin responsible for the leak of information that made it possible for the culprits to undermine the project?

Respecting her privacy, Jessie said nothing. She lifted the cloth from Rudy's head and saw that most of the bleeding had stopped. "Pretty nasty cut, but I guess he'll survive."

"He's lived through worse."

Jessie looked at him, feeling a pluck of sadness that one so young should have such an intimate knowledge of that "worse." His face was dirty, but in the midst of all the grime, his mouth was young and vulnerable. It made her sad.

Mary brought in a sleeping bag and dumped it on the floor. "I'm going to go back to sleep," she announced, leaving Jessie alone with the youth.

Jessie kicked the bag into a semi-straight line, hanging on to Rudy with one hand so he wouldn't fall over, then tipped him forward in the general direction of the bag. He landed more or less straight and crossed his arms over his chest, his eyes closed.

Suddenly weary, Jessie sank down in the chair and glanced at the flower-shaped clock on the wall. Three a.m. In a few hours, it would be light and the house would be stirring. She wondered if she ought to go back to the truck and try for a few more hours of sleep or just sit here, in case.

She heard her thoughts with a slight shock. In case of what? She stared at Rudy.

In case his breathing stopped. In case he started to be sick and wasn't turned the right way. In case—

With a crushing sense of depression, she buried her face in her hands. Would she never learn?

How often had she led her mother quietly to her room, washed her face, taken off her soiled clothes and put her to bed before her father got home? How often had she done it for Luke?

All at once she realized she had thrown on her clothes without undergarments, and her feet were stinging with goat heads. She should go back to the truck.

No.

The expression on Luke's face had been terrifying. She didn't want to face him right now, didn't want to hear what was behind an expression like that. No. She would slip into the other room and stretch out on the couch. It was the best solution—she wouldn't wake up with Luke, and she could keep an eye on this boy, too.

A school counselor had once told Jessie she couldn't stop her mother from drinking, no matter how hard she tried. Jessie accepted the advice and went to the next step—she took care of her when she was drunk. It wasn't a job most people wanted, but Jessie always found a sense of relief in it. It was something real, something concrete. No, she couldn't keep anybody sober, but she could tend them when they were drunk. She knew what to do, how to minimize the damage drinking wrought.

Co-dependent. The word whispered through her mind as she crept through the sleeping bodies in the other room and fell into a vacant chair.

Co-dependent. That's what they called it. But did that word still apply to her? She didn't know. She didn't know anymore how far she'd go in trying to shoulder the pain of an alcoholic she cared about, since it had not been an issue in so many years. She felt her actions tonight had been simply compassionate—who would leave a young man outside to freeze to death?

Shifting restlessly in the chair, she crossed her arms over the ache in her belly. Co-dependent actions or not, it was far, far better to stay here and make sure some young man didn't die in his alcoholic stupor than go out there and face Luke, who knew her, who needed her, who would engulf her tonight if she went to him.

It was better this way.

Chapter Fourteen

Luke went to the house a little before dawn broke and saw Jessie slumped in the chair. Her hair, mussed from their lovemaking, tumbled around her like a wild cape, chestnut and gold, with tendrils that clung to her porcelain cheek. Her feet were bare and reddened in spots from her run through the field. Below her sweater, he could see she wore no bra, and the gentle slope of her breasts, so vulnerable to other eyes, made him take a blanket from the couch and toss it over her.

His past drinking weighed heavily on him this morning. He had been a traitor to his people, to his family, to himself. But most traitorous of all had been his betrayal of Jessie's need to believe in someone. He, unwilling to bear that burden, had retreated into a comfortable world where no golden eyes would ask more of him than he could give.

He wished fervently now that Daniel *had* taken this woman to be his wife, that when at last Luke had learned of his daughter and the woman he had never forgotten, Jessie would have been safely and securely married to his childhood friend. With Daniel, she would have faced no betrayal.

A knot of despair tightened in his chest as he went to the kitchen, looking for coffee. There on the floor was the youth from the night before, still passed out. At the table sat Mary, her face haggard, staring at the youth as if she could make him disappear. "There's our witch," Luke said. "Will it help, do you think?"

Mary shrugged and stubbed out a cigarette. "Joaquin is gone this morning. I'm so ashamed of him. He sat through our meetings, knew exactly what we were doing...."

Luke touched her hand. "The things they did weren't serious. I doubt anyone will even press charges as long as they agree to stop."

She shook her head, and the heavy earrings she wore swung against her neck. "Joaquin will pay for the sheep he killed. It's the right thing for him to do."

"That's fair enough."

"I'm going to send him to his uncle. If he works hard for a while, maybe he won't be so bad."

"Maybe." Luke ducked his head to avoid her gaze.

"What else can I do?" she asked. "Maybe you know a little about boys going bad?"

Luke glanced at the dirty face of the youth. He sighed. "I do."

"Tell me, then, what should I do?" Strong emotion sounded in her voice and she paused, lifting her eyes to the window and the vast expanse of mesas and fields beyond. "I have no more answers."

"Maybe there are none. Maybe," he said, raising his eyes, "you just have to let him fall."

Mary measured his words for a long moment. "Maybe I do. But I'll try his uncle first." She straightened then, as if girding herself. "Let's talk about the project. I want to tell you about some of the women who will be there today, so you know who you are talking to. They will listen, but you must talk to them in their way."

In spite of his feelings that he was not the best choice for this job, Luke listened carefully. There wasn't anyone else. He would have to do what he could—for Mary and the memory of his mother and for all the other weavers who deserved more than what they were getting.

When Jessie awakened, slowly, she was exhausted. And in spite of the clear morning, with its bright sunshine and blue sky, she felt a dragging sense of depression.

Almost everyone was gone already into town for the meeting, and she rushed through washing her face and changing her clothes, only going to the kitchen for a cup of coffee at the last moment.

The youth from the night before sat alone at the table. His long hair was tangled, but he'd washed his face and hands. He still smelled as if he'd been sleeping with goats, and his eyes were bleary red with his hangover, but Jessie felt a rush of relief, anyway. He was, at least, alive.

When he saw her, he turned his face away sullenly. Jessie hesitated for a minute. His mouth was vulnerable, very young, and she saw the wounded self-respect in his pose. She wanted to sit down with him, to talk. Talk some sense into him or make him feel better.

She wanted to tell him tomato juice would put back the vitamins he'd lost, and that a couple of aspirin would open the blood vessels constricted by alcohol. That was what gave him the headache that almost visibly pulsed around him—a lack of oxygen to his brain.

Instead, she poured herself a cup of coffee. "Mary has some aspirin if you want it," she said.

He glanced up at her with an expression of such feral hatred, she backed away. "Are they gonna take me to jail?"

"I don't know. Depends on what you've done."

"I didn't do it all."

"Who hired you?"

"Told your boyfriend already—the Meeker Galleries."

"What?" The string of Southwestern galleries, run by a rich family out of Albuquerque, had pretended to take a solicitous interest in the project. She sighed. "Terrific."

Luke came in through the back door, and Jessie glanced up guiltily. He looked haggard. "Jessie," he said. "Good. I came to see if you were up."

"More or less."

He looked at the youth. "She tell you her hangover cures?" he asked without smiling.

The youth said nothing.

"Tomato juice and aspirin."

Jessie lowered her eyes, painfully embarrassed.

Luke's voice was bitterly ironic as he continued. "She'll even tell you why it works if you want to know." He shot her a veiled glance. "Right, Jess? You're the expert on hung-over alkies."

Jessie winced at his harsh words, but put her cup aside. "Let's go," she said.

"In a minute." Luke leaned on the table, close to the youth. "You like waking up like this? You like comin' to and not remembering how you got there?"

The youth's chin jutted upward and his eyes turned to flat slits. "Get outta my face, man!"

Luke straightened. "It makes me sick to look at you. Go wash up. You smell like a goat."

Appalled, Jessie almost protested—until she saw the fine tremor in Luke's hands as he whirled away. As they stepped outside into the bright fall day, she reached for his arm. "Luke—"

He yanked away violently. "Damn it, Jessie, just leave it alone, will you? You don't have to take care of me anymore."

His words seared her. "Don't take it out on me."

"Why didn't you come back to the truck?"

She looked away. In the rough pen, sheep bleated quietly and a goat, seeing the pair of them standing there, trotted over hopefully. "I don't know."

"I do." His mouth twisted. "You were in there playing Florence Nightingale, right?"

Jessie swallowed, drawing back a little from the fury in his voice, the bitterness she had never heard before. It startled her into telling the truth. "I was afraid to be with you, the way you looked."

"It's easier to deal with a drunk, isn't it?" His voice was dangerously controlled. "A drunk who can't talk or get through to you, rather than a man who might really need you, who might really ask you to be honest."

Jessie stared at him, clinging to the shreds of her collapsing defenses. "That's crazy," she whispered.

"Is it?" He stepped forward. "It was always easier for you to take care of me when I was drunk or hung over than when I was just loving you. You couldn't take it."

"You're right!" she retorted, giving in. "I didn't know how to love you the way you were. You were so good and so strong and so beautiful and I knew—"

It was this weakness in her that she feared more than anything else, some thing in her that didn't heal people who were alcoholic, but encouraged their disease.

In horror, she backed away from him. "I always thought that if you hadn't been with me, maybe you wouldn't have fallen over the line." She struggled with her emotions, but too much had happened too quickly, and they were exploding out of her. Tears washed over her face. "And when I left you, you got sober, didn't you?"

"Jessie—" he said, reaching for her.

She dodged, struggling to calm herself. "We have to get to the meeting."

He grabbed her just above the elbow. "Wait a minute."

"No," she said violently and tried to pull away, but his grip was fierce and unbreakable. "I don't want to talk about this anymore."

"Too bad. We're gonna get it all out in the open right now. You listen to me."

Jessie sighed and turned her face away, letting him hold her elbow. Passive resistance, that was the key.

But Luke wasn't having it. With his free hand, he took hold of her chin and turned her face gently but firmly to his. "Look at me, Jessie," he said when she kept her lids lowered.

When she ignored him, keeping her gaze focused loosely on the white buttons of his chambray shirt, he warned, "I'll stand like this all day if I have to. You know I will."

In defiance, she closed her eyes. But when he simply stood there, she knew she would give in a long time before he did. His stubbornness was patient, hers impulsive. She raised her eyes.

"That's it. Now listen closely." He looked at her intently, bending his head toward her. "I'm an alcoholic, Jessie. I started drinking a long time before I met you, and I knew better. Sooner or later, I was headed for a fall. You being there didn't make a difference one way or the other, except that you made me more comfortable when I'd get sick."

She opened her mouth to interrupt, but he held up a hand. "You didn't have anything to do with your mother, either. You know it, too, when you're thinking clearly."

Jessie shifted, trying to pull away in discomfort, but Luke held her steadily, firmly. "Are you finished?" she asked.

"No." His mouth tightened for a brief instant, and he shook his head. "No child should have to go through what you did, Jessie. I know it hurt you and that there are things you'll never get over, but I wish you could see yourself the way I do. I wish you could see how strong you are now. Even with that kid in there—"

"I didn't do anything this time," she protested in self-defense. "All I did was make sure he didn't freeze. Anyone would do that."

"No, not anyone. But that doesn't matter. I can't tell you anything—you have to work it out on your own." He stepped closer and brushed the tips of his fingers over her cheek. "But I want you to know that I love you. You don't have to do anything or act a certain way or pretend with me. Just being Jessie is enough."

She swallowed and looked away, unable to bear the straight penetration of his liquid gaze.

"Jessie," he said.

"I can't do this, Luke."

"We'll stand here until you can."

Reluctantly, she looked at him again.

He smiled softly. "There's nothing I would like better than to be with you for the rest of my life, to have more babies and make love every night and eat supper with you." He touched the crown of her head and smoothed a lock of her hair over her shoulder, his gaze following the movement of his hand. He took a breath and looked into her eyes again. "But I'm through giving you everything just to have you throw it back at me and run away. If you think you can come to me with a whole heart, then come. Otherwise, I'm gonna get on with my life." Very tenderly, he bent and pressed a kiss to her lips, almost as if he were saying farewell. "It's time."

He let her go without another word and headed for the truck. After a moment, Jessie followed. They rode in silence to the meeting house.

Outside, Giselle ran in circles, playing chase with a gaggle of other children. With a start, Jessie realized how much freedom Giselle had here, under the watchful eye of so many. Everyone watched the children, from slightly older children to the old men sitting on a bench outside.

Still, to delay going inside for a minute longer, Jessie whistled. Giselle peeled away from the group. "Hi, Mom!" she cried, and hugged her.

"You look like you're having a good time."

"I am!" With another quick hug, she let go. "See you later."

Jessie watched her go with a small sense of sadness. Giselle was no longer her baby. She caught Luke watching Giselle carefully, with no expression, and shrugged. "She's growing up."

He nodded, a distant expression in his eyes. With a pang, Jessie realized he meant it this time. The ball was in her court.

And she knew she would have to choose not to play. A vision of the future, dry and dun-colored as the desert, flashed over her imagination, giving her a hollow feeling.

Stonily, she went inside and took her place.

The meeting was oddly quiet. Luke gave reports to the weavers about the actual facts and figures of the project, fielding questions about specific numbers and various concerns. He also told them about catching Rudy in the act of smearing sheep blood on the truck and about Joaquin's disappearance.

He spoke in Dine, his manner quiet and respectful. Jessie sat nearby, listening as a young man she didn't know translated the words into English for her. After a few minutes, she realized she didn't really need him to do that, and whispered as much. The language, suddenly, was clicking in to the point that she only missed a word here and there. She noted the fact with a distant sense of surprise. She'd been listening to it for seven years, after all. It was bound to connect sooner or later.

As hard as she tried to concentrate on Luke's words, Jessie found her attention straying over and over again, lighting upon Rudy and Luke and her mother and the drunks in the street in Gallup.

But mostly, as she looked into the sea of women's faces, Jessie thought of her mother. Why couldn't she have been born to a woman like the ones in this room? Someone like that grandmother there, holding a baby close to her chest with the casual ease of long practice. Or that happy young woman over there, smiling and nodding enthusiastically as she listened, her bob swinging neatly at her shoulders.

Maybe if Jessie had had a real mother, someone to wash her hair and trim her fingernails and teach her to cook, she wouldn't feel so adrift now, especially in places like kitchens and quiet discussions of women's things. Maybe if she'd had a real mother, she'd know what to do in those situations.

With a little shock, she realized for the first time why her paintings were nearly all of women. She was painting mothers. Mothers canning fruit. Mothers laboring to give birth with the help of a gentle midwife's motherly hands, mothers nursing daughters...

Even the newest one she'd conceived, the weaver that had stunned her, was Luke's mother, the woman who'd raised such a powerfully gentle man.

Luke was right. Her trouble with the past went back much farther than the loss of Luke or even his drinking. It went back to the unresolved issue of her mother. In all those paintings, Jessie was searching for a mother to call her own.

She closed her eyes, feeling almost winded with the realization, unable to cope with yet another confrontation with her psyche. It seemed as if fate had conspired to force her to face her entire past all at once. And either it would break her, or she'd come out stronger.

At the moment, she didn't know which it would be. Oh, she'd survive. There was no question of survival. But if she didn't resolve the past right now, she was doomed to never being whole, to leading the same half-lost life she'd been living.

At the back of the room, the door swung open, spilling bright sunlight to the floor behind the folding chairs set up for the meeting. A whirl of children's voices danced in and died as a man entered the room, giving Luke a signal.

Jessie glanced at him desultorily and realized Luke was wrapping up the morning session. In the afternoon, they would meet again to go over some of the finer points, but first there would be a big lunch and time for talking in smaller groups.

Thank heaven, she thought. She really had a headache.

Luke avoided Jessie through lunch, which was served at long tables in the hall. He found Mary and sat down with her, aware that she was disappointed somehow in the way the morning meeting had gone. "It'll be okay," he said, trying to cheer her up.

She shrugged and turned her gaze toward the roomful of weavers and their families. "I don't think we're getting through."

"What do you think will work, Mary? Help me out here."

"I don't know." She frowned. "There must be something we aren't saying, something important that we haven't said. But I don't know what it is."

Luke swore mildly. He knew what part of the trouble was. Himself. Standing up to talk to all those elders, he had felt an imposter, haunted by the old ghost of himself, made flesh by the youth in the kitchen this morning. In spite of his pep talk to Jessie about letting the past go, he seemed to be having a little trouble letting go of it himself. "I'm going to take a walk," he announced. "Maybe it'll clear my head. If you think of anything, let me know."

The meeting hall sat at the edge of town, jutting up against a wide field pinned down with fans of yucca.

Luke gazed at it for a moment, pausing at the door to roll a cigarette, then wandered out into the desert, trying to let everything go. Jessie, Giselle, the past—all of it. What mattered was those weavers and finding ways to assure them all would be well.

He walked toward a short bluff, hearing the sounds of the clustered people in the hall drop away until there was only Luke, the silence of the desert and the wide open sky overhead. Gaining the crest of the mesa, he sat down to admire that sharp blue sky and felt the color and space of it ease the coils of tension in his chest. The air smelled of dust and sage.

Below him ran a knot of children, chasing each other around a clump of prickly pear. Luke felt a quick worry that one of them would stumble into it, especially when he spied Giselle. Did she know how hard it was to get the spines out?

With a quirk of his lips, he let the worry go. If she didn't know, she'd learn. It wouldn't take more than once, and painful as it might be to fall into a clump of cactus, it wasn't fatal.

Giselle caught sight of him and waved. Luke waved back, surprised when she didn't break free of her friends to come to him, as she'd been doing the past week at every chance. Instead, like a herd of wild horses, the group of them shifted direction and ran away to a new game.

The sight of them running so freely through the desert made him abruptly, absurdly homesick for this place. Again he lifted his eyes to the wide open sky and then toward the hazy horizon. The land stretched endlessly, subtly colored and restful to his eyes.

Home.

In his imagination, he saw the mountains around Colorado Springs, which had been his home for much longer than this land had. He thought of the way the light broke through the canyons in the evenings and remembered Jessie talking about it that night in his truck.

But she'd never seen the way the light broke here, the way the sunset stretched in violet and red and yellow fingers across the pale desert, spearing yucca and dancing in arroyos. She'd never seen rain thunder down from the hills in crashing violence, or sat with sheep on a mesa like this and listened to them murmur to each other as the sun lowered in the blazing blue sky.

With an odd sense of awakening, Luke took up a handful of earth and held it in his palm.

Four times in his life he'd known grief—the deep and shattering kind, the kind that tore holes wide open in a man's heart and let him bleed, leaving him empty. Staring at the dun-colored soil in his palm, Luke realized that the first loss—that of this land—had gone deeper than he had ever allowed. At ten, he'd lost his home, and had never quite recovered.

Then it had been his mother, for whom he'd endured the loss of the land, and then his father, who was his last link to the place.

And then he'd lost Jessie.

He let the dirt spill from his hand, watching it with a sense of power growing wider and stronger through him. He thought of his parents, and the pain of those losses was bittersweet, no longer searing. He thought of Jessie and admitted to himself that he'd done all he could to heal the rift between them. He blew the dust from his hand as if to release her completely to her fate.

He stood up. What he did have was Giselle and the land that waited patiently like a mother to welcome him home. This land and all it had given him were what he would give his child.

When he returned to the meeting house, calm and sure, he was only mildly curious about the big truck that pulled up. The children playing by the parking lot stopped their game and ran over, shouting, Giselle in the lead. The truck door opened and a man stepped out.

Luke watched as he bent and scooped Giselle up into a hug, then ruffled the heads of several other children.

Daniel.

The braid was still defiantly long, not quite black and streaked with lighter color from spending time in the sun. His cheekbones were sunburned. That was familiar, too.

But in the twenty years since they'd last met, Daniel had grown broad-shouldered and strong, and carried himself with an unconscious aura of dignity he'd once lacked.

Across the heads of the children, he caught sight of Luke. His expression shifted from open and laughing to distinctly apprehensive in a split second, giving Luke a deep sense of satisfaction. Considering the jealousy Luke had been suffering the past week, a little discomfort on Daniel's part seemed only fair.

Luke lifted his chin in greeting.

Daniel nodded at something Giselle was saying and set her down gently, then straightened. He crossed the dirt lot reluctantly, coming to a stop a foot from Luke. "*Ya ta hey,*" he said, his voice rumbling.

Luke held his gaze and nodded.

Daniel bent his head, touched his nose, kicked something in the dirt. "Guess you probably have a few choice words for me. I'm willing to listen."

"Why didn't you tell me sooner, Daniel?" Luke kept his voice low, private.

Daniel winced and glanced off toward the horizon. "A lot of reasons. None of them good ones." He inclined his head. "I'm sorry, my old friend."

"So am I," Luke said, crossing his arms. "I wish I hadn't missed all those years of Giselle's life."

Daniel bent his head, wordless.

"But I gotta tell you, man, I've been asleep on my feet for years. Today I'm awake and alive, and I have you to thank for that."

Daniel looked up, startled. He laughed suddenly and reached out to give Luke a rib-crushing hug. "Good!"

"Yeah."

A strong voice rang out into the day. "Daniel."

Against him, Luke felt Daniel's body change, stiffen. He let go of Luke and turned slowly as Jessie approached. Her eyes sparked with an expression Luke knew was dangerous, and he glanced toward Daniel to see if he knew it, too.

On Daniel's face was an expression Luke knew intimately, painfully, and he had a fleeting wish to protect this friend of his childhood, to stand between the woman approaching and the pain he saw in Daniel's eyes.

He loved her. There was a gentling on the harsh features, a shine in his eyes, a quirk of his lips as he lifted his hands, then dropped them. "Hey, Irish," he said.

She looked up at him, focused so completely on Daniel that Luke might have been made of stone. His heart pinched at the conflicted expression on her face. Maybe now Luke would truly lose her. Surely she couldn't look into Daniel's face and not see what Luke did.

But if she saw it, she gave no sign. "You weren't even sick, were you?"

He glanced at Luke, then back to her. "No."

"How long have you known that he was Giselle's father? And why didn't you just come out and tell me you knew instead of being so sneaky? And just what, exactly, did you hope to accomplish?"

"You want an answer to any particular question first?"

She shook her head. "How could you be so manipulative, Daniel? You can't go around playing God all the time."

Daniel sobered. "I was trying to help."

"Jessie," Luke said, nodding toward the curious faces of children gathered not far away. "Leave it till later."

She looked at him, and he saw the suddenly stricken expression in her clear topaz eyes. It seemed she would say something, something to just him, and her fingers closed around his hand on her arm. Then she looked back to Daniel. "I feel betrayed," she said.

Daniel nodded. "I know. I'm sorry."

"We'll talk about it later," she said, and sounded tired. She let go of Luke's hand.

Both of them stared after her, and Luke knew Daniel's eyes would reflect his own thoughts if he dared glance in that direction. He couldn't stand it.

"Hell of a woman you got there," Daniel commented.

"She's not my woman. Hasn't been for a long time." Luke shook his head slowly. "You could have claimed her anytime, all those years."

"It wasn't like I didn't try." His voice was tight.

"That's what I figured."

"The trouble was," Daniel said, turning to face Luke eye to eye, "she gave her heart away a long time ago to somebody else. He let her down."

"Yeah, I know."

Now all lightness fled from Daniel's sharply carved face. "I'm gonna tell you the truth, my old friend," he confessed in a voice not friendly at all. "I didn't send her up there for you. I did it for me. I thought if she saw you, she'd finally get you out of her system and the one damned thing in my way would be gone."

"Pretty big gamble."

"Yeah." He laughed without humor. "And it only took one glance to see I lost."

Luke narrowed his eyes. "Why are you telling me this? You think I'm gonna feel bad about it?"

"No," Daniel answered heavily. "I just wanted you to know you aren't the only one who lost something. I stole time from you, and for that I'm sorry. But I've done what I can to make it right."

They stared at each other beneath the bright winter sun, divided by a child and a woman, but linked by something rich and warm from long ago, when they'd ridden horses against the winds of the desert and run to a mountain to escape the world.

Luke stuck out his hand. "Truce."

Daniel accepted it.

"It's almost time for the meeting," Luke said. "We oughta get inside."

"You want me to take over now?"

Luke shook his head. "No. I know what I need to say."

Chapter Fifteen

Jessie found her seat in the meeting room. The post-lunch crowd seemed decidedly more energetic, she noticed and wondered if it were Daniel's arrival that had made it so.

Still caught up in her emotions, she folded her hands over her chest protectively as she sat down. She felt like a hapless fly, stuck between the window glass and the curtain, unable to find her way free to flight.

Daniel and Luke came in from the back, and she could see both of them were on guard. Uneasy. Then Luke leaned over and said something, and Jessie watched a slow, ironic grin smooth the lines of tension in Daniel's face. He clapped Luke on the shoulder.

She found herself absently rubbing her hands together as she watched them come to the front of the room. These were the two men she knew best in the world. Daniel was her best friend. He'd given her hope and something to believe in, braced her up when she fell into her sorrowing modes, pushed her when she hung back, badgered her and hugged her and been there for her.

And now he'd pushed her out into the painful circle of confronting the past, the unhealed past she shared with Luke.

Seeing them together now made her feel strangely apart, distant. She'd always thought Daniel quite handsome, but seeing him next to Luke made him almost plain. Daniel was broader, Luke was taller. Daniel's mixed blood showed in the lighter brown streaks of his hair and his pug nose. Luke had a calm about him that contrasted vividly to the restless, humming energy that surrounded Daniel.

But they were very much alike, too—male and Indian and bonded by a shared history in a place as mysterious to her as the moon. As Daniel sat down, he winked at her. Jessie simply looked at him, unable to sort her feelings well enough to figure out what the right response should be. She felt a little mean when his smile faded and he looked out over the crowd, trying to pretend his feelings weren't hurt.

And yet, what had made him think it would be all right to do this? To link her and Luke once again, face-to-face. How had he justified playing God like that?

The room settled as it became obvious they were about to start. Luke and Daniel sat side by side, waiting as Mary Yazzie made some announcements about a dance that would be held here this evening. When she finished, she looked toward Luke and Daniel.

To Jessie's surprise, Luke stood up. And she saw immediately that there was something different about him this afternoon, something strong and clean in the way he stood there, looking toward the weavers in respect.

He began to speak, and the translator looked at Jessie. "You want me to tell you what he's saying?"

She nodded. It seemed critical to understand every word of what he was going to say.

So the words came to her in stereo, parts of the Navajo slipping in before the translator gave her the English. She leaned forward, struck anew with the musical sound of Luke's clear tenor rising and falling with the lilting syllables of his native tongue. His everyday speaking voice held this same tone, but she had never realized just how deeply the rhythm of those early words had marked his English.

She was caught in the sound and didn't really tune in at first. He spoke of being the son of a weaver, who had given him respect for what she did. And he told them about Reeves, the gallery owner in Colorado Springs.

These things she knew, and only paid them scant attention. But then he began to tell a story about Coyote, the traditional trickster of Navajo legend.

Suddenly riveted, Jessie lifted a hand to the translator so she could hear the words in the original tongue, and she did miss a few words, but most of it was clear.

"Coyote, this time, isn't something outside," he said, "but something inside. He's like the worm in an apple, trying to make you believe the special gifts you were given by Spider Woman are not worthy of all they can command.

"Some people here are afraid of witches, but we found the boys who were causing that trouble. You know them, and know they are young men with problems. They were working for some of the galleries, trying to make you give up. They put on Coyote clothes to make you think you aren't worth more, but you are.''

As transfixed as the rest, Jessie stared at Luke. She had never seen this side of him before, this gently funny man, Navajo through and through. With the rest of them, she laughed when he made jokes and teased and made light of the darkness.

But it was as she was laughing over one of his jokes that she realized she *had* seen this side of him. It was this wry, strong Luke who had loved her so fiercely when she was broken and afraid as a young woman. It was this Luke who had loved her so unconditionally and completely and passionately that Jessie was able to be the kind of mother to Giselle that every little girl should have.

It was Luke who had given her the gift of her child and the tools to be her mother.

She glanced toward Daniel, who watched Luke with a glitter in his eye, a resounding and nodding approval. Daniel, too, had played his part, had given Jessie the tools to enter Luke's world, then pushed her into it, screaming and fighting all the way. Because Daniel knew her, he knew well that Coyote had had a stranglehold of fear on Jessie's life for a long, long time.

She took a long, deep breath. Oh, yes, the trickster had made mischief in her life, all right. By making her doubt herself and her instincts. By manipulating the guilt carried by most children of alcoholic parents. By making her feel she had no judgment.

With the same stunning sense of revelation she'd felt over seeing the endless mothers in her paintings, Jessie now saw something else. She'd been right to leave Luke eight years ago. It had been the only choice she could have made. In taking that step, for herself and for her child, she'd broken her cycle of co-dependency.

It might have been wrong to hide his child from him all these years. She didn't know. But the past was gone and couldn't be retrieved.

And with surprise, she thought of her behavior with Rudy the night before and realized just how far she'd come. No, not everyone felt the need to tend to drunk alcoholics, any more than everyone wanted work in a hospice. The work was too depressing for most people.

She did it because she wanted to, because sometimes there wasn't anyone else. Like a nurse, she had a need to tend the ones who were ill, to ease their pain until they could get well, or at least be one kind face in the world if they didn't.

Overcome, she abruptly stood up and walked quickly toward the back door. Luke's truck was parked in the lot, with the keys dangling from the ignition. For a minute, she hesitated, wondering where Giselle was. A high laugh sounded from the swings around to one side, and Jessie recognized the sound. Jessie whistled, and Giselle came around the building. "Hi, Mom! Is the meeting over?"

"Not quite. Tell Luke I'll be back in a little while, okay?"

"Okay. Bye."

Jessie drove around for a while, trying to rein in her emotions, the overwhelming insights that had been rocking her all day. Each one hit her anew, one after the other, in little bursts. Her mother. Luke. The tricks Coyote had played.

At an isolated spot, she stopped at the edge of the narrow highway and parked. She bent her head over the steering wheel and let go. She cried in joy and release and a certain inescapable sorrow. Mostly she cried in relief at the freedom she felt soaring into the free air, where she could breathe, where she was no longer responsible for everyone and everything in the world.

She wept because she loved Luke with every fiber of her being and didn't want to leave him. How often did it happen that the most sacred, holy, most heartfelt of dreams came true? How many people ever got a second chance?

And when the built-up emotions were spent, when she was cleansed by her tears, she lifted her head to stare at the harsh and beautiful land Luke loved so much. It was beautiful. They were all beautiful to Jessie—the coast of California, the forests of Washington, the farmland in Iowa, the mountains of Colorado.

Beauty all around me.

With a wry smile, she realized something else. Because of her unstable childhood, because she had no real roots of her own, she'd learned to embrace a feeling of home where ever she went. Her home was inside herself, a private, quiet place to which she had been retreating all of her life.

All at once, she felt an urgent need to paint her mother. Not drunk or sick, but as she had been sometimes when she went on the wagon. Oh, how Jessie had lived for those rare sober days—coming home from school to a house cleared of clutter, to cookies on the table and a fine Irish tea in the pot. In those times, Jessie's mother had spoken of the Ireland she left behind, that bleak land of the north where war still raged. It had been terribly painful for her mother to leave Ireland, a fact Jessie hadn't understood until she was grown.

Now Jessie wanted to paint her, the bright blue eyes and the benevolent, patient smile. She would paint her in Ireland, perhaps. She laughed a little to herself. Maybe if she painted her own mother, her real mother, who had done the best she could in spite of her illness, Jessie could finally move on to some other subjects.

And more. Jessie would tell Giselle about her other grandmother, the Irish one, let Giselle claim Jessie's half, too. She might even call her father, and ask him—

No, she didn't know how far she wanted to go with her father. Maybe some things were better left alone. Her father had sealed his wounds and put the past behind him. Jessie would not disturb that old pain.

As she sat there, she realized a certain urgent need to do one more thing. It made her feel a whisper of the same lost emotion it always had, but it was time for her to face down her demons. Firmly, she wiped her face and turned the key.

All this time, all these years, Jessie had been afraid of herself. She had been afraid that it was her actions that somehow led first her mother, then Luke into alcoholism, that if she'd been stronger, wiser, better, she could have somehow prevented it.

But that had been Coyote, the trickster, giving her doubts. Jessie wasn't responsible for her mother or for Luke—any more than Giselle was responsible for Jessie giving up cigarettes.

Jessie's mother had been unable to escape her demons. But Luke had. Sometimes he was afraid, sometimes he might be tempted. But she had faith, as once he'd had faith in her.

She wanted to laugh out loud. Instead, she turned the truck around on the rough, slim highway and headed back to the meeting house.

Beauty all around me.

Daniel was grinning from ear to ear as the meeting ended. "Well done," he said. "We'll still lose a few of them, but it looks like we'd better get those options in order."

Luke inclined his head. "Looks like it." He scanned the milling group for Jessie, who'd stared at him with the most peculiar expression as he talked—he kept seeing her from the corner of her eye.

"Maybe we can borrow some horses and ride, eh?" Daniel suggested.

"Sounds good."

When they got outside, however, Luke's truck was gone. Giselle galloped over with a bevy of her friends. "My mom took your truck."

Luke narrowed his eyes. "Did she say what she was doing?"

"It's all right, man," Daniel said. "I've got mine."

"Hey, kid," Luke said to Giselle, "you want to go riding with us?"

Giselle looked from the men to the children and quickly shook her head. "No."

He chuckled. "All right. You be good, and we'll see you later. Mary knows we're going. If you need anything, just tell her."

They got horses from a friend of Daniel's and rode out in the relative warmth of the mid-afternoon sunshine. Luke hadn't been on a horse for a while and felt deeply awkward at first, but his body remembered quickly enough. "You've done a good job with the project, Daniel," Luke said after a while.

"It's about done now. By spring, we'll have the money for galleries in most of the major markets. Now it will go to the hands of the weavers themselves."

"Who's going to run the galleries?"

Daniel coughed. "I've got a few people lined up already. Sort of hoped to talk to you about the one in Colorado Springs."

"Not a chance," Luke said, but grinned to show he had no hard feelings. More seriously, he added, "I'm coming back to the land."

"Ahh." Daniel nodded. "Does Jessie know?"

He shook his head.

"It won't matter."

Luke shrugged. "She has to find her own way."

"True enough." He chuckled. "What about that girl of yours, eh? She's a pistol."

This was the one thing that Luke still had not quite forgiven. "Yeah," he said gruffly.

Daniel rode silently. "I didn't know for a long time, man. Not until she painted the portrait."

"And when was that?"

Daniel touched his nose. "Four or five years ago."

"And by then—"

"By then I thought you were a jackass and didn't deserve her."

Luke lifted his chin, determined not to be offended. "You were there when Giselle was born. Didn't you see the birth certificate?"

Daniel looked at Luke steadily. The sound of the horses' hooves clomping softly against the earth and the ring of the bridles against the air were the only sounds. "She didn't put a name down," he said quietly, as if he knew the knowledge would wound. "Not then. She went back later and put it in."

Luke absorbed this without speaking, his eyes trained on the swoop of a hawk above them.

"What are the chances," Luke said, shaking his head, "that she would find you, of all the Navajo people there are in Albuquerque?"

"Very small," Daniel replied. "But big enough. Sometimes, the Creator is kind."

Luke decided he didn't want to ask to whom the Creator had been kind. "So, you live in Albuquerque now?"

"Yeah, but not for much longer. There's a peach orchard near Canyon de Chelly, abandoned and caught up in probate. I've been talking to a man about it."

"You don't miss living on the reservation?"

Daniel shrugged. "No good phone lines. The electricity is patchy, too. I have trouble with it sometimes." He looked a little sheepish as he admitted, "I gotta have my computers."

"Computers?" Luke laughed, thinking of the battery-operated bells and elaborate circuits Daniel had built when they were children, from scraps of anything he could find. "What do you do with them?"

"All kinds of things. Fix 'em, build 'em, play with 'em." Again he gave Luke that slightly apologetic look. "Went to school for programming at UNM. Teach a little now, too."

"Maybe you'll teach me," Luke said with a grin.

"Maybe. If you'll come fix the wood at the farmhouse."

Luke reined the horse for a minute. "I owe you, man," he said seriously.

Daniel chuckled. "Yeah, I reckon you do." He frowned. "Tell me how you let that woman get away from you."

Luke lifted a brow. "Someday maybe. Not today."

Daniel nodded. They rode on, content in the silence.

* * *

When Jessie got back, Daniel and Luke were gone, which made it somehow easier. She slipped inside the big hall and paused there a moment, breathing in the change of the room as young men pulled tables to one side and set chairs in a circle around the drum.

Jessie steeled herself and went to the kitchen. On the threshold, she stopped. Here were a dozen women working, as if they knew exactly how to mesh themselves together, the skirts of the grandmothers swirling against the calves of the younger women's jeans. Navajo and English spilled around them.

Swiftly, before she could lose her courage, Jessie surged forward, taking a knife from the counter. A woman was spilling onions onto the table, and Jessie scooped several toward her. The woman said, "Chop them fine for the chili," and Jessie nodded.

Next to her, another woman gave her a kitchen match to put in her mouth. "For your eyes," she said, and stuck one in her own mouth. Side by side, in easy silence, they chopped.

After the onions, there was lettuce to shred, pans to wash—a host of small things that needed doing. Jessie forgot her self-consciousness and moved along with them, feeling a quiet kind of joy in the smell and sound of the other women moving all around her, talking and laughing, teasing each other, chatting about children, complaining about husbands or sons. It was safe. It was homey.

It was exhilarating.

And because she saw the world with the eye of a painter, it was beautiful, too. Piles of chopped red tomato next to an enormous bowl of pale green shredded lettuce, the silver gleam of knives, the old hands and young hands deftly patting big angles of fry bread into shape. Women's hands.

Mary Yazzie nudged Jessie in the ribs, lifting her chin toward the wide window toward the hall. Luke stood there, watching her with a peculiar expression on his face, as if he'd been passing and had only glanced over, then been caught.

Mary nudged her again. Jessie took a breath and put down her knife. She wiped her fingers on her apron and then took it off. She glanced at Mary, who nodded at her, then walked toward the door.

"Are you all right?" Luke asked. "I was kind of worried about you."

"I'm fine. Will you come outside with me for a few minutes?"

For a moment, he didn't move, his dark eyes deep and still. Jessie reached out to take his hand. Surprised, he looked at the clasp of their hands together, and back to her face. He nodded.

They made their way toward a side door. Jessie liked the feel of him next to her, the brush of his jean jacket over her sleeve, the way their steps fell into harmony, the way he shifted his hand in hers so that their fingers were laced together. He smelled of sunshine and clean air, like the desert, and his boots were dirty. "Did you go riding?" she asked.

"Yeah."

That was all he said, and now Jessie felt a little wave of nervousness. The sun hung low on the horizon as they went outside, and she paused by the door.

He shook his head. "Let's walk."

"Okay."

He led, holding her hand, out toward a bluff not far from the meeting house. In town, lights were coming on, and the children who'd been rambling over the desert all day now hung close to the building.

On the crest of the bluff, they stopped and he lifted his chin toward the prairie. "You talked about the light in Cheyenne Canyon," he said. "I wanted you to see the sunset from here."

Jessie faced the wide sweep of desert below them. Deep shadows hung in an arroyo, making it a sharp contrast to the light above. Fingers of pale gold sunlight edged the sharp spikes of yucca and highlighted the bristles on cacti, making them look furry and friendly.

And as they watched, the world changed color. The muted colors of the land grew rich, filled with deep purple shadows and blazing red points of light, reflected in the sky. A wisp of cloud, nearly invisible a moment before, suddenly flared a bright gold edged with orange.

Jessie looked at Luke and saw in his face the shift of light, the play of shadows. It seemed suddenly impossible to tell him everything she had been thinking all afternoon. She said, "It's beautiful."

"I knew you'd like it. "

"I don't know why I was so afraid of this place. I'm sorry I didn't want to come with you before."

"It's okay."

"No, it really isn't. I've treated you badly, Luke. Often, both in the past and in the last few days. You deserve more than that."

"Jessie—"

She shook her head, holding up a hand. Now that the words were coming, she wanted to let them all out. "I tried to put the burden of proving everything on you. And it wasn't you with the unresolved issues. It was me. I had to see what my mother left me or didn't leave me."

Her throat felt tight and she turned away for a moment, taking power from the display around them. "I've been so lost without you, Luke. I managed to get through, and I convinced myself that it was a good life, but the minute I saw you, I knew it was a lie."

"What, exactly, are you telling me?" he asked, and his jaw looked hard.

She took a deep breath. "That I love you. That I'm tired of running away from you." Her voice softened. "That I'd love to have more babies and see your face at the supper table for the rest of my life."

He looked at her hand, caught so tightly in his own. "Jessie, you have to know there are no guarantees with an alcoholic."

She shrugged lightly, and smiled. "What's life without a few risks?"

"It's no joke."

"I'm not joking." She touched his cheek. "Sometimes all we have is faith that things are going to be okay. I have faith in you, Luke, more than you have. Do you know the longest time my mother was sober?"

He shook his head.

"Three months. Two different times, she made it three months."

"I understand what you're saying, Jessie, but one day at a time is all anyone can do it."

"The funny thing is, Luke, I discovered I have faith in myself, too. If I have to leave you again, I will." She smiled. "I don't believe I will have to, but if it came to that, I would. And I'd survive."

A shimmer of humor touched his eyes. "You mean you wouldn't die of a broken heart without me? I'm crushed."

"What I'm trying to say," she said impatiently, "is—"

He laughed, and the planes of his face lightened, as if the sun had struck him anew. His eyes crinkled and his brown throat moved with the sound of his laughing, and then he bent to kiss her, hard. "I told you this morning I loved you, Jessie. I want babies, too. I want you with me, always." He sobered a little and touched her cheek. "Without you, it was like winter. Finding you is like spring again."

Jessie caught his face in her hands and kissed him full on the mouth, staring deep into his eyes. There she saw the future, the way it had been in her mind so long ago— a future filled with children and noise and love. So much love. "Luke." She sighed and leaned into his embrace, drawing strength from him, feeling it circle back to him. It was, quite simply, the best feeling in the world. "I love you so much."

He pressed his cheek against her hair. "Will you mind coming here to live, Jessie? It would be good for Giselle." He lifted his head. "It would be good for me."

"As long as we're together, I don't care where we live."

"Good." He touched her nose lightly. "I think we should go tell Giselle."

Jessie laughed. "Oh, yes."

They found her and Daniel sitting on the swing set just beyond the door to the kitchen. Jessie glanced inside the door as they passed and saw Mary, who waved at her, smiling broadly when she saw Luke and Jessie hand in hand.

Luke let Jessie's hand go and went to stand before the little girl on the swing. Very seriously, he sank to a squat and took her hands. Giselle looked suddenly wary.

"Since I have no parents and no one to give me a blessing," Luke said quietly, "I want to ask you if you will give me permission to marry your mother."

Giselle's mouth dropped open. She looked from Luke to her mother, standing a few feet back, then to Daniel and back to Luke. "You mean we'll all live together in one house?"

"Yeah," Luke said.

Giselle stood up and whooped, a wild animal cry of joy, then leapt into Luke's arms. "Yes!" she cried.

Jessie blinked back tears. Daniel waited, standing quietly to one side. She smiled at him, but he didn't smile back. He looked weary, a little lonely, outcast from the picture he'd helped create, but also misplaced now from the place he'd once held. When Luke turned, Giselle on his hip, to take her inside, Jessie said, "Go ahead. We'll be there in a minute."

Luke touched her arm and nodded, then ducked inside with his child, leaving Jessie and Daniel in the stillness of the dying day. Jessie just looked at him for a long moment, seeing a kaleidoscopic whirl of images overlaying the present view of him—Daniel taking her to the hospital, Daniel bullying her into one project or another, Daniel earnestly learning computers at UNM at thirty-two years old....

She took a deep breath at the loneliness in his eyes now. "Daniel, my friend," she said in Navajo, holding out her hands—and couldn't go on.

Slowly a smile dawned on his face, one of pride and gentleness. He stepped forward and hugged her. "Ah, Jessie. I'm going to miss you."

All these years and she had never guessed, not even for a moment, that he'd ever had anything but friendly intentions. She hugged him back, fiercely. "It won't be the same anymore, will it?"

"No."

She pressed her forehead into his shoulder. "Daniel— I—" She broke off, then continued, "Thank you. I can never repay you."

"No, my friend," he said quietly and let her go, holding just her arms. "It's I who can never repay you." He twitched his lips. "Go on, now. He's waiting. I've worked hard for this. Don't cheat me of the payoff."

She tiptoed up to kiss his cheek, a quiet and simple mark on the end of the friendship that had meant so much to her over the years. She knew she wouldn't lose him, that he would always be a part of their lives, but from this moment forward, there were always going to be differences.

Then she turned quickly and headed back into the kitchen, where the women were beginning to serve the evening meal.

Chapter Sixteen

On Christmas Eve, Jessie waited on the bridge over Helen Hunt Falls. Around her, fat snowflakes drifted down from a pearlescent bank of clouds. The pines and spruce held a vast silence, a silence echoed by the gathering people below. It was a small number. Giselle, Marcia and Daniel.

And Luke. He stood at the edge of Helen Hunt Falls, his face turned toward her. He wore a suit made of soft gray flannel, and a crisp white shirt with a silver bolero. His black hair shone with the fiery gloss of recent washing, and snowflakes stuck in starry clusters in the heavy strands.

Next to him, Giselle for once stood utterly still, dressed in a soft white dress covered with lace, tied in back with a big blue sash. Blue ribbons were laced into her braid. In her hands she held a spray of white carnations.

Jessie looked at Marcia, who smiled and lifted her violin. As she began to play, Jessie shifted her shawl on her shoulders and clasped her own white carnations more tightly, then turned and began the slow descent to the foot of the stairs. The long fringes of the shawl Marcia had given her as a wedding present brushed her thighs and swung in a seductive rhythm around her hips.

She took Luke's outstretched hand, feeling a jolt at the almost overwhelming beauty of him standing there, love shining from his liquid eyes. With a sudden sense of mischief, Jessie leaned forward and so low no one else could hear, she murmured, "Alessandro, I presume?"

He laughed outright, squeezing her fingers tightly before he tucked them under his arm and turned them to face the minister.

Jessie tried to concentrate, she really did. The ceremony and setting were beautiful. It should have been sacred, solemn, holy. And it was, but she was also so blindingly happy, she couldn't stop grinning. And Luke seemed to be having the same problem. He nudged her at one point and pretended to eat the flower on his lapel, a glitter in his eyes. Jessie playfully lifted her bouquet for his perusal, and he opened his mouth—

"Do you, Jessie, take this man..." the minister said in a slightly reproving voice.

She looked up and struggled with straightening her mouth into a semblance of sobriety. "Yes," she said, and a bubble of laughter burst from her chest when she looked at him.

"Do you, Luke, take this woman..."

He turned and the same wild giddiness was in his eyes, on his mouth, but Jessie saw tears of emotion in his eyes, too. And unaccountably, she realized there were tears streaming down her face, no doubt smearing and streaking her careful makeup.

"Yes," he declared.

"I now pronounce you man and wife," the minister said. "You may—"

But he was too late because Luke had already drawn Jessie into his arms and he was kissing her, their tears mingling on their lips, with the cool taste of snowflakes. Giselle and Marcia cheered, and even Daniel made whooping noises.

Luke lifted his head. "At last."

Jessie smiled up at him, holding still her secret close to her heart. "Oh, yes. At last."

They waited, at Mary Yazzie's insistence, to hold a reception until they returned to the land. There, in the same hall in Shiprock where the meetings had been held, they had a celebration, with drums and dancing.

As Jessie sat there listening to the heartbeat of the drum, watching Luke and Giselle dance, she smiled over the subjects she had to paint now—all the weavers and the grandmothers, the young dancing girls. But also the great stretches of desert with their jagged, shadowed arroyos and the yucca washed with fingers of sunsets. Oh, yes. There were many things she wanted to paint.

The dance ended and Luke came over, one of the grandmothers in tow. He was grinning with that mischievous expression in his eyes, and Jessie cocked her head. "What do you have up your sleeve?" she asked.

Playfully, he lifted his wrists and looked down. "Nothing." He laughed. "Grandmother has something for you."

The old woman smiled and gave Jessie a weaving. Surprised and touched, she shot Luke a quizzical glance. He lifted his eyebrows, but anticipation shone in his face.

Jessie unfolded the soft weaving and saw stylized blue jays woven into the pattern. Stunned, she glanced up to the old woman, who spoke in Navajo. "You're a blue jay," she said, and laughed.

Luke explained, "I asked her to weave it before we went back to the Springs. She thought I was crazy, but told me she was happy with it when she finished." He grinned. "She started to like them after she watched them for a while."

Jessie touched the brilliant blue of the birds in the weaving and thought with joy that blue jays were the right symbol for all of them—for Luke and Jessie and even the weavers, who all began outside and had come inside a circle of warmth and love, where they had all grown sassy and strong.

Jessie lifted her head. "Thank you," she said in her still terrible Navajo. The old woman patted her shoulder.

"Come on and dance," Luke urged, grabbing her hand.

"Wait a minute," she said, tugging his fingers. "I have a present for you, too."

"Yeah? What?" He looked around for some package or something.

She chuckled and turned his hand to press his palm against her belly.

"A baby?" he whispered.

Jessie nodded.

He laughed and kissed her, then pulled back and made

a whooping sound. "Come on and dance with me, both of you."

And Jessie followed, to dance with him to a new song, a lasting song of love.

* * * * *

**Three new stories celebrating
motherhood and love**

*Birds, Bees
and Babies'94*

**NORA ROBERTS
ANN MAJOR
DALLAS SCHULZE**

A collection of three stories, all by
award-winning authors, selected
especially to reflect the love all
families share. Silhouette's fifth annual
romantic tribute to mothers is sure
to touch your heart.

Available in May,
BIRDS, BEES AND BABIES 1994 is a
perfect gift for yourself or a loved one
to celebrate the joy of motherhood.

**Available at your favorite
retail outlet.**

Only from

Silhouette®
™

—where passion lives.

BBB94

IT'S OUR 1000TH SILHOUETTE ROMANCE, AND WE'RE CELEBRATING!

JOIN US FOR A SPECIAL COLLECTION OF LOVE STORIES BY AUTHORS YOU'VE LOVED FOR YEARS, AND NEW FAVORITES YOU'VE JUST DISCOVERED. JOIN THE CELEBRATION...

April
REGAN'S PRIDE by **Diana Palmer**
MARRY ME AGAIN by **Suzanne Carey**

May
THE BEST IS YET TO BE by **Tracy Sinclair**
CAUTION: BABY AHEAD by **Marie Ferrarella**

June
THE BACHELOR PRINCE by **Debbie Macomber**
A ROGUE'S HEART by **Laurie Paige**

July
IMPROMPTU BRIDE by **Annette Broadrick**
THE FORGOTTEN HUSBAND by **Elizabeth August**

SILHOUETTE ROMANCE...VIBRANT, FUN AND EMOTIONALLY RICH! TAKE ANOTHER LOOK AT US! AND AS PART OF THE CELEBRATION, READERS CAN RECEIVE A FREE GIFT!

YOU'LL FALL IN LOVE ALL OVER AGAIN WITH SILHOUETTE ROMANCE!

Silhouette®

CEL1000

Christine Rimmer

**Three rapscallion brothers. Their main talent: making trouble.
Their only hope: three uncommon women who knew the way to
heal a wounded heart!**

May 1994—MAN OF THE MOUNTAIN (SE #886)
Jared Jones hadn't had it easy with women. But when he retreated to his
isolated mountain cabin, he found Eden Parker, determined to show him a
good woman's love!

July 1994—SWEETBRIAR SUMMIT (SE #896)
Patrick Jones didn't think he was husband material—but Regina Black sure
did. She had heard about the wild side of the Jones boy, but that wouldn't
stop her!

September 1994—A HOME FOR THE HUNTER (SE #908)
Jack Roper came to town looking for the wayward and beautiful
Olivia Larabee. He discovered a long-buried secret.... Could his true identity
be a Jones boy?

**Meet these rascal men—and the women who'll tame them—
only from Silhouette Special Edition!**

INDULGE A LITTLE 6947 SWEEPSTAKES
NO PURCHASE NECESSARY

HERE'S HOW THE SWEEPSTAKES WORKS:

The Harlequin Reader Service shipments for January, February and March 1994 will contain, respectively, coupons for entry into three prize drawings: a trip for two to San Francisco, an Alaskan cruise for two and a trip for two to Hawaii. To be eligible for any drawing using an Entry Coupon, simply complete and mail according to directions.

There is no obligation to continue as a Reader Service subscriber to enter and be eligible for any prize drawing. You may also enter any drawing by hand printing your name and address on a 3" x 5" card and the destination of the prize you wish that entry to be considered for (i.e., San Francisco trip, Alaskan cruise or Hawaiian trip). Send your 3" x 5" entries to: Indulge a Little 6947 Sweepstakes, c/o Prize Destination you wish that entry to be considered for, P.O. Box 1315, Buffalo, NY 14269-1315, U.S.A. or Indulge a Little 6947 Sweepstakes, P.O. Box 610, Fort Erie, Ontario L2A 5X3, Canada.

To be eligible for the San Francisco trip, entries must be received by 4/30/94; for the Alaskan cruise, 5/31/94; and the Hawaiian trip, 6/30/94. No responsibility is assumed for lost, late or misdirected mail. Sweepstakes open to residents of the U.S. (except Puerto Rico) and Canada, 18 years of age or older. All applicable laws and regulations apply. Sweepstakes void wherever prohibited.

For a copy of the Official Rules, send a self-addressed, stamped envelope (WA residents need not affix return postage) to: Indulge a Little 6947 Rules, P.O. Box 4631, Blair, NE 68009, U.S.A.

INDR93

INDULGE A LITTLE 6947 SWEEPSTAKES
NO PURCHASE NECESSARY

HERE'S HOW THE SWEEPSTAKES WORKS:

The Harlequin Reader Service shipments for January, February and March 1994 will contain, respectively, coupons for entry into three prize drawings: a trip for two to San Francisco, an Alaskan cruise for two and a trip for two to Hawaii. To be eligible for any drawing using an Entry Coupon, simply complete and mail according to directions.

There is no obligation to continue as a Reader Service subscriber to enter and be eligible for any prize drawing. You may also enter any drawing by hand printing your name and address on a 3" x 5" card and the destination of the prize you wish that entry to be considered for (i.e., San Francisco trip, Alaskan cruise or Hawaiian trip). Send your 3" x 5" entries to: Indulge a Little 6947 Sweepstakes, c/o Prize Destination you wish that entry to be considered for, P.O. Box 1315, Buffalo, NY 14269-1315, U.S.A. or Indulge a Little 6947 Sweepstakes, P.O. Box 610, Fort Erie, Ontario L2A 5X3, Canada.

To be eligible for the San Francisco trip, entries must be received by 4/30/94; for the Alaskan cruise, 5/31/94; and the Hawaiian trip, 6/30/94. No responsibility is assumed for lost, late or misdirected mail. Sweepstakes open to residents of the U.S. (except Puerto Rico) and Canada, 18 years of age or older. All applicable laws and regulations apply. Sweepstakes void wherever prohibited.

For a copy of the Official Rules, send a self-addressed, stamped envelope (WA residents need not affix return postage) to: Indulge a Little 6947 Rules, P.O. Box 4631, Blair, NE 68009, U.S.A.

INDR93

INDULGE A LITTLE
SWEEPSTAKES

OFFICIAL ENTRY COUPON

This entry must be received by: APRIL 30, 1994
This month's winner will be notified by: MAY 15, 1994
Trip must be taken between: JUNE 30, 1994-JUNE 30, 1995

YES, I want to win the San Francisco vacation for two. I understand that the prize includes round-trip airfare, first-class hotel, rental car and pocket money as revealed on the "wallet" scratch-off card.

Name_____

Address _____ Apt. _____

City_____

State/Prov._____ Zip/Postal Code_____

Daytime phone number_____
 (Area Code)

Account #_____

Return entries with invoice in envelope provided. Each book in this shipment has two entry coupons—and the more coupons you enter, the better your chances of winning!
© 1993 HARLEQUIN ENTERPRISES LTD.   MONTH1

INDULGE A LITTLE
SWEEPSTAKES

OFFICIAL ENTRY COUPON

This entry must be received by: APRIL 30, 1994
This month's winner will be notified by: MAY 15, 1994
Trip must be taken between: JUNE 30, 1994-JUNE 30, 1995

YES, I want to win the San Francisco vacation for two. I understand that the prize includes round-trip airfare, first-class hotel, rental car and pocket money as revealed on the "wallet" scratch-off card.

Name_____

Address _____ Apt. _____

City_____

State/Prov._____ Zip/Postal Code_____

Daytime phone number_____
 (Area Code)

Account #_____

Return entries with invoice in envelope provided. Each book in this shipment has two entry coupons—and the more coupons you enter, the better your chances of winning!
© 1993 HARLEQUIN ENTERPRISES LTD.   MONTH1

Subscribers-only Sweepstakes

INDULGE A LITTLE—WIN A LOT!
This month's prize:
A VACATION FOR TWO
to SAN FRANCISCO!

Are you the lucky subscriber who will win a *free* vacation to San Francisco, California? The facing page contains two entry forms, as does each of the other books you received this shipment. Complete and return *all* entry forms—the more you send in, the better your chances of winning!

Then keep your fingers crossed, because you'll find out by May 15, 1994, if you're this month's winner! And if you are, here's what you'll get:

- Round-trip airfare for two!
- 7 days/6 nights at a first-class hotel in the heart of glorious San Francisco!
- Rental car to explore neighboring Sausalito, Muir Woods, the Sonoma wine country and more!
- Plenty of pocket money (as determined by the enclosed "Wallet" scratch-off card)!

Remember, this is a random drawing *not* open to the general public. And the more times you enter, the better your chances of winning!

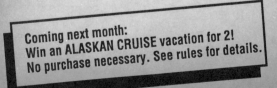

Coming next month:
Win an ALASKAN CRUISE vacation for 2!
No purchase necessary. See rules for details.

M1-IND93

SPECIAL EDITION

WALK IN BEAUTY

Once, Luke Bernali's proud Navajo
blood and strong carpenter's hands
made genteel Jessie Callahan love him
with youthful abandon. But, to his endless
regret, Luke faltered and he let Jessie down.
Hurt, Jessie left, with a broken heart...
and unaware that she was pregnant
with Luke's child.

Now, eight years later, Jessie was back—
with a darling daughter in tow. Luke was
older—and wiser—and determined to
recapture the beauty lost. Could a fierce,
desperate long-ago love soar anew
on the delicate wings of a child?

ISBN 0-373-09881-2

09881

0 65373 00350 8

SILHOUETTE
BOOKS®

PRINTED IN t